A LETHAL DOSE

BOOKS BY GENE RONTAL

The Police Surgeon

Sterile Justice

The Cruelest Cut

A Pre-existing Condition

A LETHAL DOSE

A Detective Ben Dailey, M.D. Mystery

GENE RONTAL

CAVEL
PRESS
Kenmore, WA

A Camel Press book published by Epicenter Press

Epicenter Press
6524 NE 181st St.
Suite 2
Kenmore, WA 98028

For more information go to:
www.Camelpress.com
www.Coffeetownpress.com
www.Epicenterpress.com
www.generontalbooks.com

This is a work of fiction. Names, characters, places, brands, media, and incidents are either the product of the author's imagination or are used fictitiously.

Design by Scott Book and Melissa Vail Coffman

Previously published by Sterling House

ISBN: 978-1-60381-791-2 (Trade Paper)
ISBN: 978-1-60381-792-9 (eBook)

Printed in the United States of America

To my parents, Rose and Joe.

Healing is a matter of time, but it is sometimes also a matter of opportunity.

—*Hippocrates*

PROLOGUE

THE CLACK OF MY WORN-OUT WIPER beat an annoying cadence as it dragged across my windshield. It barely let me see the light from the small strip-mall poking out of the darkness. Accurate Rehabilitation Services. Just what I needed—a rehabbed doctor getting rehabbed. What did I care? If it got me in to see Claudia Fraser and, from there, out of Toledo, it would be worth it.

I pulled my foot off the pedal and eased my ten-year-old beast into a parking space in front of the small storefront operation. A moment of gloom passed over me as I rehashed my reason for being here—a favor for Bruce Sanderson, insurance man. *Get off it, Dailey. That may pass with someone else, but the truth is you like the work. A doctor investigating crime.* I hadn't learned my lesson yet.

I had arrived in downtown Toledo around five o'clock and immediately gotten lost. I was looking for St. Anthony's Rehabilitation Unit, off I-275. Two gas station attendants and a $2.50 map later, I had found my way to Ottawa Hills; another stop for directions, and I pulled into a medical mall that hospitals used to capture suburban clientele. The place was a series of low-slung, one-story buildings—emergency walk-in, urology, dermatology, and down on the far end, off by itself, pain management.

I got out of my old Wagoneer and made for the door. I had almost the whole parking lot to myself. I parked at the edge of the building, rather than taking the physician's spot at the front door. Inside, I found the receptionist and told her I was looking for Claudia Fraser.

"Do you have an appointment?"

No, but I had a bad back. "Sort of," I said.

She had long, dark hair and big eyes. When she scowled, it was not very becoming. Uncongeniality will do that to you.

"Do you have a medical referral?" she said.

"Well, I'm a doctor. I know my way around the forms."

"Let me see if Claudia can see you."

I waited a few minutes, scanned a couple of the magazines. It was an all-golf office. Magazine selection and patient motivation. I'd never thought much about it. When the receptionist slipped back to her desk, I saw she was tall and thin.

"If you want to wait, she can see you."

I nodded and began filling out the forms.

The wait lasted about an hour. A few patients came from the back, made appointments for their next visits, and left. Old guys. Judging by their pants and cardigans, golfers. After the last one had left, the receptionist closed up shop, shut off most of the lights, and watered an abundant philodendron by the front window. She gazed at me, all big, tired eyes, and then tucked her purse under her arm. Wedged between the front door and the rest of her life, she told me Miss Fraser would take care of everything.

What did I have to lose?

About fifteen minutes later, a slim-waisted woman around twenty-five appeared at the door. Full lips, a little purple eye shadow, blonde hair with that permanently tousled look. Disarray on purpose. I looked at her hands. No rings. The only jewelry I saw was a pair of half-carat diamond post earrings. Rich boyfriend or a trust fund. I guessed the former.

"Dr. Dailey?" she asked.

"Yes."

"What can I help you with?" she asked. She held up a chart, glanced back and forth between it and me, and smiled just a little. I wondered what time that morning she'd started work.

"Back pain," I said. "Nothing serious. I saw your sign and figured you could help."

"Let's see if I can," she said. She led me back to a treatment room. The place was empty except for the two of us. There were six other rooms. All of them were dark. We took the first one, and I took a seat up on the bench.

She said, "I'll feel your back and see if I can pinpoint the spot. Slip off your jacket and shirt."

Once my shirt was off, she started probing my lower back. She knew what to look for. She found the spot, just above my L5-S1 vertebrae. She said it felt knotted, like a spasm. Mild? Yes, I said. Medium mild. All right then. She palpated the area again and said I should slip off my clothes, down to my shorts, and lie down on the table with a sheet over me. She left the room.

I hesitated. Did I want to do this? Somewhere along the way, I'd decided against the direct route. I could have asked a few questions and been on my way. I unbuttoned my trousers, thinking of the old guys in their green pants, the golf magazines up front—healthy men on fairways, victory shining in their very healthy faces. It didn't feel right at all.

I hated golf. I'd been an offensive lineman.

I lay face down on the examining table with the sheet over me and looked around. After a few moments the door opened behind me.

"We're all set. I just had to get a few things."

I looked over to my side. She had taken off her white coat. She wore a sleeveless, white shirt. I noticed her breasts, tight behind the shirt, nipples pushing outward. They didn't make physical therapists the way they used to.

"Head on the pillow, please."

She pulled back the sheet and applied oil to my back, then began kneading the tight muscles of my lower back. She was good. She worked it a little hard, but she knew where to find the muscles and what to do with them. She stopped. I heard something rustle behind me. Then she replaced the sheet on my back and lifted it off my legs.

"Been doing this long?" I asked.

"About six years." Her hands worked the muscles on my lower legs.

"Always been at St. Anthony's?"

"No, I move around. My family's near here, in Perrysburg."

Her hands moved up my thighs. The massage got closer and closer to my groin. This might be more than just a massage.

"Hey," I said.

"Hey what?"

"You know."

"I thought that's what you wanted."

I turned on my side. Her blouse was off. So were her pants. She was standing over me, breasts bulging inside her bra, her black panties revealing just the hint of hair beneath them.

"New approaches to rehabilitation," I said.

"The approach is old." She hooked her thumb in the band on her underwear and lowered them, letting me take a look. "But the techniques are new."

"What's new?"

"Chains. Handcuffs. Hot wax." She pulled her panties back up, snapped the band on her hip. "I've got everything."

An alternative approach to pain management. I was rising to the challenge.

"One session, a hundred bucks." She unsnapped her bra, her breasts dropped down in my face, her nipples only inches from my nose. She pushed a hand inside my shorts and started rubbing my erection to check my interest level. When she was convinced, she said, "Just wait one second, honey, I forgot something in the back."

I watched her slim body walk toward a storage closet. The little head was doing some big-time talking. The big head couldn't seem to respond.

How did I get myself into these situations?

A doctor investigating crime. I hadn't learned my lesson.

Was I about to?

CHAPTER 1

"SUPPOSE WE PUT GOD IN A WHITE COAT, Dr. Dailey. Suppose we gave him a stethoscope. Would *God* be above the legal system?"

I was starting to dislike this guy.

Kenneth Ellenby, premier personal injury lawyer of Dellsburg. He lifted his chin. His darting eyes and pointed teeth gave him the charming grimace of a jackal. He looked as if he wanted to tear the flesh off my bones.

"I'm a physician," I said. "Not a theologian." Or a lawyer, I thought. Thank God.

"Let me rephrase the question. Do you believe in justice?"

"Justice in its pure sense?"

"Don't chop logic, Dr. Dailey. This isn't semantics. This is a court of law." He was warming up. He smelled blood. He said, "When malpractice is committed, it should be punished. Or do you disagree?"

"It would depend on the standard of care."

"The standard of care." He turned toward the jury and gestured grandly. "Dr. Dailey, please tell the court exactly what you do."

"I practice most of the time."

"Most of the time?"

I shoved a hand into my jacket pocket. What was I fishing for there? I didn't know. I was starting to panic.

"I do research on the voice box or larynx and treat diseases of the head and neck. I see patients three days a week."

"Have you ever been sued?"

I pulled my hand out, empty. Calmly, I thought. Say this calmly.

"Yes," I said. "Once."

"And the circumstances of that suit?"

"A young boy died after surgery. His parents sued me."

It sounded simple enough when I said it. It wasn't. Five years of exile from the profession I loved wasn't simple. The loneliness wasn't simple. All because of a murderous plot to discredit me. And Ellenby wanted to talk about justice.

"Isn't it true you were found negligent in that case?"

Mike Valon, Coastal Life's defense attorney, rose to his feet, a little slowly if you asked me. He objected, "Dr. Dailey was subsequently found innocent of all charges. He was exonerated by the hospital at which he had practiced."

The judge roused himself. He was awake after all. "Sustained," he growled. He leveled a crooked finger at Ellenby, narrowed his eyes, and nodded his head twice. He knew Ellenby, probably too well. "I've read the report on Dr. Dailey, Mr. Ellenby. I forbid further mention of anything to do with that trial in these proceedings. The jury will disregard the comment."

Disregard.

Ellenby looked back at his notes with a smug look on his face. He had gotten what he wanted. Discredit the witness. Do it at any cost.

I can tell you a thing or two about justice.

I turned away from Ellenby, from the judge, from it all. I glanced at the drab, beige walls of the courtroom, wishing for a window to jump out of. It was a Friday afternoon, a beautiful day in late autumn. The sun would be slanting down toward the Delaware River, and New Jersey beyond. Somewhere nearby, early one winter morning in 1777, Washington had made his decision to cross the ice-filled water to Trenton. We all have our troubles.

I came back into the courtroom.

Don't take it personally, Dailey, I thought. The case had nothing to do with me. It was about the two and a half million dollars. As expert witness for the defense, I was the only thing between Ellenby and the biggest paycheck of his life. That was the only justice Kenneth Ellenby was searching for.

It had looked like a slam dunk for the plaintiff - at first. A routine tonsillectomy. A doctor accused of killing his patient by placing a suture in the carotid artery. And it had been a lock, until I had found a toxicology screen on her stomach contents. The screen was buried in the back of the autopsy report. Traces of ibuprofen, usually a harmless drug, but in this case, a killer. Once on board, the medicine acted as a blood thinner. And the patient took it on her own, ignoring the doctor's orders.

End of discussion. No prescription from her doctor, no responsibility.

Ellenby looked down at his yellow legal pad. He knew about the screen, of course. He was working the case, undermining the witness. He was a lawyer.

He said, "Do you often testify in malpractice cases?"

"I've done so a few times, yes."

"A few times. Do you always testify for the defendant doctor?"

"No, sometimes I testify for a plaintiff." In workers' comp cases. I tried to be on the right side when I could. But what did he care?

"Dr. Dailey, you came all the way from Detroit to testify in the Permonti case." The name rolled off his lips. He made a show of it. I wondered if he'd practiced saying it. He crossed his arms over his chest, waiting, letting the pause work. "For the money, I assume?"

He didn't really expect an answer.

"How much do you get paid, Dr. Dailey, for your services?"

"Five hundred dollars an hour."

"Five hundred dollars." Another pregnant pause. "Five hundred dollars an hour. So, if you do this a few times a year, you have a tidy little sum. Don't you?"

"It doesn't make any difference to me."

"A very tidy sum, I would imagine."

"I give the money to charity." It was the truth. After what I had been through, money was of secondary importance to me. It was a convenience. That was all.

Ellenby stared at me, then gazed down at his three-hundred dollar Gucci loafers. Maybe he felt something. Maybe he was capable of feeling remorse. He touched the lapel of his Armani suit, fingered it lovingly. No, he was regrouping. He'd just violated rule number one in the lawyer's handbook: never ask a question you don't know the answer to.

Ellenby knew what I knew. He knew he would lose. He retreated to his chair, unbuttoned his jacket, and sat down.

"No further questions, your honor."

I stepped down from the witness chair. The judge sat back and scowled. At the defense table, I caught Valon's concealed smile. It was the smile of the victor. He was feeling good. He could barely contain himself and his lawyerly joy. I didn't feel like a winner. There was the ghost of a dead patient in the room. That fact hung over the proceedings. A good doctor feels such things in his gut. Every goof and slip, every unforeseen accident that causes a life to end, is personal to a doctor. Even when it was someone else's patient, you share in the horror. I saw nothing to celebrate.

Next to Valon sat the client, Dr. Connely. He was well tanned, a little on the heavy side. I knew something about his plight. My life had been on the line in the courtroom. But my B.S. radar zeroed in on his core of materialism. I saw the Mercedes, the condo in the Caymans, the temperature-controlled wine cellar. The vanity and self-indulgence. There wasn't that much difference between him and Ellenby.

Most docs know the feeling - that special relationship with death. I wasn't sure about Connely.

THE TRAVEL AGENT HAD BOOKED ME back to Detroit on a white-knuckle special, a twin propjet Brazilian commuter plane. Fly one once and you become
grateful for 737s. You actually appreciate riding cheek-to-jowl on one of those
hulks; probably the reason customers try to avoid commuter flights.

As I boarded, the pilot sat hunched over a clipboard in the cockpit, his back
to the passengers. A stewardess said something to him, and he swung around
in his seat. He looked all of twenty-five. I found 6A and made peace with my
God.

Once we were in the air, I thought back over the day's proceedings. A trial
wasn't supposed to be about the truth, I knew. That was a naive idea. But I
couldn't get Valon's satisfied look out my mind. Or the sound of Ellenby's self-
righteous voice. I wanted the truth.

Do you believe in justice?

A physician's dislike for lawyers starts in med school, with the first innocu-
ous joke a professor makes. *They're criminals who want to avoid prosecution.*
That sort of thing. Cruel statements. Some of them prescient. Doctors and lawyers share a natural battleground. Doctors have malpractice policies; lawyers
have law. For a sharp attorney it's easy money. So doctors think in adversarial
terms. They practice defensive medicine. Dot every "i," cover every base, be
wary of the doctor-patient relationship. It is an unnerving necessity.

We leveled off at 25,000 feet. The engines whined. A dip here and there.
Otherwise I was comfortable. I opened the Detroit Free Press on my lap and
turned to the sports first. Old habits die hard.

I played football in college. I can still see the team taking the field, the
tunnel in front of me, and I can still hear the rhythmic clatter of metal cleats
against asphalt. In the muted light of memory, we hang in a vapor trail, a hundred juiced-up men in still life, pawing the ground, answering a call to battle.

If that's the call, my grandfather would have said, *Tell them they got the
wrong number.*

He was from the old school. He escaped Vilna just before Hitler invaded
Poland. It left him with a cold realism about life. He knew something about
adversaries and battle, but he never understood football.

"Why do you waste your time with this foolishness?" he would say. To first
generation Americans, education was the ticket to success.

"I love it."

"It's a game. You could get hurt. And then you won't be a surgeon. Have you
thought of that?"

"I could get hit by a truck walking across the street."

"Tell me three Jewish men that ever became famous playing football."

"Benny Friedman."

"Yes?"

"Sid Luckman."

"Yes?" I hesitated. "One more, smart guy."

"And me."

He laughed.

"I'll do it. You watch, Pop."

He'd been gone thirty years. I was a doctor, not a football player. But I was playing defense for all I was worth. Frankly, I was a little tired of it. I wanted to reach out and hug the grandfather who had been gone for thirty years. I wanted to tell him what I was doing. I wanted him to know that it had to do with healing. And justice.

On the ground at Metro in Detroit, I made my way off the plane and into the terminal. People rushed down the tacky, narrow concourse. It was crowded and hot. Airports are a foretaste of hell. By the time I had exited the airport, retrieved my car, and hit the Ford Freeway, I'd had it. This legal day-tripping stuff was making me nuts. To top it off, I'd returned just in time to hit rush hour, road crews, and angry motorists. Detroit has two seasons, winter and road construction.

Stopped in traffic, I searched my Wagoneer for CDs. I needed "Side by Side" with Johnny Hodges and Duke Ellington. A few minutes into Hodges' sax against Ellington's improvs, I started to relax.

Eventually I was in the northwest 'burbs, coming home to the hills and lakes. It was beautiful. A hard, November sky made everything clear. Forget that shyster and his cheap tricks, I thought. Ellenby was just another opportunist making a living off people's misery. Frank Connely didn't seem much better. He gave me the creeps.

At the townhouse, I slipped the key in the door, opened it, and stepped inside the foyer. No noise. Everything the way I'd left it. The scent of flowers on the Baker side table in the entrance hall. Sarouk runner on the cut limestone floor. Coat hung on the gentleman's stand—metal art deco, Jordan's touch. Not, of course, that my values were materialistic. My appreciation was purely aesthetic.

I heard a keyboard clack in the library. I hadn't expected her home this early, especially on a Friday. The U.S. Attorney's staff usually wrapped things up and moved the staff meeting to Galligan's or the Rhinoceros. But here she was. I turned the corner and entered the oak paneled room. Jordan looked up from the computer, swallowing a shriek. A hand jerked to her cheek.

"You scared me!" she said. "I didn't expect you until tonight."

She was blushing. She looked back to the computer, punched a few keys, hard, as if in anger. The main menu flashed on screen. I'd surprised her before. I knew she hated it. And I had no gift to propitiate her. What do you buy in Dellsburg, Pennsylvania? I was going to apologize when she turned toward me, opened her mouth, and tilted her head, ready to say something. What? I looked into the two most beautiful eyes I had ever known. Jordan Dalkind, my friend and confidant, the only woman I had ever truly loved.

"Disappointed it's me? Expecting someone else?"

"No, but you scared me. Don't do that." She glanced back at the computer, then lifted her five-nine frame from the chair, came over and wrapped her arms around my neck. Her hair flowed against my cheek. She had wonderful, auburn hair. An auburn-haired beauty. Auburn in autumn. There was a jazz piece there, I thought.

"Rough ride?" she said.

"Define rough." Tension was easing out of my body. She pulled herself closer, inched up, lifting her chest against mine. The thought of a ride was getting more appealing. I told her about the propjet. "It starts its ascent," I said, "the wings feel like they're going to fall off the plane, and I think I'll never see you again."

Over her shoulder, I looked at the computer.

"But here you are," she said. "Was it grueling in court?"

She was online.

I ran an index finger down her spine. "Trying to save on long distance calls?"

"Office work," she said. "We're investigating Internet crime. I'm checking out chat rooms. Seeing what they consist of." She let herself down and smiled up at me. "So. How was it?"

"Bad case. The doc should get off with no cause. It's hard to blame a physician for something out of his control. The patient died ten days after surgery."

"What happened?"

"What's your screen name?" I said.

"What do you care? Are you going to write to me?"

"I want to meet you in a chat room," I said. "I want to have a chat."

"Actual love is better than virtual. I'm a traditional woman."

"I love tradition." I lifted her up and kissed her three times; two short, one long. It was our code.

But she wanted to talk shop. Obediently, I told her how the patient bled to death. The plaintiff's attorney claimed the surgeon placed the suture in the wrong place. Turned out she had taken ibuprofen.

"So?"

"Causes bleeding. I think that's why she died."

"What did the defense say?"

"We proved the case pretty well. The plaintiff's attorney gave me a hard time, especially about what happened at St. Vincent's."

"You were proven innocent."

"Nothing is sacred in a courtroom, especially reputations. You know that.

He wanted to cast doubt. The judge stopped him. But he made his point. I was almost an unscrupulous character—such as the ones you meet in chat rooms."

She was traditional in a modern kind of way. A top trial attorney in the federal prosecutor's office. Go figure. All my nightmarish dealings with the legal profession, and I had fallen for an attorney. Without her, I might never have pulled myself out of the muck.

I went upstairs and showered. Jordan went back to her computer. We had all night. No rush. And then the weekend. So much to look forward to.

Over wine in the kitchen, I glanced at the mail. A letter from T. Pearson. Todd Pearson. A blast from the past. One of Jordan's old flames. He was introduced to me at a party once as an ex-quarterback from Stanford. I'm suspicious of people who need to be ex-anything. It tells me nothing good has happened since. And he wore his ex like a laurel, like a whole pile of laurels.

Or could I be honest with myself and say I was jealous?

I got hurt playing football in college. A broken nose, a concussion. Something changed for me after that. On game days, I still got excited, but my excitement was tempered with realism.

Since then, I always felt I was holding something back. A scar, an anger that ran deep and ugly inside my brain, deeper than the small, white line on the bridge of my nose. The slightest thing dredged up this anger. Like Todd Pearson.

Jordan appeared in the kitchen doorway. "Reading my mail?"

"Tired of your chatroom?"

"Ben?"

"All right, yes," I said. "Only when it's from someone who has an emotional attachment to you."

"Had, Ben. Had an attachment. He's president of Stanford's Alumni Association. I'm on the committee for academic endowment."

"How petty can I be?" I said.

Jordan poured herself some apple juice. Odd, she'd usually have wine. She was a good sport. She rarely piled on. She didn't need to.

"I had an academic endowment," I said. "It was called a summer job."

"Tell that to a youngster in the inner city who has to raise thirty-grand for a year's room and board."

"Not everyone has to go to Stanford."

"Denying qualified students' opportunities for lack of money is short-sighted for the whole society." She swirled her juice. I had to admit—I liked this lawyerly repartee. But only with her.

"Enter Todd Pearson," I said.

"Do I detect a trace of resentment?"

"I'm too unscrupulous to be resentful, and I'm too old to be jealous." It was a lie. When it came to her, I was jealous. Or just insecure.

"You know, Dailey, when I was in college, I always wanted to shack up with one of those guys that went to med school. Men of science. In control of their emotions."

"We're just as corrupt as everyone else."

"Maybe, but I'll settle for the one that's here," she replied.

"Is that a cue?"

She swirled her juice again and looked down into the glass. "Would you be mad if I said no?"

"Not mad. Just disappointed," I said.

"I just don't feel there right now. You know?"

No, I didn't know. Twenty minutes in the house and I had already screwed up. Too anxious.

Or was there something else?

I take boxing three times a week at a small studio in a suburban mall. Al, the guy I work out with, keeps telling me I could be a contender. I tell him, yeah, if I was fighting in a nursing home. One of my friends, Jerry Brooks, works out there too. Two over-the-hill ex-jocks. I told Al we'd have a match, invite everyone to come. We'll call it the Geritol Brawl in the Mall.

So I'm semi-tough. But it doesn't make any difference. I have no defense against Jordan. The year and a half we had been together, she had thrown me more than a few times. She kept me off balance.

And she knew it.

She asked me big questions when I was defenseless. Not the marriage question. We never discussed that. How could a universe expand forever? How much insurance did I have? Hadn't I ever thought about having kids? Shouldn't we drop everything and sail for a year? What did I think about at the moment I cut a patient open?

I wondered what was coming as I came downstairs the next morning. I heard Jordan rummaging around in the refrigerator. Relaxing over the paper, I'd be an easy target. Pay attention, I thought to myself. I poured coffee and eyed the front page of the sports section. It seemed there was a football team, down the road in Ann Arbor, and in another week, a huge game.

"Lose something?" I asked.

"Almond rice shake."

An almond rice shake at 7:30 a.m.? Strange new appetite. A suspicion crossed my mind. Nature abhors a vacuum, and accidents did happen. First, my overture rebuffed last night. Call that a mood swing. Now, an odd hankering. No, no, no, it couldn't be *that*.

"Six bottles, all vanilla," she said, her head still inside the pantry. Something toppled over. She swore. "I want the almond one."

"Pull up a wheat germ and sit down."

"Seriously. I was talking to Jan at work. She says a rice shake is one of the most complete foods you can eat. She eats three or four a day with granola. No cholesterol."

"I thought that's what Cap'n Crunch was made for."

"Here," she said. "Rice shake. I said healthy, not heathen."

I took the bottle from her, opened it, and handed it back. It was too early for me. And I was still suspicious. Had I missed any signs?

"See this?" she said. "A rice shake has two hundred calories and only four grams of fat. Add it to granola, and it's great. There are lots of great foods we all ignore."

"Like what?"

"Olives for one."

"I know they're good. Especially in martinis."

"Don't laugh it off. My grandmother said it kept her skin smooth. She lived to be ninety-two." She took a swig of her shake, poured the rest in her cereal, and then sipped some coffee. I gagged slightly.

"Uncivilized," I said.

"Doctors have the worst nutrition. I don't think they teach you anything about it in medical school."

"No. That's not true. I just slept through the class."

Without warning, the sudden mood swing.

"Do you ever get lonely when I'm away?"

Here we go, I thought. "Yeah, sometimes. How about you?"

"Most of the time. That's why I was thinking." She poured coffee. Coffee and granola. Granola and lifestyle. It was too horrible.

"You were thinking."

"I'd like to have something between us," she said earnestly.

Marriage I could handle. Maybe. I'd failed miserably the first time. I didn't want to ruin things with Jordan. Or was this about children? I'd never had children with my first wife. She didn't want them. Or was it me she hadn't wanted? I got up from the table and went over to Jordan. She lay her head on my shoulder. Auburn hair. The autumn of your life. Not yet! I could do this. Be a husband or a father. Whatever she wanted. It was something new, something that would bind us forever.

I kissed her cheek. "Something between us?"

"Like maybe a puppy."

A puppy. Was she kidding? I hung on, tightened my hug, tried to hide my surprise, or disappointment. Or whatever it was. "A puppy?"

"We need something, Ben. Something animated. Something wild."

"A puppy." Who said we need something?

"I knew you wouldn't mind."

She spun free of my arms, swirled around, and laughed. Animation. I liked that part. I opened my mouth to say something stupid. *It's a big responsibility.* But it wasn't that. It was a damned nuisance. It wasn't what I had expected.

She'd done it again!

Jordan slipped into the back room. I could hear her laughing back there. It was Jan's fault. Wheat germ. A puppy. I was going to have to talk to Jan. I sat back down, pulled up the sports section. We had to talk about this. Something between us, yes. Definitely. But a dog? Definitely not a dog.

"Ben," she said.

"Look, Jordan," I began in my most reasonable tone.

"Say hello to Buck," she said happily.

She had a furry little ball cradled in her hands. The look on her face was, well, childlike. Irresistible. The ball yipped and squirmed. It would pee and chew and keep us up at night. It would have melted Ebenezer Scrooge's heart. She rushed across the kitchen to me.

Something between us.

"What is he or she?" I asked, petting the ball's head.

"A yellow Lab. One of the smartest breeds."

Then the dog was in my lap, licking my face. And the phone was ringing. Little licks, sharp teeth. Jordan, I thought, I love you but. The phone rang and rang. He liked me. It was definitely a he. And I was insanely jealous. I handed the ball off to Jordan and went for the phone. Jordan cradled the dog, nuzzling it. There went the weekend, and then some.

I got to the phone on the fifth ring.

Chapter 2

"**B**EN, YOU'LL NEVER BELIEVE THIS." It was Bruce Sanderson, regional manager of Coastal Life Insurance. Bruce was merely hyper on a good day. Discommoded in any way, he got apoplectic. I could hear a manic whine in his voice. This was something big. "Ben? You there?"

"Good morning, Bruce."

Buck was spinning his wheels, running circles on the kitchen tile. My new son. I wasn't yet sure how I felt about him. At least he wasn't a cat.

"That case you testified in? We lost it, Ben. Big time."

"Dellsburg?"

"Dellsburg's down the tubes. I mean it, Ben. It's down the goddam tubes."

I scooped up Buck and held him under my arm. His tail whacked me against the ribs. Maybe I could get used to him over time.

"It was a slam-dunk, Bruce. The ibuprofen caused the hemorrhage. The doctor should have gotten off with a no-cause. Open and shut."

"Connely caved on the stand. After you left, he got up and testified. He said he thought he had screwed up. He broke down. It's going to cost us millions." He muttered something, and the phone line crackled. He was eating. I'd talked to him only two or three times when he wasn't eating. Maybe it was Pavlovian; take a bite of cheeseburger, call Dailey. "I can't believe it," he moaned. "He just went to pieces."

"What's for breakfast, Bruce?"

"Thought he'd screwed up. Those were his words."

"Tell me it's something healthy." Like wheat germ, I mouthed to Jordan.

"Danish." I heard him take a bite. "Danish with apricot. These people, I tell you. They know I don't like apricot. We've been over this a hundred times. Just once I'd like to find a peach Danish." He was in the deli next to his office. He hated them; they hated him. It was a marriage of inconvenience. I heard something clatter on the tabletop.

"How am I supposed to eat at a time like this?"

"Forget it, Bruce. Sometimes you have to pay one. Make up for Dellsburg on the next case, on your next investment."

"It's not that simple. We have to go to our secondary carrier on this one. They're mad as hell. Too many bad cases. Too many bad risk docs. This one could take us down."

Buck's legs were pumping. I set him on the floor, and he spun out. He scooted between Jordan's feet and slid into the door to the back room. "I feel for you, Bruce, but I'm only a doctor."

"You're not just a doctor, Ben. Remember the Burkinette and Scotten cases? You're the best damn investigator we've got."

Reminding me of two near-death experiences was not great strategy. And what did he mean, "we've got?" I was an independent operator. A lone wolf. No one had me. Except Jordan. And, what the hell, Buck.

"Ben?"

"I have to go, Bruce."

"Listen, Ben. Just for a second, will you listen?"

"I'm a doctor. I practice medicine. The investigating business was a sideline. I'm retired."

"It won't take much. Just a little review of the case." Buck was circling in the kitchen corner.

"Review?"

"The doctor changed his story. In deposition he said one thing, but on the stand he said something completely different. It was mind-boggling. It was like an emotional meltdown. There's something going on here. All I'm asking is look over the depositions again. Check him out. Then go back into retirement."

Buck lowered his little rear end to the floor.

"Okay, I'll think about it."

"I'll send you the file."

"I said I'd think about it. I have to go."

"Ben!"

"Enjoy the Danish. Talk to you later."

I hung up. It was too late. Buck was relieved. He scratched the floor, covering his dirt, at least theoretically. Then he took off running, tail wagging. I was too late. Just once I'd like to be early.

Jordan came back into the kitchen and shook her head

"He'll be house broken in two weeks. The vet promised me."

"Just like me, huh?"

"Darling, the day you get trained will be the day I streak during the Ohio State vs. Michigan game."

"I can't wait."

"Who was on the phone?"

"Bruce." I watched the corners of her mouth go down.

"Why do you talk with him? Trouble flows from him like a barrel over Niagara."

"I feel as if I owe him. He was the only one who would give me work when I needed it."

"Your sense of obligation has almost cost you your life twice."

"Emphasize the almost, please."

"I don't like his tactics. Roundabout investigations. Innuendo. When my people investigate, we go at it directly."

"This is just a malpractice case that went bad."

"Just be careful."

I hadn't learned my lesson. Yet.

I GOT DOWN TO MY OFFICE AT ST. VINCENT'S a little earlier than usual on Monday. The Connely case was making me feel bad. It resurrected the same odd emotions I'd had when Jimmy Scotten died. The lawsuit, the disgrace, but most of all poor Jimmy, lying cold and white on the dissecting table with the yellow tag on his big toe. I don't think I'll ever get over that sight.

After my reinstatement and the settlement, my practice had been altered. Three days a week, mornings only. Life is too short; I now focused more on my first love, voice work. I'd always enjoyed music, playing with Sid down at The Pipeline Club, so studying the larynx came natural to me.

That's why I ran a voice clinic. Mondays were my day to work on the neurological stuff, especially spasmodic dysphonia. A queer disease, uncontrollable movements of the vocal cord producing a halting and unintelligible voice. It was thought to be a psychiatric disease until some smart neurologist found similarities between it and other movement disorders. There was never any treatment for it, until the discovery that injecting into the vocal cord a purified toxin from the bacteria that causes botulism would control the symptoms. It works great. The only problem is that it wears off, requiring repeat injections.

I had been lucky. Before my problems, I had done research on the technique. When the FDA approved it, I was one of the few people in the country who knew how to do it. Which is why my Monday waiting room regularly had patients waiting for their injection.

"We've got a full morning, Dr. Dailey," my nurse, Randy Phillips, interjected, snapping me back into reality. "The first one is from New York. He has to catch a plane at noon."

"No problem."

I got up from my desk and walked into the first examining room.

A forty-year-old man in a black, collared, knit shirt got up from the examining chair. He was trim and athletic, standing over six feet, with big shoulders.

"Steve Waring, Dr. Dailey." He spoke in a halting, somewhat high-pitched voice.

"Ben Dailey. Nice to see you." I stuck out my hand and shook his. I like shaking hands. It tells me a lot about the other person. In this case, he had a firm handshake, a little sweaty in the palm. Not unusual for someone about to get stuck in the neck with a needle.

Waring sat back down, and I started my usual dialogue. By this time Randy had the microphone in place, with the patient hooked up to the video machine. I asked him some routine questions about his loss of voice. While we talked, I studied him for a moment. Gray hair at the temples. High cheek bones, an aquiline nose that gave him a patrician look, and dark, haughty eyes.

As he answered, I could detect the tremor in his voice that garbled his words.

"I wonder if you wouldn't mind singing for me?" I asked.

He looked puzzled.

"Any song you like. People with spasmodic dysphonia are usually able to sing, though not talk. It will confirm my diagnosis."

He smiled for a moment. "Okay, you asked for it." He sang a stanza from "Kansas City." His voice was strong, almost with a country western twang.

I laughed. "Fifties stuff, huh?"

"It was the first song that came to my mind."

"Well, you certainly fit into the spasmodic category. If you'd like, we can do the injection today."

"That's what I'm here for."

The first thing I did was a videostroboscopy. Record the view of the larynx for posterity. Interesting. Pretty standard test for a patient with spasmodic dysphonia: only a small discoloration on the right vocal cord.

After anesthetizing him, I attached the flexible laryngoscope to the television camera and passed it through his nose. Reaching the back of his throat, I angled the light source down onto his vocal cords. Suddenly, the cords came into view.

"Okay, Randy, take hold of the scope, and I'll get the needle."

I picked up the syringe with the needle attached to an electromyography unit. Then I felt for the soft spot beneath his Adam's apple and inserted the needle through the neck. I looked up on the video screen. There, poking into his airway, like the Alien, was the needle tip. I angled the tip up into his vocal cords and confirmed I was in the right place by asking him to say "eeee." As he did, a crackling of electrical activity came over the screen, indicating I was in the right place. I injected 1.25 units of Botox into each side. After the last drop went in, I pulled out the needle and the scope.

"All done, Mr. Waring. Call Randy next week and let her know how you are doing. I plan to see you back in three to four months."

He thanked me. I was just about to talk music with him before he left, when Randy interrupted.

"A Mr. Brooks on the line for you, Dr. Dailey."

"Randy, tell him that I'll meet him down at Sid's tomorrow. I'll be there around two." By the time I finished, Waring was already headed toward the desk.

When I came into the library at the townhouse that afternoon, a present was waiting for me. Before Jordan had left for the office, to defend the people against chat rooms, she'd brought in the package and left it on the foyer floor. A huge stack of papers from Bruce. Mostly things I had seen before: Connely's deposition, his curriculum vitae, a pile of hospital records. Transcripts of his testimony at trial.

I got a mug of coffee and settled into an easy chair. I glanced at Connely's CV, threw it aside and began shuffling through the transcript. Buck was asleep in his crate in the back room. We were all safe for the moment.

So, our doctor hadn't stood up to Ellenby's onslaught. Halfway through his testimony I read the cross-examination.

Q: *"Do you always suture the tonsil?"*
A: "Not usually. There was a fair amount of bleeding at the time of surgery."
Q: *"A fair amount of bleeding. Would that make it difficult to see?"*
A: "It can. Yes, I guess I did have a little bit of trouble."
Q: *"If you can't see, how do you know where you put the suture?"*
A: "You do it by feel. You see with your fingers. Ask any physician."
Q: *By feel. But what if you feel wrong?"*
A: "You don't. I mean, I suppose you could, but I thought I could see."
Q: *"Thought. That's not much to go on, Dr. Connely, when it comes to someone's life. Is it, Doctor?"*
A: "At times like that, it's all we have."
Q: *"But this is life and death, Dr. Connely. Life and death. If you were unable to see, and I mean see with your eyes, you could have put that suture in the wrong place, couldn't you?"*
A: "Possibly, but not likely."

Q: "But it could happen, couldn't it?"

A: "Yes, but..."

Q: *"Just answer the question. The wound is filled with blood. By your own admission there was a fair amount of bleeding. It obstructs your view. You put a suture in. You don't know exactly where that suture is, do you?"*

A: "I suppose that's correct."

Q: *"Could you have put a suture into this patient's carotid artery?"*

A: "I suppose it could have happened..."

Q: *"Thank you, Doctor."*

It could have happened. That was all Ellenby needed. It was a foot in the door. He could build a case around, "I suppose it could have happened." A doctor who had been coached properly, a doctor with a little legal savvy, could have helped himself. He would have said he was too cautious to let that happen. He would have said that in his hands it wasn't a risk.

He could have shut Ellenby right up.

I pictured Connely on the stand. Perspiration glowing on his forehead, neck bulging above his shirt collar. Maybe he had just choked. Maybe it was just that simple. But then again, maybe it wasn't.

AT ABOUT FOUR THAT AFTERNOON I called Craig Lasky in Philadelphia near Dellsburg. He was part of my medical, old-boy network. I'd worked with him on a few committees for the Academy, and we'd had a couple of dinners together. Late ones. The kind where, if you're lucky, the showboating stops, doctors become humans, and colleagues become friends. Lasky was refreshing. He could actually stop talking about his practice.

He was surprised when he came to the phone. "Where have you been, Ben?"

"Self-imposed sabbatical."

"I read about your research, but I haven't seen you at the meetings."

"You will know me by my works.'"

"Well, what really counts is dinner. Remember Monterey?"

We ran down the menu together, and the wines, and the waves on the beach we wandered onto afterward, the jazz in a hotel bar. The old-dude blues in the morning. It was good to talk to him again.

"So, what can I do for you?"

"Have you heard of a doc in your area, named Frank Connely?"

"I know Frank. He practices at one of the hospitals I work out of. They call him 'The Apostle.' The other docs hung that moniker on him after his wife died. He found religion."

"What happened to the wife?"

"She died from an accident on a plane. I can't remember the details. All I know is that Frank and his wife were returning on a flight from an anniversary trip to the Bahamas. You know what happens. People suffer a loss, they change their lives in radical ways. He turned to God."

And he'd done it in a big way. It wasn't enough for him to convert, Lasky said. He wanted everyone to see the light. God saved him so he could save others. He left Christian conversion material in his waiting room. Patients, hospital personnel, parking lot attendants. No one was safe.

I shifted in my seat. The computer was on. Buck was now sleeping between my feet. He'd had lunch, played a bit of chew-the-shoe, and was now resting before an evening of activity.

I asked Lasky if he knew about the malpractice suit.

"Sure," he said. "It makes sense in a twisted way. He probably felt guilty as hell about that patient dying. So he gives the money to the plaintiff. 'Give everything away and follow me.' It's God's work."

Wind was coming out of the west, sweeping leaves across the lawn to the neighbor's. A good system. I could picture Buck romping in the leaves. "What else can you tell me about him?"

"One of the toughest men I've ever met. You'd see him change in the surgeon's lounge, all rippling muscles, a six-pack. He made the rest of us look pretty flimsy. Word is he used to play football in college."

The Connely I'd seen seemed a little more sybaritic than Lasky's description, but then I had never seen him in the locker room.

"So he worked out at one time."

"Tough, Ben. Aggressively tough. He wouldn't back down from anyone or anything. I saw him once in the emergency room. A family member questioned him over the care of his daughter. It got a little noisy. I happened to pass by and saw Connely turn on this guy. I mean turn on him. The look in his eyes was something I won't forget. He's complex, Ben. In a schizoid kind of way."

"So a lawyer wouldn't have scared him in those days."

"Are you kidding? No one messed with Frank Connely. Now look at him. Docile as a lamb, never a word. All due to his wife's death."

"Gone a little flabby, too."

"His mind's on spiritual matters," Craig countered.

"Anything else you can tell me?"

"What's this about, Ben?"

"Nothing, really. I testified for his insurance company. They had a few questions about him."

"And they use you for information."

"You might say that," I said. I didn't feel like going into my second career. Because it wasn't a second career. It was an accident. Just a prolonged mistake, one that had nearly cost me my life. I was no detective.

"There was one other thing," he said. He'd lowered his voice. I pulled a pencil from the drawer. He said, "Connely had a rep with the ladies. Way back, I mean. Before he saw the light."

"A rep?"

"A fling, Ben. At least one that's definite. Maybe others. The one we know about, he was fooling around with a hospital employee. This was a few years ago. It happened, then he broke it off."

"What happened to her?" *Girlfriend*, I wrote on a pad.

"She left her job. Then left town, I gather."

"And Connely stayed on. He was rehabilitated?"

"Yes."

"Would you have a name?"

"You'd have to check with someone at the hospital."

I wrote, *Girlfriend + Frank Connely. Wife's death. Finds God.*

I told Lasky I might see him at the meetings next fall. He was a good man. I'd enjoy another evening with him - with a little less wine and a little more jazz. He said he'd be looking for me.

"Don't just say it, Ben," he urged. "Do it. Come, let us know what you're doing."

I said I would. I tried to sound convincing. Then I hung up the phone and looked at my notes. So Connely had choked on the stand to atone for his sins. He must have something big to make up for.

But what?

CHAPTER 3

Next morning, I drove through a cold, Michigan drizzle to Coastal Insurance. I was met by Sheila Pryzbycki. In the district office of America's forty-fourth largest insurance company, her presence was nothing if not matriarchal. She was a big woman with big hair, a dyed-blonde coif curled and piled with exquisite care.

She had her hand in a purse big enough to fit her head inside. She didn't look up from her search. "Back so soon, Ben?"

"It's nice to be wanted."

"I sent you your check."

There was a distinctive fragrance in the air. I stepped closer to the desk and breathed it in. Yes, Doublemint gum. I pictured her with an identical twin in a TV commercial, bows tied in their abundant hair, laughing and folding sticks of gum into their mouths.

"Didn't you get it?" she demanded, still not looking up.

"Money can't buy you love, Sheila."

She glanced up, gave me a blank look. Then she blinked. "That was a song."

"You should try out for Jeopardy, Sheila."

"You really think so?"

I nodded. "Is he in?"

She motioned with head and hair in the direction of his office. "Eating lunch."

I might have guessed.

"Was he expecting you?"

"He must have been," I said.

Propped up on both elbows, Bruce Sanderson was leaning over his desk, eating a fried egg and cheddar cheese sandwich on a salt bagel. Food was a deep comfort to him, a reliable refuge from the insurance business.

"Sit down," he said.

"Ever heard of the Atkins diet?"

"My grandfather in Kentucky smoked Luckies, drank Jack Daniels, and had Crisco for lunch. He lived to be ninety-two." Jordan's grandmother had also lived to ninety-two, but she'd done it on olives. Would Crisco and olives together take me to one-hundred-and-eighty-four?

"Anecdotes, Bruce, should not be confused with science. But it's not you I'm worried about. You're going to kill everyone who watches you."

His underchin wobbled a little as he laughed. He said, "Right now, the only dead person I'm worried about is me, if Coastal has to pay the settlement on this case. Tell me something good."

"There's no witness so terrible as the conscience of a man's heart."

He took a long drink of iced tea, eyeing me down the length of the bottle. "Huh?"

"Polybius. He was a Greek philosopher."

"You read too much. I can't eat and think at the same time."

"Connely lost his wife. I don't mean to upset you, but it was some kind of airplane accident." Bruce shook his head and locked on the sandwich. "He was filled with remorse after her death. It isn't all that uncommon. Someone you love dies, you live, you feel responsible. The sins of the world became his."

"Religious guy?"

"After the fact."

Bruce took a drink of tea. "So, ridden with guilt, and mentally unstable, he finds religion and confesses to doing something wrong."

"That's about it."

"It sounds too pat."

"Maybe he snapped," I said.

"I can't swallow it." He set the last of his sandwich down and wiped his chin. He took a deep breath and continued. "This case is going to cost us ten million dollars. I'm supposed to assume he just lost his cool? Nope. Sorry. I need more facts."

"Ten million." I whistled. "I thought it was two and a half."

"They added punitive damages. Hospitals have deep pockets."

"How about a lie detector test?"

"Can't do that without the patient's consent."

I told him about my conversation with Craig Lasky, about Connely's philandering. Bruce turned in his chair and lifted a leg up to rest on an open drawer. He leaned back in his chair and looked out the window for a moment, his chin resting on his chest. It looked like napping posture.

"Talk with Dr. Connely. I'll try to find out the girlfriend's name," he said. "We need to find out what she knows."

"We?"

He reached over, picked up the last bite of sandwich, and tossed it in his mouth. He chomped on it happily, revived and restored. "Find both of them. There's got to be some reason behind all this, Ben."

"I'm a doctor, not a gumshoe."

"Don't be so self-effacing. You did more with that Burkinette case than ten professionals could have."

"And almost found myself in the morgue."

He smiled. Or maybe he was licking his teeth behind those sealed lips. "If something happens to you," he promised, "I'll get the company to donate to the charity of your choice."

"How much?" I was sick of negotiating.

"A generous sum."

"The Stanford Alumni Association?"

"Done."

"Just one thing," I said. "I'll talk to Connely. But no threats, no confrontations. I want to help this guy."

"Why's that?"

"I've been sued. It's the worst thing a physician can go through. Part of me is on his side." I remembered how long it had taken me to vindicate myself, to restore my reputation. I hoped that wouldn't be Connely's fate.

Bruce scooped up the few crumbs still lying on the wrapping paper and dropped them in his wastebasket. "Check out the girlfriend. You can be objective about her, can't you?"

"I'll try, Bruce."

CHAPTER 4

A FOOLISH CONSISTENCY IS THE HOBGOBLIN OF LITTLE MINDS. One of my professors used to quote Emerson's proverb to me every time I stopped thinking. I thought about that on my flight to Philly. Why was I doing this? Out of a sense of duty? By the time I was in the rental car and heading to Dellsburg it was too late. Fatigue was setting in, so I decided to take the first motel I saw. It was a Motel 6 along the freeway in Dellsburg.

I assumed Sanderson would appreciate the economy. It was a truckers' motel. In the windows of the attached restaurant hung enlarged, laminated photos of trucker-sized servings of eggs and potatoes. Next to breakfast were shots of the 38-wheeler buffet. In the motel office were posters of trucks, calendars of trucks. On the entrance just inside the front door lay a mud mat shaped like a truck.

It was hot in the office. About eighty degrees. The kid at the desk wore a black, pocket t-shirt. He had a pudgy face and skin the color of milk. When he glanced up at me, I saw a twitchy, studded eyebrow and pierced lip. Maybe he was just saying no to trucks. I was too tired to think much about his incongruity with his surroundings. I asked for a room upstairs, hoping to avoid the noise. No problem, he said, shaking his head.

From the parking lot, the sound of truck engines penetrated the motel walls. It was a convocation of diesels. Trucks arriving. Trucks starting, idling, revving. None of them seemed to be leaving.

I dropped on the hard bed, switched on a light, and called Jordan. No answer. I watched some local news and called Sanderson. I asked him if he'd gotten a contact at Dellsburg Baptist Hospital. I'd wakened him. He was groggy and cleared his throat several times. He'd have the name for me in the morning.

He complained about how late it was and said I was overzealous, which, now that he thought of it, was exactly what he wanted me to be. By the time I hung up, he was wide awake and hungry.

After Sanderson, I tried Jordan a few more times. Nothing. It was midnight when I gave up. I looked around the nondescript motel room and wondered what she was doing. Something told my fragile ego that I needed to be back home. What now, my love? I found an extra pillow in the closet, lay down, and instantly fell asleep.

I dreamed I was in the stadium tunnel. I knew the dream immediately, feeling myself take on that weird vantage point you undergo in your dreams, both spectator and participant. Someone beat on my shoulder pads. It was Jerry, my pal on the hamburger squad. We stood next to each other all season, on the sidelines. He was fourth string quarterback, and I played both ways, tight end and defensive end. The team surged toward the end of the tunnel. I know what's next—the explosion of light and sound as we take the field. It's November in the Big House. It's a hundred thousand screaming people.

The dream tumbles forward, answerable only to its own logic. There's a coin toss disappearing into the air, becoming the high arc of a spiral pass that lands in a player's outstretched hands, hands that multiply and push into our huddle for a halftime cheer just before we take the field again. We're losing. Nothing goes right. I'm dizzy in the dream, rolling on the field, feeling sick to my stomach. Red jerseys everywhere. There's a roaring in my ears that I can't shake. Through the roar I hear my name, as if spoken down a length of pipe, and I'm up and running across the field. My feet are leaden. I can't run a straight line. Finally, I reach the huddle. On the bench the coach is an inch tall. He motions a play, telling me something.

He's yelling at me.

What is it?

Wolf right, zone.

I hear the words but don't recognize them. We line up. What am I supposed to do? I've waited four years to get here. I'm defensive end, six-three, two-fifteen, too small for this red wall that's about to collapse on top of me. I take my three-point stance, looking up and down the line. I see stringy, blonde hair beneath a helmet. Dull eyes lock on mine. He says he's going to take my head off. Next to him, another monster with venomous eyes glaring beneath bushy eyebrows. I see his mouth contort, forming words. My stomach is inside out. I feel like I'm going to tip over, fall forward flat on my face.

The quarterback starts his call, bobs his head. Suddenly, my head clears and the game speeds up. I know what to do. My key is the running back.

Trap left!

The linebacker's voice. I move to fill the hole.

The center hits me. I raise my hands up.

Horns blaring.

The running back is coming, knees lifting and dropping. Horns, again, blasting in my ears, and I'm swimming back into consciousness. Not yet! I think. I fight it, trying to stay focused on the game to see what would happen. I've never got this far into it, but I can't will myself back into the game. The horn is too loud. It must be end of the quarter. The end of something.

A truck horn blasting, right outside my window. That's it.

I'm awake.

I roll over, wet with perspiration, my heart pounding. In bed, alone. I roll on my back and look up at the ceiling. I hear the drone of an engine, just outside. It was the game I got hurt in, last game of the year. I got creamed defending that trap play. I know it's the game I've lost all these years.

THE ALARM CLOCK WENT OFF AT SIX. I looked out the window. The beast that had wakened me was still parked outside my room, engine running. I got up, showered. I love truck stops. Honest food and plainspoken people. I had the trucker's special—fried eggs, hash browns, and coffee.

I called Jordan again. She was home, of course, at 7 a.m. I wanted to ask her where she'd been last night, but I held back from being that transparent. So we talked about Buck, her acting as if nothing at all had happened. Maybe nothing had. I told her I would be back soon.

Bruce had arranged a meeting at ten o'clock. The first thing we needed to do was to find out who Connelly's ex-girlfriend was. I'm not usually punctual, but this morning I got to Delaware Baptist early. It was Dellsburg's only hospital, a new facility, built on the hills overlooking the Delaware River. A storybook hospital in the suburbs. This scenario I found myself in was beginning to feel like a soap opera. Except the ten million dollars was real. And so was the death.

My first appointment was at Human Resources. The director had a cubby-hole office in the administrative wing. Her name was Frances Cobbleton. She was a tall woman with short, brown hair. She had the chaos-friendly look of someone who lives with too much paperwork. She was sitting at her desk when I walked in. She peered at me over two piles of applications.

"Regulations, affirmative action, sex discrimination, Americans for Disability," she said. "You name it, I got it."

"And now me," I said. "You thought you might get off easy today."

"You want to know about a personal relationship that Frank Connely had with an employee when she was employed here. Is that right?"

"Right."

"In connection with the lawsuit?"

"Right."

"I don't see a connection," she said. "And furthermore, I don't see how it's going to help matters. Dr. Connely lost." She pointed at a fat file on top of a cabinet. "Nothing in there will change that fact."

The lawsuit had shaken the hospital. It was their first. And a bad one. Moreover, Frank Connely seemed to be a regular pillar of the hospital community. After what had happened to him, he'd made a remarkable change in his life.

"You mean after his affair?"

"Yes," she said. "And then he lost his wife tragically."

"Can you dismiss an employee for an affair with a doctor, sexual harassment law being what it is?"

I saw a muscle wobble in her jaw. There was a limit to her appetite for chaos. She reached around, picked up the file, and handed it to me.

"This is her file. I've been instructed by Mr. Sherman to give this to you. You'll also find the Board of Trustees minutes."

I opened the file and read the name, Claudia Fraser. Mrs. Cobbleton laid a form on top of the documents.

"The hospital lawyers have asked that you sign this. You agree not to divulge any material herein, all deemed confidential."

I signed the form.

"I can't let the original file out of the office. You can sit in our conference room, copy it, and read through it, if you like. If you have any questions, we can talk."

I moved into the adjoining room, picked up the file, and started scanning it. Minutes of a meeting of the Board of Trustees with Frank Connely in attendance. He stated that he'd had a brief affair with Miss Fraser. When he'd tried to break it off, he claimed that she had threatened him with exposure, for "forcing her to perform certain acts." There was a break in the transcript.

Unseemly acts deleted.

Claudia Fraser had signed a document disavowing any connection between Dr. Connely and her letter of resignation. All pretty neat stuff. Dellsburg might be a small-town hospital, but they had big league lawyers. I stepped out into Mrs. Cobbleton's office.

"So it was blackmail. Dr. Connely was a victim. You succeeded in stopping her."

"Everyone felt for him. People make mistakes."

"Yes, they do."

"And blackmail is just plain dirty."

"There was a page missing from the record," I said.

"He was so humiliated." Her tone was not that of someone uttering a *non sequitur.*

"Why the missing page?"

"There's a legal agreement with the doctor not to divulge the information."

"And where's Claudia now?" Hadn't she had any legal advice at all?

"We've gotten requests for references from a number of places. She went to New York, then Toledo. I spoke to her there."

"About what?"

"She claims our response regarding her employment prevented her from working as a therapist. She's now an aide in a rehab unit."

"Did you prevent her from working as a therapist?"

"We didn't distribute any adverse employment records. There was an agreement between her and the hospital not to do so." She was fingering through Claudia's record.

"Did she work anywhere else?"

She held up a document. "East Coast Airlines. She interviewed for a job as a stewardess in a few years ago."

Nothing here to illuminate the motive of Frank Connely's self-immolation on the witness stand. Had he simply caved and that was that?

"Is there someone I could talk to about the missing page?"

"I was told to show you up to Mr. Sherman's office. He's executive vice-president. He answers to the board."

More bureaucrats, more questions.

ALDEN SHERMAN'S OFFICE WAS UP ONE FLOOR, in a corner of the building. It was carpeted, wood paneled, big enough for two or three important men. Lots of plaques, photos, appreciation litter. Sherman sat behind a polished wooden desk the size of a Chris-Craft. He had plenty of windows and a view. It was a beautiful view—the rolling, green hills of the Delaware River basin. In the long run what mattered more, patient care or administrators' perks? Delaware Baptist knew where to put its money.

Sherman was a little older than I. He had a round, cherubic face and was totally bald except for a tonsured fringe of hair. A modern-day Friar Tuck.

He motioned me to the leather chair tethered to the hull that was his desk.

"Nice view, isn't it?" he said, motioning toward the window.

"Currier and Ives couldn't have done better."

"Evidently they did some of their work in this area. Maybe right on the spot we're sitting." He studied me for a moment. We weren't here to talk about inspirational painting. Both of us knew that. He was a big man. He was probably used to getting his way. I was not a welcome interruption to his day. We held each other's look for two or three beats. It was an oddly eerie silence. Then, as if he'd flipped a switch, he turned on his administrator persona. With nearly audible unction he asked, "And what can I do for you?"

"I'd like to know why Frank Connely lost this case."

"Of course. I've spoken to Mr. Sanderson about your visit."

"Big settlement," I said.

"Yes, big," he nodded. "But we'll get through this."

I noticed the "we." It was the imperial "we." It was his captain-of-the-ship "we."

"Dr. Connely had some troubles," I said. "He strayed from the fold, you might say. And like others who have strayed, he paid a price."

Sherman touched his fingertips together and nodded. "Frank Connely made an excellent recovery," he said. "We at Delaware Baptist are both confident in his work and proud of his affirmation of the moral life."

I'll just bet you are, I thought. "One thing bothered me. What was in the page that was torn out of the employment record?"

"I'm not sure what you're talking about."

"What was Frank Connely accused of?"

He glanced down at his desk. There was nothing on it. No real evidence of work. On his computer screen, the star field simulation rushed at him. Something about that image of vacant outer space seemed dead on.

"He was accused of a variety of things. None of them provable. None relevant to Dr. Connely's unfortunate lawsuit."

"You know this for a fact?"

"Claudia Fraser recanted all of her testimony."

That didn't mean that nothing had happened, I nearly said aloud.

"'Forcing her to perform certain acts.' I believe that's the last phrase before the gap in the testimony."

"The woman was looking for a ticket to ride. She seduced Frank and then tried to blackmail him. We all assumed nothing had really happened, and that's what we found when truth came to light. She fell apart, and her story went to pieces. That was the end of it."

First Claudia Fraser falls apart. Then Frank Connely falls apart. People around here had a way of coming unglued.

"Do you think he gave up on this case because of his moral and religious inclinations?"

"What other reason could there be? The hospital is alarmed at the size of the settlement. But we're a God-fearing organization, dedicated to the work of Jesus Christ. Man is made in God's image, but man is not perfect. We'll pay the verdict and recognize that we need to do better."

Sherman stood up and smoothed the front of his jacket. He placed both hands on the empty desk. If I'd been the thin-skinned type, I might have suspected an effort to dismiss me.

"Has Dr. Connely ever had any other suits?" I asked.

Sherman shook his head. "It was the first and only action ever brought against him. He has an excellent reputation. Dr. Connely will continue to practice at this institution."

I got up and shook his hand. He wished me a speedy conclusion to my investigation. I said I hoped for the same, but that, like most physicians, I tended to take my time. I enjoyed the lessening of his smugness at the answer so much, I added that I prized thoroughness above all else.

At the front door at the hospital I lingered for a moment. The hospital's mission statement was embossed on a bronze plaque that hung on the wall. It read:

This is a Christian hospital serving our Lord Jesus Christ, who gave his life to cleanse our sins. We are committed to assist in his work of healing the sick by providing the very finest in health care.

So that's who the "we" was.

No wonder Claudia Fraser was gone.

SHERMAN'S CLAMMY HANDSHAKE AND SMARMY MANNER told me he was, at the very least, committing a sizable sin of omission. Maybe Frances Cobbleton too. I could have talked to her again, but it now it all seemed beside the point. The wagons were circled, the case was settled. I was cursing myself for coming here at all. All I had to do now was get through my interview with Connely, and I was out of here.

Frank Connely's office was on the top floor of the hospital's affiliated professional building. It looked out over the parking lot and the hospital beyond. When I walked in, there was one patient in the waiting area and three uniformed women behind the desk. His office was open for business. But was the doctor in?

A middle-aged woman with henna-dyed hair greeted me.

"I'm Jan Werner, Dr. Connely's office manager. His patient hours begin at eleven," she said. "Do you have an appointment?"

"No. I'm just here to speak with him."

I told her my name. She said that she was expecting me; Sherman had called and asked her to show me around. We walked back into the inner examining area, where I was handed off to the nurse, who introduced herself as Susan Werner. She was long limbed and willowy, with fine, brown hair knotted on top of her head. When we shook hands, I noticed a wedding band on her left hand. Also her alert eyes. I imagined that Connely loved her—for her efficiency and intelligence. She took me back to see the four examining rooms, an operating microscope, and a laboratory. On the wall going to his office was a photo of what I assumed was Connely and a nice-looking woman in her forties.

"That's the doctor with his wife, Mary Jane," Mrs. Werner said. "They were college sweethearts. She was a fine woman. It was all so tragic."

"Did he ever remarry?" I asked.

"No."

My next question was carefully worded. "Do you think he ever found any closure?"

Mrs. Werner was a pragmatic woman. "Well," she said briskly, "There was supposed to be a lawsuit against the airlines. I think there was a moderate settlement. He never talked about it. For a doctor, he lives a pretty frugal life. He still lives in the same house as before. He takes a few trips a year. Mostly fishing and skiing."

Just as she finished speaking, Connely walked up to us. He looked different in his starched, white coat than he had on the stand. A Ben Casey type. Big, impressive, ruggedly handsome. Bedroom eyes. Definitely a woman's man.

"Dr. Dailey. Nice to see you. I wanted to thank you personally for helping out on my malpractice case. Sorry it didn't turn out the way we had hoped. What brings you out here?" He spoke confidently—remorse didn't seem to be bowing him down.

His office was at the end of the gray carpeted hall. We walked in and sat down in a pair of cloth-covered Breuer chairs next to a blonde maple desk devoid of papers. A pen and pencil set and a peculiar paperweight in bronze that looked like a small pear with leaves on it. Next to the pen set was a photograph of Connely and the same pretty, middle-aged woman from the hallway at some ski resort.

Connely saw my stare.

"My wife," he said. "She died a few years ago." He didn't go into the details.

"I'm sorry."

"It was hard for a while, but with the help of the Lord, I'm back on the right track." He put his hands in front of him; big, wide hands with blonde hair matting the backs and knuckles of his hands. Offensive lineman's hands.

"I feel a little funny talking with you today. I was sued and lost a case myself. I know how you feel."

Connely nodded.

"I just couldn't face the Lord with the possibility that I had lied on the stand. It was possible that I'd made a mistake. I have to stand up to my failures. The only thing that matters to me now are my patients. Trying to do the best I can."

I glanced at a magazine rack, which held a couple of religious publications.

"Do you read the Lord's Word?"

"Probably not as much as I should."

"Can I send you material on finding Jesus?"

"You're probably working on unpromising material. My relatives pray in a synagogue."

"Ah, Jewish. They are the chosen ones. God's people. But there's always room for conversion."

"It would be hard to convince a family whose forebears died in Auschwitz."

I looked around his office. Through a doorway I saw a Kay videostrobe.

"I see you're into voice work," I said, trying to change the subject.

"Yeah, I got the strobe a couple of years ago. I'm starting to get into Botox work."

"Have you done any yet?"

"Just a couple of patients. I've had a little trouble knowing when I'm into the vocal cord."

"I've had some experience in it. Do you have any tapes? Maybe I could look at your technique."

"Sure. I was hoping I could pick your brain. I read your article on spasmodic dysphonia in the *Annals*. You are that Ben Dailey, aren't you?"

"One and the same."

"At first I didn't make the connection. How come you're doing this kind of work?"

"It's a long story and not very interesting. I'm doing it for a friend."

"Well, I'm sorry you got tangled up in an unfruitful endeavor. Meanwhile, I would appreciate any help you could give me. I've done several procedures. Some didn't turn out as I had hoped. Let me show you a tape."

We went across the hall and into his voice room. He put a cassette in into his VCR. Soon a pair of vocal cords came into view. While he went through the recording of the patient's voice, I looked at his equipment. State of the art.

"Okay, I've got it on the screen. See how the needle went in? It was just as you had described in your article. But after a week there was no response."

"Did you hook him up to an electromyogram?"

"No."

"That's the problem. Without electrical evidence of being into the muscle of the vocal cord, you may not have injected him in the right place."

Connely looked irritated with himself. Doctor or sybaritic, rich professional? Right now, he looked like the former.

"I knew I should have done that. But it seemed so clear that I was in the cord on the video."

"If you want, I can take your tape and edit it with one of mine. You'll see the difference. Can you make me a copy?"

"Sure. I'd be grateful."

He got Mrs. Werner to make a copy and label it.

While we waited, we talked some more. My initial impression in the courtroom had possibly been wrong. Listening to him talk, he didn't seem like the man Craig Lasky had described. Maybe he had reformed himself.

"I don't think there's much else I can tell Coastal. You did what you thought was right."

"In the end we can only be judged by the Lord. I hope he judges me by my intentions."

Mrs. Werner walked up with two tapes and gave me the copy. I slipped it into my briefcase.

She was about to walk back to the file room when the intercom squawked. Pick up on line four.

Connely took the call in the hallway. He nodded without saying anything and hung up the phone quickly.

"I've got an emergency at the hospital. A bleeder after sinus surgery. Tell the patients, Jan. Can you get my headlight for me? I should be back in about an hour." She set the tape down on her desk and scurried into the back room.

When she returned, she had a black suitcase and some instruments. Connely turned to me.

"I've got to run, Ben. Sorry I couldn't be of more help. Sue, help Dr. Dailey with anything he wants."

After he left, Mrs. Werner opened the refrigerator to put a bottle of partially used toxin in the freezer. As she did, I looked inside. There were a dozen Styrofoam packages of toxin. I picked up one of the unopened bottles and held it up to the light. Nothing was visible.

"Amazing, isn't it?" I asked. "It's a fine powder. Less than the human eye can see, but it gets the job done."

"At $300 a bottle, it had better be worth it."

"Is this all the Botox Dr. Connely has in the office?"

"We don't keep a lot of inventory. It's expensive, but easy to get."

I asked her where it came from.

"Newark, New Jersey," she said.

It was a clean operation. He was using a cutting-edge therapy. He was helping people. I had to admit, it was good work. But all that leftover Botox bothered me. I made a mental note to ask him about that after we talked about Claudia. And also from which supplier he got his Botox.

Mrs. Werner put away the toxin and straightened up the room. It was a cue: the tour was over.

"I had a couple more questions for Dr. Connely. Should I wait in the outer room?"

"If you'd like."

I went back out front and took a seat in the waiting room. It was now 11:45 a.m. The room filled with restless patients. I sat next to a man wearing a cardigan sweater and a felt hat. He had wispy, white hair and thick glasses. He must have been at least eighty years old. I made the mistake of nodding hello. Immediately seizing the opening, he introduced himself as Bernard McPherson, telling me how he had carried rural mail all his life. He'd also farmed a section of land outside of town. And kept livestock. And raised two sons, one of whom would be about my age and was a bookbinder in Philadelphia, the other killed in Vietnam. He held up five fingers. He had five doctors. In his retirement he'd begun to have back problems. And feet problems. And now his thyroid was on the blink. He smelled of Bengay. Bernard McPherson was eager to tell me his medical history, beginning with his feet and moving upward.

I picked up a *Newsweek* and made a show of reading. There was a note on Michigan football in the sports section. The reference didn't make current sense. I looked at the cover; the magazine was a year old. Bernard McPherson continued his sociable confidences. He poked a blunt finger into his ear, bored into it, and squinted at me as he talked. Thyroid made him jumpy. He soaked his feet in Epsom salts. He'd been waiting an hour and a half this morning and didn't mind. He said he'd wait all afternoon for Dr. Connely.

But he was surprised. He'd never had to wait for Dr. Connely before. Did I want to know what his urologist had told him?

Actually, no.

I set the magazine down and looked at my watch. I couldn't wait any longer. Not unless I wanted to forego the jet and take the eggbeater home again.

But as I left to prevent Jordan's spending two nights in a row without me, a nagging, cynical little voice reminded me of every surgeon's time-honored way of getting rid of an unwelcome, persistent salesman.

An emergency at the hospital.

CHAPTER 5

THE FACT THAT JORDAN WASN'T OVERLY ENTHUSIASTIC about eating out that night didn't help the paranoia Todd Pearson's letter had set off in me. I wanted to go to Louie's for a burger, sit in one of the back booths, and talk about us. But she had a sudden craving for health food. So we ended up at the Health Nut, an open-air restaurant in one of those three-story shopping malls in the suburbs.

How could anyone get off on bulgur? What kind of romance can you have eating alfalfa sprouts and tofu? I was defeated before I sat down. There was no meat to the conversation.

"When did you start eating this stuff?" I asked, watching the chef chopping and cutting vegetables I'd never heard of.

"I've been reading some articles. This stuff is good for you. Low caloric intake, low fat, no additives. You should appreciate that as a doctor."

"I'm from the holistic school. No calories, no fat, no taste."

"I think it's fantastic. I crave this kind of food."

It was hopeless. How could I convince her of the benefits of cholesterol? She had that missionary look in her eyes, out to convert the heathen. The only distraction I could come up with was the unwelcome subject of my trip to Dellsburg.

"Why does Bruce have you going after this?"

"It's insurance money. He treats it like it's his own." I had ordered the veggie burger. Chewing on it was the closest I could get to the Louie burger's bacon and Swiss.

"I think there's more to it than that."

"How's that?" I asked, sipping my carrot juice, wishing it was a Labatt's Blue.

"I think Bruce needs you more than you think. You are his link to credibility."

"Come on, Jordan. He gave me a job after the Scotten case. Do you think he was impressed with my status then?"

The same old wrangle. The bottom line for me was that Jordan had never had her hands dirty, and I had. I didn't find it as easy as she did to look down my nose at Bruce Sanderson. There but for the grace of God -

"You think you owe Bruce something for helping you. I think he calls you for these cases because you represent something he thinks he's lost."

"What would you do?"

"In the legal world we have a word for it."

"What's that?"

"*Res ipsa locquator*."

"Which means?"

"Let the fact speak for itself. What does Bruce want you to do?"

"He wants me to follow up on Connely's ex-girlfriend."

"My point exactly. He wants to show his bosses that Connely was a lousy risk. The kind of policyholder they shouldn't have taken on. And who does he put up in search of the truth? His ace detective, the good Dr. Ben Dailey."

"Do you think I should tell him to forget it?"

"It depends on how much you want Bruce as your friend."

I thought about my grandfather, telling me one friend is worth a hundred enemies.

"I'll check out Claudia Fraser and then be done."

Jordan raised her beet juice and clicked my glass.

"The little trouble in the world not due to love is due to friendship."

"Huh?"

"An old English saying."

"Any particular meaning?" Todd Pearson flashed across my mind.

"Just make sure your need to repay Bruce doesn't get in the way of your common sense."

Jordan was hard to argue with. Even in The Health Nut she looked voluptuous in a tight t-shirt, with full lips and a red glow to her cheeks that made her face sensuous in the light. But the voice was stern, serious. Her eyes bore into me with the same look she gave the jury on a closing argument. There had been a bite in her voice.

I watched the chef again, beating on his vegetables. My eyes went to the beautiful woman across from me, wishing it was my carrot she was cuffing. The look I got back told me it wasn't going to happen tonight.

CALLING CLAUDIA. IT SOUNDED LIKE A movie title. I was considering it my final duty for Coastal.

I had her Xeroxed file from Dellsburg in my briefcase. I took it home with me, frolicked with Buck for a few minutes, and got down to work. According to her file, she'd graduated from a school for medical technicians and then trained in physical therapy. Dellsburg Baptist Hospital was her first job. She'd stayed three years. Always on time. The only negative was a letter of reprimand concerning an undisclosed disciplinary action. Shortly afterward she'd submitted a letter of resignation.

She was twenty-three when she left.

She must have had it out with someone. Probably Connely. She'd never had a chance. If it were just an affair, the doctor would win. It was a virtual certainty. The hospital would want the doctor's case revenue, and the aggrieved party would be quietly paid if she were lucky, and shown the door.

Her file showed queries from other hospitals, checking her employment record. Through these letters, I followed her by phone to Philadelphia, from there up to New York. She had worked at a hospital in Queens. When I mentioned her name to Delois Jackson, the human resource manager at the hospital, she seemed anxious to get off the phone. But I'm not easy to get rid of.

"This is no big deal, Mrs. Jackson. Claudia Fraser is looking for employment at a hospital in Detroit. We need to find out a little more about her."

"She was with us for a short period of time. She had a problem with absenteeism. According to her record, she showed up late for her shift on numerous occasions. She said she was working a second job. We can't have that. After we told her, the problem continued, so we let her go."

"Any idea where she went?"

"We have a letter from St. Anthony's Hospital in Toledo, Ohio."

"Anything else?"

"Nothing I can talk about," she said, then excused herself. I sat back in my chair and wondered. What else was going on with Claudia Fraser?

I looked at the dead computer screen in front of me. Chatrooms. *Hi, my name is Jordan. What's going on in here?*

People got caught up in things they thought they could control. Sometimes they were wrong. Maybe Claudia was just a kid who had some growing up to do.

St. Anthony's personnel department was next. Claudia had arrived two months ago and worked in their outpatient physical therapy unit near Toledo. So far, nothing else.

I hung up and sat there looking at the phone. Toledo was close to home. Familiar ground. But I had an uneasy feeling. This was familiar ground, all right.

Ground that might give way and suck me down.

EVERYONE NEEDS A PLACE TO RETREAT. Bruce's refuge was food. Mine was jazz. I was due to visit Sid Blanton down at The Pipeline. His club was in the warehouse district. It was a safe harbor, a quiet place to think on a Tuesday afternoon. Sometimes I got a chance to play. It was just past one o'clock when I walked in. A good time of day. If some of the boys showed up, and if I smiled real nice, they'd let me sit in.

"What's up, Sid?" I asked, strolling through the back door. Sid was behind the bar. He waved and shook his head. I'd treated him for cancer a number of years ago. After the radiation, he sounded like Louis Armstrong. When he played sax, you heard Sonny Rollins and Paul Desmond. He had a nice touch with the horn, but I always joked that with a voice like that, he should sing. He'd make millions.

"Who's on tonight, Sid?"

"Marcus."

Marcus Belgrave. A very good horn. After a night of Marcus and his quintet, you went home thinking Clifford Brown was alive and well.

He poured me a cup of coffee. We talked about business, about the district, the casinos moving in. Land was selling off for top dollar. A sinkhole on the riverfront was worth a million bucks. He said he was afraid his landlord was going to cave in. Who wouldn't?

"Consortium wants to tear this building down. Make a high-rise."

A high-rise in place of Sid's. Why not tear down Mariner's Cathedral?

"I got options," he said. "I'm waiting to see where they fall out." He took a drink of decaf and looked up at me. "What's with you?"

"Headaches."

"So go to the doctor," he said. "Don't you know any?"

"None that I trust," I said.

I told him it was football all over again. I'd gotten knocked out in the game of my recurring nightmare, really creamed, lost all memory of a big chunk of time; a few hours before the game, a few weeks after. It was my senior year at Michigan. Last game of the season. Last game of my career. For a long time, I'd felt cheated. I'd always wanted to remember that game. I'd wanted to savor it. I tried everything—the neuropsychiatrist, hypnosis. I'd watched clips a hundred times, hoping to recover just a few seconds of my time on the field.

"We lost the game," I said. "In the clips, everyone's jumping up and down in fits of anger. They're dying down there on the field. We've lost the last game; they can't believe it. And there I am, just standing in a daze."

"Who won?"

"Ohio State."

He rolled his eyes. "And that was that?"

"For me, yes. But I wasn't going to do anything with football, Sid. How many Jewish football players can you name?" I asked, parroting my grandfather. "I had a much better chance making it as a doctor."

"Forgetfulness can be good medicine. My cousin down in Tennessee, he forgets a little something every tax season."

"Does it work?"

"It did." He laughed. "They were pretty good to him, once they caught on. They worked out a special payment plan."

"If he can just manage to remember it," I said.

Sid raised his coffee mug. "When I get a splitter, I just play and play." He stepped out from behind the bar, crossed the floor to the stage, and dropped into a chair. Next to it was his alto, in the case. "You up to it?"

I nodded and hustled to the piano. "*Garden City Blues*?"

He nodded.

We started in, a little slow at first, then blasted off. It was the Duke and Johnny Hodges. Me and Sid. I could see them on the front cover of the album I played until it was worn out. They battled each other for supremacy, the great piano man, the great sax. Duke had charisma; Johnny could play like no one else.

In the end it was no contest. Charisma wins every time.

We wailed for a few minutes, trying to keep it tight. We knew each other's moves and anticipated them. We both knew enough to mix it up, throw in some surprises. The surprises made it sweet. In the end, it was just good, honest music—melody, rhythm, chords.

When we finished, Sid looked at his hands. "See, Doc," he said. "A little music calms your nerves."

It was good medicine. You couldn't bottle it and put a price on it. That's what made it so good.

Long live Sid's, I thought. Damned casinos.

I looked up and saw Jerry Brooks, my friend from the college team and the nightmare. Sometimes coincidence scored a touchdown. He looked at me, then down at his watch, and then up at me with a huge smile.

"Man, for a doctor, you sure can play."

"It's *gestalt*, Jerry, *gestalt*."

"Quit using them big words on me. Don't forget I played four years next to you. You only used those big words when you were trying to obfuscate the coaches." He laughed.

"The whole is more than the sum of its parts."

"I get it. Like football, huh?"

"You're like a steel trap, Jerry."

I stood up and gave him a hug. Jerry and I had played on the hamburger squad for Michigan. You don't play that long with someone, laughing and suffering, and not develop a lasting friendship.

"You know Jerry, don't you, Sid?"

"What do you mean, do I know Jerry? The man is a legend around here. Before he got married, he held The Pipeline record for the most in-the-sacks of any of my ex-jocks." His eyes twinkled as he patted Jerry on the shoulder. "Look at that suit, Jerry. Business must be good, huh?"

"Economy's good, lots of building. People need wood, and I'm their man."

After graduation Jerry hooked up with a local lumberyard, and now he owned it. Not bad for an African American whose father left home and whose mother raised him. The first in his family to graduate college. As far as I was concerned, such a success story was the most tangible benefit of playing football.

I sat down at the bar and asked Charlie for a Diet Coke with a lime.

"What'll you have, Jerry?" He pulled out a handkerchief and gave a real honk.

"Jesus, Jerry, you're going to blow your brains out."

"Stupid dog. My old lady bought one. I'm allergic as hell, but I don't have the guts to tell her to give it back."

"Every day it stays, it gets harder to get rid of."

"How do you know?"

"Because Jordan just bought a dog."

"Oh, yeah, what kind?'

"A yellow Lab. She calls it Buckeye, Buck for short."

"You have to be kidding. You're going to have to spend the next fifteen years with a Buckeye in your house?"

"I thought it was a cute name."

"Depends on what time of the year it is. Are you ready for it?"

"For what?"

"The worst fucking week of the year. Michigan and Ohio State."

"Come on, Jerry. It's just a game. College football. Kids. Enjoy the game and go home. It's not life and death." I regretted my words the moment they came out of my big mouth. For Jerry it was as close to life and death as it got.

"If it wasn't for Timmy, maybe I'd say you were right."

Jerry had been coming back to Ann Arbor the night after the Ohio State-Michigan.

Jerry didn't come back with the team after the game. Instead he drove back that night with his best friend, Timmy Steel. According to Jerry's story, a couple of Columbus guys in a Bonneville spotted their car and started taunting them. Jerry didn't pay any attention, until they started playing chicken with him on US 23. The roads were icy. The Bonneville nudged Jerry's front bumper just before an abutment. Jerry lost it and crashed his car. Remarkably, he only had a couple of bruises. Not so with Timmy. He snapped his neck on impact. That's about all Jerry remembered. They never found the guys that caused the crash, and Jerry never lost his hate for Columbus and the game.

"Sorry, Jerry. I didn't mean to be so callous, but you're just punishing your-self. It was thirty years ago." I could see the flash in his coffee-dark eyes.

"I wouldn't take that from anyone else. Coming from you, I can accept it."

"Forgiveness is the attribute of the strong." I held up the peace sign.

"Come on, flower child, who said it? You're not that smart."

"Gandhi. I said that to myself every day I went through my own ordeal." Jerry knew; he'd been one of the few people to stick by me.

"You're probably right. It's just an ugly reminder every year. I've transferred my anger to the game."

"Sociologists would love you. Have you got tickets?"

"Catch this. One of the coaches called me. Wanted to know if I wanted field passes. As many as I want. Seems as though they picked a lottery and my name came up. Like to be my date?"

"You know, Jerry, I always thought there was something weird about a quarterback sticking his hands under some other guy's ass for sixty minutes."

"Different strokes, baby, different strokes."

"Count me in." In spite of everything for both of us, being on the field for the Ohio State vs. Michigan game would be a treat.

We talked with Sid for a while, and then I left. The sun had warmed the sidewalks enough that a few places were serving people at outside seating, down across from the riverfront. The people looked about in amazement. You couldn't live in Michigan and not feel a special longing for sun, the way some people feel about the lottery. Next to one island of multi-colored umbrellas, I stopped. At a table in front of me were two figures leaning over the table, close enough to administer CPR. The woman held an olive in one hand, her other hand was outstretched across the table.

Auburn hair.

I spun on the toes of my shoes and took off in the opposite direction. I felt my hands start to shake, my heartbeat race. What was she doing? The olive, her hair—it could have been Jordan, or any other woman. Say hello, I told myself. There's a reason she's sitting there. But I couldn't go back and look. I didn't want to know. Across from her had sat a man; the golden-boy face, a man I might have seen before. Pearson? It could've been. The ex-quarterback from Stanford. But that was years ago. I didn't know what he looked like now.

Yes, I did. So smooth.

And charisma wins every time.

I had suffered through one bad marriage. At the time, I'd told myself it was the Scotten case. The death of a young boy, evidence implicating me, and all the while, a string of false accusations from my wife. She'd wanted status and money, and before she could get it, I lost it. All of it.

It had taken five years to come back, to rebuild—and to find Jordan. I wasn't going to do anything stupid. I backtracked to the corner and stood there a full five minutes. When I finally turned back and passed the umbrellas, ready to be nonchalant, they were gone.

I was angry when I got home. A couple of minutes of reflection and I knew I was angry with myself for letting my guard down and allowing myself to be taken in. Angry with Jordan. Three in the afternoon and dallying around with Mr. Stanford.

I didn't want to think about that.

I didn't know what to believe. I'd either seen her out in front of McGeachey's, or I'd seen someone who looked just like her; and whatever was going on between her and that guy, it was friendly, real friendly. All I could think about was olives. Jordan's hands reaching across the table. Olives were good for you. Impaled on a cocktail sword she held out to that guy, whoever he was. Whoever *she* was.

Inside, everything was in place. No letters I cared about on the end table. I went into the library, scooped up my file on Frank Connely, and put it in the old, leather briefcase I used for legal business. I ran upstairs and looked around the bedroom for a few moments. I was a jealous, middle-aged man. I was too insecure to allow this dynamic woman to have a conversation with another man. Get over it, Dailey, I thought.

I opened a dresser drawer and found a couple of shirts still folded from the cleaners. I threw them into my overnight case, collected some toiletries, and tossed them in too. I was hurrying. What was the rush?

Back down in the hall, I wrote a note to Jordan saying I'd be gone for a couple of days, tops.

Then I walked out. Jordan had her legal verbiage, and so did I. I'd taken an oath. To do no additional harm. So far, I was the only one that seemed injured.

After everything that had happened to me, I wasn't waiting around for a goodbye song. If she wanted to be with Todd Pearson, I wasn't going to be a roadblock. Leave town, talk later. I got in the Wagoneer, drove out to Old Woodward and then over to I-75. It would be two hours before I got to Toledo.

Chapter 6

Next thing I know, Claudia Fraser's naked breasts were in my face. Claudia began to slowly undulate, her swaying, upright nipples mesmerizing. I looked at her face, the pretty upturned nose, rosy cheeks. I could see her running out on the playground, young and innocent. Some father's daughter. I wondered what he would have thought.

Jordan was going, or gone, and this girl stood over me, with what Jerry and Sid would have called her good stuff in my face. What did I have to lose? Nothing tangible. But I had this stupid hang-up called scruples. Until I knew better, until it was over for sure, I owed something to Jordan. I decided I'd better get to work, investigating. Wasn't that why I was here?

"Wait a second," I said, my bigger head suddenly back in control. I moved her hand away from my crotch. "Can I ask you something?"

"Anything you want."

"Have you ever heard of Frank Connely?"

She took a deep breath and stepped backward.

"Is this a bust?"

"Relax." I sat up and reached for my pants. "I'm not a cop."

"Then who are you?"

"My name is Dr. Ben Dailey. I'm investigating Frank Connely, a case he's involved in. Your name came up."

"Doctor?" She gathered her clothes. "What did he do, rape an old woman?"

"This is about malpractice. He lost. He shouldn't have, but he did. The company I represent will have to pay a lot of money. You and Dr. Connely had a relationship. I thought you might be able to tell us something that would help."

"I've got nothing to say."

"Suppose the police heard that a woman was running a sex shop in a medical facility?"

"Suppose you tried to rape me and I fought you off."

"It'd be pretty hard to defend yourself, Claudia. Given your record in New York City and Philadelphia."

She buttoned up her blouse and picked up her pants.

"He did this to me. I was a good physical therapist. We had an affair, and he turned on me. He made me sound sick."

"Were you?" I asked.

"I liked the sex. Nothing else."

"What else was there?"

"I've had enough, okay? You want to turn me in, go ahead. Otherwise I'm leaving." She leaned against the wall and pulled on her pants, zipped them up, then slipped on her shoes. A rich guy like Frank Connely could make her appear to be anything he wanted.

"I'm not going to turn you in," I said. "I need information. Why don't we start over?"

Tears were gathering in the corners of her eyes. I pulled a fifty out of my wallet and put it in her hand. She nodded her head and tucked the bill inside her pants pocket.

"So how did you meet Frank Connely?"

"He came down to PT one day looking for a patient. We struck up a conversation. I saw him in the cafeteria. We had lunch." As we spoke, I glanced at her arms. They had a peculiar reddish hue. She noticed my look.

"I'm sensitive about my arms. I spilled hot water on them when I was a kid. My worst feature."

I'd seen enough of the rest of her. I could only agree.

"How long did you see Connely?"

"Over a year and a half."

"Did his wife find out?"

"She caught us at a motel outside of Philly. She'd hired an investigator. It was messy."

"Did he promise anything?"

"The usual—he'd dump his wife, we'd live happily ever after."

"But it didn't happen."

She nodded. "After the wife caught us, everything came crashing down on me. He went to the Board of Trustees and made a complete confession. He accused me of seducing him. But it wasn't true. He was all over me. They needed him more than they needed me, so I was gone." She was crying softly now. "I had to leave. They made me sign a letter of resignation."

"Why didn't you get a lawyer?"

"I didn't know anything. I figured that's the way it was done."

I asked her what kind of guy Dr. Connely was.

"He seemed decent, at first. We had fun. Went to clubs, took a couple of trips to Atlantic City. The sex was good," she said.

"Did he have other interests?"

"Other interests?"

I shrugged. I didn't know what I was looking for. I wouldn't know until I heard it.

"Computer cafes. You drink coffee and dial up the Internet. We'd go to New York City and sit in a few of these places. He called himself The Apostle and got into discussions with people in chat rooms. He liked to put them on."

Chat rooms. I thought about Jordan. She'd be home by now. Between chat rooms and Pearson, I didn't know what she was mixed up in. She would have seen my note by now. She would be thinking I was still clueless. If everything was all right. And here I was, with this girl's breasts in my face. A total stranger. At least Claudia hadn't called the cops. I'd have had some explaining to do.

I told Claudia about the case. The operation, the misplaced suture and the bleed, the patient who'd died. How the case was ours until Connely had choked on the stand.

She shook her head in disbelief. "He wouldn't cave. I don't believe it."

More or less what Lasky had said.

"Have you talked to him since you left Dellsburg?"

"I couldn't bear it. Because of him, I've been hurt at every hospital I've worked at. That letter and my record hurt me real bad."

"So you turned to this?"

She nodded.

"What about clinics?"

"I'm an aide. I worked this thing out with Janine, the receptionist. If a guy comes in late in the day, she makes him wait. She leaves, and I'm alone."

We went out to the front of the clinic. It was dark outside. The fluorescent desk light above the receptionist's desk illuminated the room. Traffic hissed on the road out front. I hated these places. Strip mall medicine. At this hour especially, there was a terrible sadness about the room. I reached in my pocket for another fifty for Claudia. She held up her hand and declined.

I thanked her, gave her my card, and asked her to call me if she thought of anything more. Maybe not a great idea, her calling me. One more potential complication at home, but at least we were beyond the sex thing.

I stared through the rain-soaked windshield at the road and watched the line of muted lights wandering down the highway. I wondered what problems those strangers had. As bad as Claudia Fraser's? Then I thought about myself. What the hell I was doing here anyway? Searching for a truth I didn't seem any closer to.

I pulled into a station to change my wipers. While I was there, I saw a family restaurant up the road. I wanted something wholesome, a blue plate special—Swiss steak, potatoes and gravy, bread and butter. I wanted food that was connected, however indirectly—and I knew it was the longest of long shots—to someone's mother.

I took a chance and drove over. They had booths with red, worn plastic coverings and a menu with a hundred and fifty items, almost all containing eggs. Fortunately, I found Swiss steak on the last page.

The waitress was in her fifties. She was a big woman. Not obese by any stretch of the imagination. But not a stick, either. Substantial with a definite grace. She might have laid down a hundred plates that day. Mine was delivered with care. Some unhurried words, a few light pats on the shoulder, splash of coffee to refill.

My mind was tumbling.

The come-on. I hadn't anticipated that.

And Claudia's corroboration of Lasky's take on Connely. A take-charge guy. He didn't sound at all like the doc I had met in Dellsburg. He'd been mean enough to get her blackballed and ruin her for good. Then why had he choked? Add to that his infidelity, the kinky sex, and phony Christianity. It didn't add up.

I got up from the table and asked for a phone. It was in the back. It seemed like I had enough back rooms for one night. Thank God I'd been cool. I wouldn't forget Claudia hovering over me, pulling her bra off. I dialed and waited. Four rings. Then came the answering machine. Where was Jordan at eight at night?

I stayed at the Holiday Inn that night off I-75. I didn't sleep well. I got up around two. Looking around I found a couple of those sample bottles of Jack Daniels in a basket next to the TV. I turned on an old Bogart movie and downed both of them.

Toledo at two o'clock. The makings of a headache. Was I any further ahead? What had I accomplished? Cheap sex offered and declined in a rehab office. Trashy confessions in a Baptist hospital. Tabloid stuff. A complete waste of time.

At about five in the morning, I got up and showered. An hour later I had my Wagoneer pointed toward home. I wasn't any closer to the truth than when I'd left. I was only disgusted with myself. I should have stayed with Jordan. We had work to do on our relationship, and I was running away from it. And toward what?

The ride home reminded me of how cold and gray I felt. The industrial heartland bristled with smokestacks. The ore ships still plied the waterway, waiting for the ice of December to close them down.

I reached home at about one in the afternoon. I was surprised to see Jordan just getting ready to leave. My thoughts of a confrontation evaporated when I saw her.

"Ben, you look like hell. How was your trip?"

I wasn't in the mood to divulge my experience at the rehab center. It was bad enough to think of her cavorting around town with Todd Pearson, let alone admit that she'd been right about my doing Bruce's bidding.

"How come you're home?" I countered.

"Just came home to get some papers I left on the desk."

I was tempted to say something. Something told me to listen.

"Ben, someone named Miss Fraser called." I cringed with regret that I'd given her my card.

"She's the person Bruce wanted me to talk with in Toledo, the physical therapist I told you about."

"She said she has something to show me. She wants to meet with me tomorrow. What could she have to show me, Ben?"

I was afraid I knew. How much would I bet myself that Claudia Fraser had videotaped our encounter?

God, I was stupid. Too stupid to deserve to keep Jordan.

"Stay away, Jordan. There's amazing bad here. Real bad. I can sense it. Listen, we need to talk." She looked at me strangely.

"I'm in a hurry to a meeting. We'll talk when I get back tonight."

"Where's Buck?" I recalled, as she moved to the front door.

"I didn't know when you'd be home, so I left him with friends."

"Are we bad parents? Leaving him like that at an early age?"

"I'll be back home around seven. Maybe we'll go to Louie's." She picked up her bag. At the door she turned around and kissed me on the cheek.

"I missed you, Ben."

"I missed you too."

SEVEN HOURS LATER, TRAFFIC BLEW PAST ME on the expressway. There were hearts etched all over the traffic signs. Ink faded. A carved heart would last. The phone call from Jordan's hysterical secretary replayed in my head unendurably. She had passed out at the office. They called EMS. When they took her to St. Vincent's she was still unconscious.

I must have violated every traffic law in the city on the way to the hospital. When I reached the emergency room, I parked in the on-call physician's spot, and rushed in. The guard gave me a scornful look. Screw you, buddy. Jordan's in a coma.

I staggered into the ICU. Brand new and state of the art. Individual enclosed glass cubicles circling around a central nurses' station. Outside 405 stood Phil Lindstrom. After being around doctors all my life, I could tell what was going on just by their faces. I didn't like the look on Lindstrom's face.

"She has a bad infection," he said. "It looks for all the world like botulism."

"Jesus. What happened?"

"Apparently she missed a meeting. The door was closed to her office. Her secretary knew it wasn't like her. When she opened it, they found her with her head slumped down on her desk with a high fever, nausea, and abdominal distention. She was in and out of consciousness."

"Did she say anything?"

"She just kept calling your name."

A flash of guilt bolted through me.

"How far are we into this?"

"A couple of hours, I'd say."

"How bad?"

"We're covering her with antibiotics, antitoxin, and steroids, but you know it can be touch and go."

"I thought that botulism didn't cause a coma until late in the disease."

"That's what's puzzling about this case. Something's very strange."

There was a long pause.

"Ben," he said. "There's something more you should know."

I felt weak. I leaned against the counter for support. "What?"

"Jordan's pregnant."

Granola and rice milk in the morning. Did I ever get lonely? Something between us. Health food. My God, Jordan. Why didn't you just tell me?

I looked down the hallway near the main entrance to the ICU. A few people I recognized waved and said, "Hello, Doctor." I waved back, a stranger to myself. At that moment, I wasn't a doctor. I wanted to cry but couldn't let myself. I wanted to be the doctor who takes charge, solves problems. I wanted to be where we were yesterday and live with Jordan for the rest of my life.

I looked back at the room. A couple of nurses dressed in scrubs whispered to each other; one held a hand up to her face and laughed quietly. Their stethoscopes gleamed. They were talking about patients. I wanted back into that world. I had to steel myself for what I would see. She would be intubated, on a respirator, unconscious, suspended between life and death. Maybe even beyond the sound of my voice, the touch of my hand.

I walked into her room.

Yes, it was Jordan. No prayed-for mistake.

I kissed her cheek and said her name. Her face was pale. Her left hand lay open, palm up. I laid my hand over it. A nurse I knew was there, by the bedside. Flannigan. I couldn't remember her first name. She'd been an ICU nurse for twenty years. I should have known her name. A technician was drawing blood.

"Well?" I said. Jane, I remembered.

"She's holding her own."

Holding her own. Patient talk. I'm a doctor, I thought to myself. Tell me the truth. I didn't have the guts to say it. I pulled a chair up to the bedside and sat. The IV dripped. On the monitor, her blood pressure read normal. We were going to have a baby. This intelligent woman, so sensible and argumentative, so giving, she was going to be a mother. I wanted that to happen to us.

I just sat. Thirty minutes or so had passed when Phil Lindstrom came in. He was a small man, compact and muscular, with short, brown hair and a mustache. He stood in the doorway, hands at his side.

"I never imagined this," I said. I caught his eyes for a second, then turned back to Jordan on the respirator.

"Of course you didn't," he said.

I folded her fingers around mine. "What about the baby?"

He said they had called Jim Rathberger in. He was the best perinatologist in the area. I knew that. Rathberger said it was still too early to tell. She was probably only a few weeks pregnant.

"Is that bad or good?" I said.

"The smaller the fetus, the better the chance of survival."

I looked at Jordan's freckled face, the endotracheal tube. This must have come on suddenly. She seemed frail compared to the voluptuous woman I had parted from eight hours earlier. More guilt, more self-recrimination.

"What are the infectious disease people saying?"

"They're trying to track it down."

"Where do they start?" I asked.

"Do you know of anything unusual she might have eaten? Maybe in the house?"

"I don't know," I said dully. Health food? My mind was on a cure not a cause. "Is there an antiserum?" I asked.

"We're trying. We have a number of them. It takes time to figure out if one works or not."

"We don't have time, Phil."

"We have to do this according to the book, Ben. Otherwise we get into a mishmash of treatment, and no one knows what's going on." He ran a finger across his mustache. He said, "Come with me down to the laser lab. It'll take your mind off things."

I didn't want to take my mind off Jordan.

"I want to show you some things we're doing."

We walked to the elevator and took it down to the basement. As we did, Phil talked about the disease. In a botulism crisis, there was always a moment when the body's own defenses had to take over. Treatment was one thing, but without a good intrinsic defense mechanism, the battle could be lost. The better the protoplasm, the better the survival.

And if the protoplasm won, the doctor got the credit.

We got off the elevator, went through a few doors I hadn't ever opened, down a few halls I didn't know existed. We were in the research wing, following a corridor I hadn't explored. I put one foot in front of the other. It was all a dream, a bad dream, I thought to myself. As I did, an image from that football dream flashed in my memory. The OSU player across from me on the line, his mouth forming words. We turned a corner at the end of the corridor, where Phil opened the door of a lab filled with experimental equipment.

"Welcome to the laserium," he said.

I had used carbon dioxide lasers in the operating room. But the equipment he showed me, I had never seen before. The Neodymium YAG laser. He called it YAG for short. The YAG laser, he said, was the big daddy of the bunch. Strong enough to put a hole through you. They were using it in conjunction with a substance called protoporphyrin, which localized itself in cancerous tissue. Given high concentrations of inhaled oxygen, the protoporphyrin activated the cancer cells. The laser was shone on the activated tissue, now light sensitive.

"We deliver the YAG and the Argon laser through a fiber," he said, "either by holding it directly or putting it in a holder." He opened a cabinet drawer and produced a black plastic holder. He slipped the fiber through it. It looked like a gun. Then he turned the machine on. There was a sound of water rushing through the apparatus.

"Watch this," he said.

He went over to the refrigerator in the corner of the lab and pulled out a piece of raw steak. He put the meat on a metal table and handed me a pair of yellow-tinted glasses. He turned on the wand-like laser.

"Let's try eighty watts," he said.

He dialed a number and then put the foot pedal down on the ground. When everything was in place, he pushed on the pedal. Smoke rose from the beef. A neat, deep white line in the tissue emerged. The smell of burnt meat filled the air.

"This baby cuts."

"Deeper than the carbon dioxide laser," I remarked.

"Some of these cost over a hundred thousand dollars. It's state of the art stuff. That's why I brought you down here—to show them to you. I want you to know that everything is being done for Jordan."

I nodded, trying to look appreciative. Everything is being done. It sounded so melodramatic. I wondered if I'd used that awful expression before with a patient. Didn't we do everything possible for every patient?

He put the YAG fiber down and walked back to the carbon dioxide laser. "If she doesn't respond to the antiserum pretty soon, Ben, I'd like to inject her with protoporphyrin and hope that it goes to the diseased tissue."

I looked away from the meat on the lab table. I would have preferred to read about it.

I said, "If this is experimental, do you think it's smart to try it on Jordan?"

"It would be a last resort. I just wanted to show it to you. Sometimes faith needs a little help. Don't give up hope."

We walked out the door and back to the elevators. By the time the public health department found the source of Jordan's botulism, it would probably be too late. My faith needed all the help it could get.

WHEN I REACHED THE TOWNHOUSE, I wished Buck were there. Any touch of life would have been comforting.

I thought about Jordan. I knew enough about botulism to be terrified.

Clostridia botulinum. Usually ingested in food. The organism produces a toxin. It's the toxin that gets you. And there isn't just one toxin. There are various types. Depending on what kind, a specific clinical course is required.

I knew this much, and a little more.

The toxin is absorbed through the intestinal tract. It enters the circulation and winds up in the muscles of the body. It blocks the transmission of chemicals that allow muscle function. The so-called anticholinergic effect. The result is a progressive paralysis of the body's musculature, leading to respiratory paralysis and death. Treatment involves support of the respiratory system and the administration of antiserum. Antiserum has to be matched with the toxin to prevent progression of the disease.

A strange toxin. In low doses it was therapeutic; unchecked, the fatality rate was around seventy percent.

Don't go there, I thought. Not yet.

When I was a resident, I'd worked on a guy named Gabe Nielsen. He'd come in from a car crash nearly in extremis. The raccoon eyes. You could sink a fist in his chest. Deep coma he'd never come out of. Six tubes and you're out, we said. Well, he was out. He had a broken cheekbone that another guy and I decided to fix up. It wasn't completely futile medicine. We needed the practice. So we did the job, fixed him and stitched him up, and walked away.

A month later I walked into the St. Paul County Hospital, and there he was, getting off the elevator. *Gabe*, I said, *I can't believe it's you*. Against all the odds, the guy had simply wakened one day.

People did just wake up.

I went into the study and dropped on the couch. I was tired. So much churning thought and emotion. I couldn't sleep. I went over to the stereo and looked at the disc inside. Johnny Hodges, the Verve collection. I pulled out the disc cover and looked at Hodges, sax in hand, fierce eyes—eyes that said I'm too damned independent to be under the shadow of anyone, even the Duke. I lay back down, pulled on some headphones, and listened to the wail, the drawn-out notes only Hodges could play. Poor guy. He died in a dental chair having his cavity filled.

I closed my eyes, wondering if I'd drop back into my football nightmare. What was going through Jordan's mind? She'd be angry. Or she'd just be scared. She'd need me. I hoped so. I'd asked Gabe about the coma. What had it been like? Did he remember anything? He looked at me with improbably bright eyes and thought for a minute. It was nothing, he said. Just nothing. Deep, empty, bottomless sleep.

Damn.

The next thing I knew it was four in the afternoon. I rubbed my eyes and shook myself awake. Hunger was gnawing at my stomach. Then I called the hospital to see how Jordan was doing.

No change.

I opened a cupboard and took out a glass. I pulled out a half-empty box of graham crackers and finished them. I was about to throw the box in the trash when I noticed a strip of blue ribbon on the countertop, such as you would use to wrap a present.

So he'd given her a gift.

I picked up the ribbon and felt my face get hot. Jordan never threw away a bow. I ran the ribbon through my fingers a second, decided to save it, then changed my mind. I opened the door under the sink. There in the trashcan was the partially open gift box. Beside it was a sheet of wrapping paper, ugly shiny blue foil, which Jordan had carefully folded and inserted into the trash. The box was empty.

I laid the ribbon on top of the trash, shut the cupboard door, and went to the refrigerator, looking for something to eat. There were apples and oranges in the fruit bin, a bottle of white wine that hadn't been opened. Next to them were a couple of opened bottles of green olives, some mayo, mustard, and several unopened containers of specialty foods, the kind you find in those fancy food boutiques.

I pulled out a loaf of bread and some deli meat and laid them on the counter. That's when my gaze shifted back to the olives. The baby - that's why she'd craved olives, I thought. I set down the food and took out the bottles. One of them said San Marino. I took the cap off and looked in. Held it to my nose. There was no odor, nothing abnormal.

Or maybe there was.

Jesus, I thought. Maybe the source was right here.

I quickly closed the bottle, grabbed all the other containers off the refrigerator shelf, and put them each in a separate, sealed plastic bag. Though my hands were trembling, I carefully put them in a box and ran into the garage. I laid the box carefully beside me on the seat of the Wagoneer.

It was a fifteen minute ride to the hospital, and another fifteen walk to the lab. There was a tech I knew in bacteriology, Yvonne Jensen. She worked afternoons. I had operated on one of her kids once and helped save her father's life when he almost died from a throat infection.

I set the box down on the counter. I cautioned her not to open anything until she was sure she had proper control.

"What's inside?" she said.

"A bunch of food from my refrigerator. I think we've got a botulism source here."

"Some of them are unopened," she replied, quizzically.

"Leave those for now. Let's check the olives, mayo, and mustard."

She took out rubber gloves, put on a mask, and then dipped a swab in the liquid inside each jar. She smeared each applicator on a separate agar plate. Then with a heated metal loop, she stroked the plates with multiple lines. When she was done, she took another swab from each bottle and placed them on individually labeled slides. Once it was dry, she stained them and took them over to the microscope.

She lowered her eye to the microscope, spun the focus knob, and changed the power on the lens. After a few minutes of looking at each slide, she took her protective glasses off and turned around to face me.

"There are spores on this slide." She pointed to the last slide she had looked at. It was the one labeled San Marino. "You may have the real thing here, Dr. Dailey."

"Call the pathologist, whoever's on call. Tell him what you've got. I also want you to contact the public health officer for the hospital. He'll know what to do."

"Where did you get this?" she asked.

"I don't know, Yvonne, but I'm about to find out."

I drove back home and looked through the garbage. I had to find out where the bottle came from. When I found the wrapping paper and the package, I spread them out on the kitchen table. I unfolded the paper. Jordan hadn't torn so much as a corner when she'd unwrapped it. There was a typewritten note on the unaddressed, attached card. It said, "Thanks for everything. Hope you enjoy the treats...." Part of the card was torn along with the sender's name. By Jordan, who never tore even a gift-wrap? I didn't want to read any more. And maybe I hated the guy, but I also didn't want to believe that Todd Pearson had anything to do with this business. Why would he send her a basket of food with botulism in it?

On the bottom of the card was the name of the store. The Gourmet Place.

I had been there dozens of times. It was smack in the middle of a trendy shopping center near our house. Specialty foods, wine and beer from around the world. Coffees.

Ten minutes later I was there, searching up and down aisles, past cases of wine, crackers, cookies, and candies from every part of the world. At the end of an aisle next to the gourmet spaghetti sauces were the olives. I found San Marino green olives. I took one of the bottles and went up to the store manager.

Ray Carmichel was one of those people who was meant for his job. He loved food. When I handed him the bottle, he held it up to the light.

"World famous," he said. "We get a couple of cases of these a year. When they're gone, that's it. They come from Sicily. Anyone who knows olives, knows San Marino."

"You send out gift boxes, don't you?"

"I'm the guy that makes them up."

"Have you sent out any recently?"

He nodded his head. "Last ones I sent out were two days ago."

"Can I get a delivery name and a purchaser name?"

"Sure, unless one of the kids sold some while I was on vacation last week and didn't mark it down on the computer. They're supposed to do that for future reference." he said.

He looked through his order book. "Here it is. St. Vincent's Hospital Auxillary. It was paid with cash. Bought it from Pat over there."

"Is that something you could double check?"

He went over to his computer, spoke with Pat, and punched it in. "The man that bought it said it was from the Board of Trustees honoring doctor Ben Dailey. Is there a problem with something you bought here?" he asked nervously.

I told him Jordan was sick. That's all I said—sick. I realized I'd have to get used to talking about it. It wasn't an adjustment I wanted to make. I said I was just trying to figure out if it was something she'd eaten.

"Well, you let me know," he said. "Any problems, I need to know."

"I will, Ray."

I bought the olives. I walked out the door to my car, wondering if I should have told him more. A food scare in a store like his could ruin him. I decided to wait until this bottle was tested.

Yvonne was still in the lab. I handed her the new bottle and asked her to run a second culture. She gowned up and went through the plating ritual again. When she was done, she took another swab and stained the juice from the olives. This time when she glanced up from the microscope, she had a different look.

"No organism, no spores."

"You're sure."

"As sure as my eyes can tell." A thought occurred to me.

"Yvonne, check the unopened bottles, and see what's in them."

She repeated the process. It took about thirty minutes. While she was working, I paced the room. I think I looked at every book she had on her shelf.

After she had examined the last slide, she took off her glasses and looked at me.

"I think you've got a real problem here, Dr. Dailey."

"Why?"

"All of those unopened bottles are positive for spores."

My heart pounded from fear and anger. I walked out of the lab, took the elevator to three, and made my way back to the intensive care unit to see Jordan.

No change.

"I'm doing something," I said to her. "I'm doing everything I can, Jordan." I sat with her for a while, holding her hand and talking to her. How often did we tell family to talk to comatose patients? You never knew what got through to them. It had to make a difference. So we said.

So I talked. My voice, strangled with emotion. Did she know I was there?

I was sure the botulism threatening Jordan's life had not originated at The Gourmet Place. Nor did I believe my rival, Todd Pearson, had poisoned the woman he wanted to take from me.

Jordan had not been the intended victim. I had been the intended victim.

And, almost certainly, still was.

CHAPTER 7

C OPS ARE A LOT LIKE DOCTORS. That's one thing I've learned from expe-rience. They solved people's problems, but it wasn't cops and robbers; medicine is a science, a methodology. Another thing I've learned: don't ig-nore their knowledge. Like doctors, police have methods. They have access to resources. I had a woman named Claudia Fraser. I needed methods and resources.

That's why I knocked on Lieutenant George Sennett's door late that night. He lived in Sherwood Forest, a comeback community in the city. It had lived through the '68 riots and, after that, through white flight and urban blight. Some of the classiest homes in the city were there. It was integrated-profes-sional-chic, a genuinely good place. When he moved back from Ann Arbor to the Detroit police force, George Sennett had bought a bungalow that was worth more every year. There was no better barometer for a city's recovery.

I stood on the porch, knocked, and waited. Knocked again, harder. George pulled open the heavy, wood door and looked at me through the screen. Reading glasses hanging down from the tip of his nose, padded slippers on his feet. Beneath the sleeves of that polo dress shirt were rippled, brown arms. I'd seen him knock heads more than once. He was one of the toughest homicide lieutenants on Detroit's police force. I'd known George since the Scotten case. He'd bailed me out of some tough situations. With his help, I'd resurrected my-self and met Jordan. Now that good life was falling apart.

"Ever hear of storm windows, George?"

"Ever hear of 'kiss my ass,' Dailey?" He pushed the screen door open and held out his hand. "What's got you out in the middle of the night, coming to see me? You working nights again, or is this a social visit?"

"I wish it was that simple," I said. I told him about Jordan and his demeanor instantly changed.

Still shaking my hand, he pulled me into the house. I followed him into the living room and sat down in a wing chair next to the fireplace. He took the chair across from me. On a television set in the corner of the room, the eleven o'clock news droned on. George muted the sound, tossed the remote on a stack of newspapers, and leaned toward me.

"Any suspects?" he said.

I broke down the last few days for him. The case in Dellsburg, where I'd flown in as witness, the unexpected turn of events in the case, and my attempts to find out what was going on. Yes, I was doing some investigative work. No, there was no point in his offering me a job. Then Dellsburg, where I got to know a little more about the seamy side of the good Christian doctor, and back to Toledo and my encounter with Ms. Fraser. I had the beginnings of a hunch, I said. I also mentioned Todd Pearson and the food gift. The one thing I didn't tell him was my anger and jealousy. Some things are better left unsaid.

George ran a big hand over his scalp. "What are you after?"

"A malpractice case, Claudia Fraser, that's a start."

"Why the malpractice case, Ben?"

I told him that Connely's wife had died in an accident on an airline.

"So?"

And Claudia Fraser may have done some work with the airlines.

"Okay," George said. "Maybe more than coincidence. What do you want me to do?"

"We got a ticket with St. Vincent's name on it. But I can't believe a place like a hospital would leave a box of gifts loaded with botulism. Claudia Fraser is running a scam in a rehab clinic. Draw a male client in, entrap him with sexual favors, and then threaten to call the police. I would bet she's where the action is at."

He smiled and shook his head. "Toledo used to be a nice town. We'll check her out."

"She's getting ready to do me, I get up and walk out. I tell her if she wants to find me, I'll be at the police station telling them about new approaches to rehab. Then I talk to Jordan, she tells me someone named Claudia called. Wanted her to look at something. Probably, she has a tape of my visit?"

"Never argue with the power of electronics." The TV flickered with the Saturday sports news. Both of us watched for a moment. All football, all local.

"I've been involved in the past with the use of botulinum toxin," I recounted patiently. "Frank Connely works with the same drug. Claudia Fraser, a medical technician, knew Connely intimately. I ask questions and Jordan contracts botulism. Do you see my point?"

Sennett said all signs pointed to Claudia Fraser, but not conclusively. "It's not a case, Ben. It's a hunch, like you said. Hunches can be tough to prove."

I stood up. "A few questions from a law enforcement official might help."

"Ordinarily, I'd say you're crazy. But you're not ordinary, Ben. I'll give it a shot tomorrow." He got up and walked with me to the door, a hand on my shoulder.

"What about the hospital?"

"I'll assign someone to talk with them. In the meantime," he said, "watch out for Jordan."

I told him I'd try and keep the faith. Sennett told me his take on faith: it was an antidote to helplessness.

Helplessness is life's most frustrating emotion.

CLAUDIA FRASER DIDN'T HAVE A CHANCE. The next morning, when I met George at his office, he had three printed sheets on her. Every byte of information available, right down to her last root canal and her most recent credit card balance. So he'd done some looking. The only thing he couldn't find, he said, was Claudia Fraser herself. The clinic reported that she'd quit the day before and left no forwarding address.

"We've got to find her," I said.

He held up a handful of papers. "You see these? Every one of these is a message. Every one needs answering. I don't answer, I get a hundred more messages. I want to help you, Ben, but I've got stuff on my desk."

I pushed my chair back and jumped to my feet. His office door opened. Knudsen, his sergeant, handed him a pink sheet of paper. Knudsen was blonde, six feet tall, a body builder, and a very soft-spoken cop.

George took the paper. He said, "Don't run away mad, Ben. I care about Jordan. And I think your hunch may be right. But get me a little more to work with. I get paid the same for a wild goose chase as I do for a solid case. I prefer the latter."

Knudsen stood in the door stroking his goatee. He pointed at the message. "You'd better look at that, sir."

"Thanks," George said.

I sat back down. The door clicked shut, with Knudsen outside.

"Listen," I said. "I visit Claudia and get caught in a set-up. Claudia calls Jordan with some tapes. The next thing I know Jordan is suffering the effects of botulinum toxin."

"Was Claudia Fraser on the flight that this doctor's wife died on?"

"She applied for a job with East Coast Airlines."

"Did she get the job? Was she on the flight?" George looked through the window in his office door, gesturing to Knudsen, who was still hovering just outside. "The boy is zealous," he said, and laid the message on his desk.

A few calls later, we'd learned that employment records had Claudia Fraser working for East Coast. She flew Philadelphia to the Bahamas. Another call placed Dr. and Mrs. Frank Connely on a flight to the Bahamas. George called the East Coast employment office back. Bingo. Claudia Fraser had worked that flight.

"You're in the middle of something, Ben."

Knudsen was still outside, big as a billboard.

"The woman's killing people," I said.

"Motive?"

"Frank Connely jilts her. The wife dies, and he lives."

"And you start closing in on her, so she goes after you next."

"Then leaves town."

George glanced down at his desk. "We can't send out a nationwide search for her," he said. "We don't have any grounds." I heard tapping on the office window. Knudsen's urgent knuckles. He *was* zealous. George picked up Knudsen's message, studied it, then tossed it on the desk. He motioned to Knudsen. It was a cop signal I didn't understand.

George said, "You're a hell of a nice guy, Ben. But for some reason, trouble seems to follow you like a bad rash."

"You mean a bad penny."

"Whatever," he said. "We've got Claudia Fraser. Her body's in an alley down on the Cass Corridor. Throat slit, dead as a doornail."

ALLAN DAVIS, THE MEDICAL EXAMINER, talked as he took us back to the shop. He'd just gotten back from Puerto Vallarta. Margaritas, sun, family time. So good to get away. He was tall, thin, and balding. Went there with his daughter and son-in-law. His daughter was about Claudia Fraser's age. They'd just had a baby. I pictured him sitting by the pool, making chitchat with a thirtyish lady accountant from Scranton. *And what do you do for a living?*

He talked as he led us into his office, mainly to Sennett, which was all right with me. *Allan Davis, M.D.* was stenciled on the glass door. Davis and I had a history. I didn't like his style, but we differed on much more than that.

Davis's undertaker's personality was perfectly matched to his job. He met us in the outer hallway and then opened the door to a cold room with green tile walls and floors, fluorescent lights, and the smell of disinfectant fighting a losing battle. A flourish of hands and his grin said: *this is it.* It was an act, I knew. But he seemed to relish it. He pulled on a jacket and gloves. Did we want coffee? He was drinking from a lab beaker. Both of us declined.

"We have two customers today," Davis said. He stepped up to one table and pulled the white cover back a few inches, revealing a head: female, with blonde hair. Bulging eyes that had seen the face of violent death.

"That her?" Sennett said.

"Yes," I said.

I'd seen dead people. People massacred in car wrecks. People drowned, shot, wasted by illness. I'd been trained to look at death with the eyes of a scientist, which meant closing my eyes to the part of death I couldn't reach. But I couldn't look at Claudia Fraser through my physician's eyes. I'd seen this woman, been touched by her. And then she'd tried to kill me.

"Are we connected to the deceased?" Davis said to me.

I said I knew her.

"She's part of an investigation Dailey's doing," Sennett said.

"Hmm." Which expressed Davis's opinion of me.

He pulled the cover down the length of her body. She lay with her hands at her sides. Her skin was pale, almost yellow. Purple bruises stood out on her cheeks, and along her rib cage. Her mouth had been smashed by a blunt object, her nose horribly broken. Four horizontal imprints around her neck. In the hollow above each clavicle, a shadow. Her belly was flat, the skin slack, rubbery.

"I thought her throat was slit," Sennett said.

"Strangled." Davis pointed at her throat.

"Got it," I said.

Davis folded his hands and began. "Multiple traumas all over the body. These could be individually inflicted lesions. Here next to her nipple is what looks like a cigarette burn."

I made myself look. Saw the spot.

"On the other one, it looks like a piece has actually been shaved away. Whoever did this enjoyed himself."

"S and M?" Sennett asked.

I nodded and then shifted back to her eyes.

"Exactly," Davis said. "I've seen this before. One last month, also found down on Cass." He turned the body over, examined her buttocks, talking as he worked. This time of year, he said, there were good rates for Puerto Vallarta. But then, Mexico also had good value. Always. He pulled her stiff cheeks apart, peered over his glasses at her anus. We should see that grandkid of his swim.

"Forced entry," he said. "Maybe a splinter of wood. We'll find out for sure. This woman was in a lot of pain when she died."

"Torture or sex?" I said.

He glanced up at me. "Not always an easy distinction. Here, I believe, the two became one."

"I'm due for a vacation," Sennett said. He glanced from Davis to me, gave me a sheepish look and shrugged.

Davis said without looking up, "I can help you."

"Thanks."

Davis moved down to the groin. "In cases of S and M, there sometimes is a sign on the body. A tattoo, for example. It identifies the individual with the group. An insider. This instance is rather unusual."

"Tattoo?" Sennett said.

"Yes, in the genital area. I've never seen this." She was supine. He examined her vagina. He took a razor and shaved away the curly, soft hair. "Here," he pointed, "above the clitoris, there is a mark."

It was a crudely shaped flower.

Davis straightened, inspected the length of her right leg, lingering over Claudia's knee. She was bruised there too.

"The tattoo," Davis said, "looks like the work of an amateur. Could be part of a rite."

"Rite?" Sennett said.

"Initiation. Say she belonged to a club, the tattoo would be her card." "Some calling card."

"The papers said she was found off the Cass Corridor?"

"In a dumpster," I said."

"There may be more." Davis pulled off his gloves and tossed them in a bin. He asked me if I was seeing patients these days. I thought of Jordan. I'd have time to stop and see her after this. I told Davis I was about to make my rounds.

"So who's your travel agent?" Sennett said.

CHAPTER 8

SENNETT HAD FRIENDS IN LOW PLACES. We were in his tan Lexus in search of one, crossing block after block of dilapidated housing, boarded up stores, vacant fields of weeds sprouting through broken concrete. Late Friday afternoon; dead as Sunday morning. Whole sections of the Renaissance City were still waiting to be reborn. Sennett ignored the speed limit. He said a nice car was an essential tool of the trade. People in this town respected a nice car more than the law. There were no red and blue lights, nothing to identify it with the job. Just style. He kept a few tools in the trunk. Among them, an army blanket he could lay over the backseat if he had a transport, which he rarely did. That was Knudsen's job. Knudsen had the company car.

We crossed town east to west on Grand Boulevard, hit Cass, and jogged north toward the Corridor. Home of prostitutes, drug dens, illegal gambling, and some of the worst sex clubs in America. You could find anything in the Corridor. Anything. Everyone knew it, but the cops looked the other way.

Sennett parked on a side street, in front of a red brick apartment building flanked by a party store and a peep show house. A guy with shoulder length hair and amputated legs rolled down the sidewalk in a wheelchair and came to rest by the Lexus.

"Hey, Lieutenant." He wore an army jacket. He had a scraggly blonde beard. His stumps, crisscrossed with surgical tape, jutted out from his pant legs.

"Trying to walk on those things again, Bradley?"

"Rollerblading," he said in a gravelly voice. "I'm into wheels."

"You eat anything today?"

"Too busy," he said.

"I'll get you a sandwich, you watch my ride while we go see Harry?"

"I don't like Harry," Bradley said.

"I don't either," Sennett said. They smiled. It was a deal. "You watch it close, all right?"

"All right."

Sennett slipped into the party store and came out with a brown paper bag. A quart of milk, a sub, a couple of cigars. Bradley rolled back from the street, parked by the storefront, and began unwrapping the sandwich. We made our way down the street to Harry's Hard to Find. When we walked in, a ping announced us. Harry was in the back with three of his friends. He had his fists clenched in pantomime. Someone was getting a beating. When he glanced up at the lieutenant and me, his funny face froze in a tight mask.

"My man," he said. The mask relaxed, one hand fidgeted at his side.

Sennett wagged his hand to the left, and the other three men made for the door, their backs bumping against walls covered with magazines and ribbed condoms.

"How's business, Harry?"

"You know, Lieutenant. I get a little, I sell a little."

"That's cute, Harry. You ought to print that on your business card."

Harry was about five-six, with a thin goatee, a straight mustache, and a silver cross at his throat. He couldn't have weighed much over a hundred pounds. Dressed in a satin shirt and tight, black jeans he looked very much the part of a Cass Corridor entrepreneur. A man who knew his product.

Sennett lowered his head and looked inside the glass case. "A very impressive array of dildos, Harry."

"Fuckin' A, Lieutenant."

"People got needs, Harry."

"Yeah."

"And you just meet those needs. Don't you, Harry?"

"Fuckin' A."

"I got needs, too, Harry. I need some information."

Harry took a step back, crossed his arms on his chest, and lowered his head. His shoulders started to bounce. I thought he was laughing, but it was a cough. He coughed hard, looked up at us through teary eyes, and smiled. When the coughed eased, the laughter started. It was more attitude than laughter. Sennett smiled and shook his head. When Harry was finally settled, he hocked up a wad of phlegm, picked up a Styrofoam cup, and spit in it.

"They found a white girl in the alley last night." Sennett began conversationally.

"I ain't your whore."

"Harry?"

"You come here to fuck me? I don't know nothing about a girl."

Sennett moved a little closer, his face inches from Harry's. "I got needs, Harry. You're in the business of meeting people's needs. So meet my needs, Harry." He reached down and clapped a hand on Harry's crotch. "Every day of the week, you're selling shit to minors. You know it. I know it. I look the other way because every now and then I need a little cooperation. Now my friend is going to show you a picture, and you're going to give us some information. You give us that, I let you go. Get a little, give a little, Harry."

I held up the picture. Harry lurched forward as Sennett squeezed.

"I didn't hear that, Harry. You know, I just can't get it right, squeezing some-one's balls. I hate it when they squish out between my fingers. What's happen-ing down there, Harry?"

Harry coughed, tears running down his cheeks. "Let it go. I'll tell you any-thing, just let go my manhood."

Sennett backed off, stood in front of him. He took the picture from me and held it to Harry's face. "Let's start over. The girl that was left in the dumpster. What do you know?"

"She came in here last night. Bought some stuff. Spiked nails, handcuffs. She went to a place down the block. Small bar called Eddie's Easy. They got a room downstairs. They do shit down there."

The door opened, pinging again as a draft of cold air blew in. One of Harry's friends came back. He saw Harry and Sennett and me, turned on his toes, and walked right back out the door.

"What kind of shit, Harry?"

"The bad shit," he said. "Live shows. Chains and stuff. Up the ass."

"Kind of refreshing to get an honest answer. It is an honest answer, isn't it?"

Harry dragged a shirtsleeve over his cheeks to mop up the tears. He picked up the cup and spit again. His fingers scrabbled at the countertop, tugged a cigarette from a pack, and raised it to his mouth. He lit the cigarette and blew smoke at the floor. He didn't look up.

"Now don't go anywhere," Sennett said. "Because what if I don't find what I want? You understand, don't you, Harry?"

Harry took another drag on the cigarette and nodded his head. "Fuck you, Lieutenant."

"Right back at you, Harry."

ONCE WE WERE OUTSIDE, I started breathing again. Bradley was still there, drinking the milk, smoking a cigar. It was almost 6:30, already dark. Two hook-ers had appeared on the street corner, huddled together in the cold. Across the street from them, a Mercedes was parked, a well-dressed man behind the wheel. Minding his merchandise. We walked up the street to Eddie's, found the door locked. We went around back, and found that door shut tight.

We walked back to the hookers. One tall, one short, both with short-slit skirts hiked up to their crotch, both wearing long, black boots. Sennett approached the taller of the two. Behind the dark purple eye shadow and thick mascara gleamed a pair of fearful eyes.

"Safety in numbers?" Sennett asked.

"Huh?"

"Do you always work in pairs?"

"Tonight we do, honey. Looking for a quick one? Twenty-five for a blow. I'll do the two of you for forty."

"We're not looking for action," Sennett said. "We need information."

"Cops."

Miss Short made a hand signal to the car, the door opened, and a big man in a slouch hat and overcoat started to get out of the car.

"Call him off," Sennett said. "Or you're both in jail."

Another hand signal, the man returned to his car.

Miss Tall leaned against a parking meter, looked at her nails. "I'm clean, I got no drugs."

"Last night, we found a woman in the back alley," Sennett said. "Tortured, then strangled. A broomstick up her ass, a nipple cut off. Her pretty face smashed. You know it. Otherwise you wouldn't be working together."

She snapped open her bag and pulled a tissue from it. She blew her nose, then carefully folded the tissue.

"Eddie has a downstairs room," she said. "It's for the queer shit. Women doing it to women, butt stuff. Once in a while someone from the audience gets it. Last night a new guy came in. Messed up one of the girls bad."

"What girl?" Sennett said. He reached into his pocket for the picture.

She put the tissue back in her bag, took out a lozenge and began to unwrap it. Sennett held up the photo. She shook her head and nodded toward the car across the street. "The girl who got hurt works for Roy. He'll tell you."

"What about that one," I said, pointing to the picture.

"Never seen her."

"All right. You be careful now," Sennett admonished as we left them.

We crossed the street to the Mercedes. Roy had the radio cranked. Bass notes throbbed, a few phony horns blared, someone was yelling lyrics. Sennett unbuttoned his coat jacket, then tapped on the window a few times. After a long pause, the window ran down a few inches.

"Roy?" Sennett said. "Can you turn the music down, please?" A wash of synthesized sound, more bass, more yelling. "Roy?"

The window ran down a few more inches. Roy cranked the radio up, smiled a did-we-dig-it smile, then turned it down.

"Lieutenant George Sennett, police department. Please get out of your vehicle."

Roy eyed him for a moment, then opened the door. He set his $400 Bally's down on the pavement and oozed out of the car. Fully extended, he was about six foot seven, I'd guess two hundred and ninety pounds.

Sennett asked to see his driver's license. Roy reached into his pocket, and, as he did, he lunged at Sennett with the other hand. It would have caught Sennett in the face if he hadn't stepped back almost in boredom. In the same motion, Sennett brought his Maglite down across the larger man's arm.

Roy doubled over. "You broke it," he said. "You broke my fucking arm."

"The doctor here will look at it later if you're still crying. Why not be cool and answer a few questions? The girls said one of your employees was messed up last night."

"That's why I made the move on you. I didn't think you were a cop." Roy straightened up, rubbing his arm. Inside the car, a new track was on the system. It was slow, three voices rising together, blending. Nice. Then that bass thing again.

"What's the girl's name?" Sennett said.

"LaShonda Wright."

"What happened?"

Roy dropped his arm to his side. He had fists the size of sledgehammers. "What happened is a big ass, honky dude. What happened is he wanted to do some shit on her, she didn't like it, and he put a world of hurt on her. She's going to be out of work for a month. Busted her up something good."

"Where can we find her?"

"Elm Grove Apartments. Number 12. End of the street. But she ain't talking much right now."

"Roy," I said, "a woman got killed down here last night. Do you know anything about it?"

"Dangerous place down here. Ain't no place for a white bitch."

"Do you know anything about it?" I said. Sennett held out the picture.

Roy studied it. "I know it happened. I never saw her." He grabbed the picture and looked again. "Pretty thing. You guys better find that motherfucker. People are going to be scared to come down here."

The economy down here was depressed already. Now this.

"We're working on it, Roy," Sennett said. "Take care of that arm."

We crossed back to Sennett's car. Bradley had smoked his cigar down to within an inch of his face. He said he needed cab fare, if Sennett didn't mind. And he'd like to get a new pair of roller blades, fast ones. He smiled up at Sennett, then me. He had a mess of bad teeth. Across the street, the whores had stepped up to a red minivan. Roy was bopping in his car again, keeping watch. I pulled a ten out and handed it to Bradley. Sennett made it twenty. Bradley tossed the cigar butt in the street, folded the bills, and tucked them in his jacket pocket.

We drove the three blocks down to Elm Grove. It was a five-story struc-
ture. Christmas lights circled a second-story window, blinking peace on earth.
Someone was rushing the season. Or they'd been up all year. Either way, good-
will seemed like a good idea. Across the street was a park lit by a single streetlight. A few cars whispered past, dragging the Corridor for action.

Sennett opened his coat and loosened his shoulder revolver.

"You sure you want me along?" I said.

"Sit in the car or go with me."

If he wanted me along, who was I to refuse?

The gate to the apartment complex was open. We walked down a hallway,
past two tied-up stacks of newspapers someone had forgotten to deliver. We
counted the doors until we came to number 12. Sennett pulled his gun and
motioned me to stand behind him. Three hard knocks.

"Police, open up!"

No answer. Three more knocks, then he tried the door. He was about to
break it with the butt end of his gun, when he tried it and the knob turned easily. He pushed the door open, and we stepped into a dimly lit room.

A radio was playing low, tuned to the local news station. I smelled perfume
or a fancy soap. In the front room was a couch, a knit afghan neatly folded
over the back cushion. On either end of the couch were plastic end tables, one
with a brass lamp on it. Next to the window was a television on a metal stand.
Beneath it, the radio dial glowed. Sennett flicked on a light. He held his gun up
near his chin, slid along the wall, poked his head around the corner. He slipped
down the back hall, motioning me after him. The bedroom door was straight
ahead, open.

She was in her bed.

Under a thin, blue blanket, a light-skinned black woman, no more than
nineteen or twenty, gripped the blanket with long thin fingers. There was a
plum on either cheek, the kind a fist makes. Her lips were puffy and red. Her
head was shaking, her whole body convulsed in fear.

Sennett shushed her, showed her his badge. He walked over to the bedside
and switched on the lamp.

"What do you want?" she whispered.

"LaShonda?"

She nodded.

"Lieutenant George Sennett. And this is Dr. Dailey. We're investigating a
homicide. We need to ask you some questions."

She raised one hand to her mouth, shrank into the bed.

"She's in no shape, George."

"Just a few questions." He was asking me to take over, his eyes on mine, ac-
cepting my medical judgement. "Please."

I moved to the bedside. Her eyes were feverish, and perspiration dripped down her face. I said we'd talked to Roy. He'd told us what had happened. I touched her wrist to check a pulse, looked at her pupils, asked where she hurt. When she drew back from me, I told her that another girl may have been with the same guy, and the other girl was dead. Every girl on the Corridor was a potential victim.

"Help us," I said, "you might save a life."

"You a real doctor?" she said.

I opened my wallet and showed her a hospital identification card. She squinted at it. Satisfied, she nodded at Sennett. She nodded again. When he didn't get it, she twirled a finger. Would he please turn around? He rolled his eyes. "Please," I said. He backed up to the doorway and swung around, facing the hall. I waited until she was settled, then pulled the blanket down to her waist. She wore a light blue nightgown that tied at the shoulders. It was stained with blood. Burns glistened on her arms, and the skin between her breasts was red and raw. I checked her shoulders, forearms, wrists, and hands. When I asked her to lower the top of her gown, I had to help her untie the straps. She let it fall and looked down. Her right breast was covered with a blood-soaked dishcloth she held in place. I asked to look, she turned away. I checked her ribs, pressing gently, and she sucked in a breath. I figured a couple were broken. He'd really worked her over.

She'd met the guy at Eddie's. They'd had a couple of drinks downstairs, then left together. He paid her fifty at a corner hotel. It looked routine until he got rough. Handcuffs. Putting his thing in her face. He lit a cigarette and started to burn her, straddling her, getting harder every time he touched her with the ash. Liking it so much, he put a washcloth in her mouth to keep her quiet. When he came, she thought it was over.

"He waits about ten minutes," she said. "Smokes another cigarette, then starts again. Pulls out a knife. Starts stroking it up and down my chest until he gets here." She touched her right breast, sobbing now. "He cut me. That son of a bitch, he cut me so bad." I knew. We'd just seen Claudia Fraser. She pulled down the towel. There was an open wound where her nipple used to be.

I put my hand on her arm, motioned for her to cover it. I tied the gown straps up again and told Sennett to turn back around. She kept talking through sobs. She was telling it now, getting rid of it. Saying it wasn't a life she wanted, it was just temporary, and she knew the risks. Roy roughed up the johns that stepped out of bounds, but this guy was evil, devil-from-hell evil.

"Name?" Sennett said.

"Vic. Vicar. Something like that. He was a big guy. Body-builder chest and arms. So strong I never had a chance."

"Young or old?"

"Age of the doctor." She pointed at me. "Tattoo on his shoulder. A little flower."

"Anything else?" Sennett asked.

She yanked a handful of tissues from a box and snuffled into them. "One other thing," she said. "He kept saying something over and over, like he was preaching at me. 'Vengeance is mine,' he said. Cutting me up, he puts his face right up next to mine, whispers, 'Vengeance is mine.'"

I was thinking about blood loss, the danger of shock. I told her we should get her to an emergency room. Detroit Medical Center was close.

"I'm not going anywhere." Her eyes clicked to the wall, then down. A sound. Something was there. Sennett reached for his piece. "I got a baby," she said.

I walked around the foot of the bed and looked. On the floor, in a basket. Maybe six months, tan skin, dark ringlets.

"I can't leave her," she said.

Sennett reached for his cellular phone and went into the living room. I heard talk, the refrigerator open and close. Within a couple of minutes, he brought a bottle, bent down, and picked up the infant.

"EMS will be here soon. So will Protective Services. They'll take care of you and your baby. Get you out of this place."

So she tricked at Eddie's to stay close to home—to be near the baby.

I thought of the baby inside of Jordan. We lived in another world from LaShonda Wright, a world just twenty minutes away, a world that was crumbling while I looked for answers. George stood in the door, the baby in the crook of his arm. I wondered what kind of father I would be, if I got to be a father at all.

CHAPTER 9

I NEEDED A MEDICAL LIBRARY. The closest one was connected to Great Lakes Medical Center. I drove there from police headquarters, thinking about Jordan. If she recovered, we'd get married. I didn't want to wait long. We could do it within six weeks; plan the wedding, something small, invite friends. Neither of us had much family. She'd be strong again, her old self. If she recovered. So I'd begun to think in those terms. When I thought of her at that moment, I saw her in the hospital bed, not at home, sitting across from me in the kitchen, with Buck squirming in her arms.

Oh Lord, the damn dog.

After a few calls I located the friend Jordan had left Buck with, Shirley Taberall. When I told her what had happened she felt terrible about having to ask me to take Buck back. She was going out of town.

I'd have to find a kennel. Or maybe a kind-hearted person who would do me a favor. There was only one person I could think of calling. She was a long shot. I'd try her later, when I got home.

It was late in the day at the university. The library was crowded with med students and nurses. They looked haggard and serious, exams not far off. I found an open seat at a terminal and started searching for articles on botulism. The first few told me what I already knew. The bacteria, toxin, and paralysis failing to treat effectively with antitoxin was a very bad prognosis. They also mentioned its medicinal qualities. Even quoted my article. It gave me a hollow feeling.

A nursing student was standing next to me in her scrubs, trying not to look impatient. A shock of blonde hair fell in her face. Just another minute or so, I told her. She was in her early twenties, thin-boned and delicate. After what I'd seen that day, I couldn't help feeling frightened for her. I tried to put the image of Claudia Fraser's mutilated corpse from my mind. Focus, I told myself. I reviewed an article on culturing bacteria and thought of Yvonne Jensen. Enough time had elapsed, she might know something. I cleared the screen and gave my seat to the young woman, thinking, *Please be careful.*

In the downstairs lobby, I found a phone and dialed up the St. Vincent's laboratory. Yvonne was on duty. She said she'd been trying to reach me.

"What did you find?" I asked eagerly.

"This is a strange one," she said.

"I thought it was *Clostridia botulinum.*"

"It is, but not exactly. It's a different strain, something no one has seen before. We sent it to the CDC for identification. It takes a week."

The Center for Disease Control in Atlanta.

"I don't have that kind of time," I said.

"I know, Ben. All I can tell you is that it looks like a laboratory strain. A bug like this doesn't surface in the population very often."

I hung up the phone. An unusual laboratory strain. Where would Claudia have gotten such a thing? She had a way with men. She must have known someone in research.

I went back to a terminal and logged on to GratefulMed, searching for information on tattoos. There were twenty-six articles, nothing helpful. A higher rate of social malevolence was associated with tattooed individuals. Well, thanks. I had a textbook case of malevolence.

It was almost midnight when I left the library. I decided to stop at The Pipeline, visit Sid. When I walked in, there was a piano and string bass playing, so slow and cool and quiet I hardly wanted to breathe. A hush of brushes on the snare. Then a sax. It sounded like "Audrey," Brubeck's piece for Hepburn. The place was almost empty. At a table near the stage, a woman whispered to the two men she was with. Their table was covered with glasses.

Sid was sipping a Coke at the bar, talking jazz with his bartender.

"Ain't that right, Ben?" he said when he saw me. "It was Duke that started it all. He brought the black man's music and the big band sound together. Made jazz respectable."

"The music commanded respect," I said.

The bartender handed me my club soda. The woman had stood up. She had long, brown hair, a high laugh. She was trying to get one of her men to dance. The one with his hand on her ass.

"But the men playing it," Sid said. "They needed respect. What's the first thing you think of when you meet a musician? Good hobby, hard to make a living. Who makes a living playing the piano, even today? Nobody." He pointed at the stage. "Look at those guys. Teacher, draftsman, cook. And I don't know what. With bass players, you never know."

"Poet," the bartender said.

The woman had taken his hand off her ass and pulled the man to his feet. He put his arms around her. Pure grace.

"Poet," Sid said. "People think a musician is lazy and dumb. Talk to him, listen to his ideas. Smart people. You'll find a poet?"

"Really," the bartender said. "Some of the dumbest people I know are musicians."

"And doctors," I added.

She hung an arm around his neck. They hardly moved, rocking in place while the sax player blew. I closed my eyes. Jordan, smiling, looking at me from across the table, chin cradled in one hand. Intelligent loving eyes. I didn't want to move. I had to call the hospital. I had to get home. I had to chase down a laboratory strain of botulism. I had to find someone to look after my dog.

The band was easing out of the song, a long finish. I opened my eyes. On the dance floor, the woman lay still in her troglodyte's arms, her head dropped back, exposing a fine, white neck. Now what? I thought. The one sitting at the table lit a cigarette, drained his glass, then emptied two more glasses left on the table. The woman's partner did something wonderful. He dipped her, almost to the floor, let her hang there, then pulled her back to her feet and held her through the last bars, long after the song was done. Just held her. Maybe he wasn't a Neanderthal. I couldn't understand anything.

Sid wasn't finished. "A musician understands where people live—in here." He touched his heart. "They read notes, interpret the music, create different moods."

He must have seen me watching the couple on the floor.

"Where's that girlfriend of yours, Ben? I miss her."

I told him where she was, and about the food poisoning. How the botulism was meant for me. I could have said more, but I was trying not to think. I was tired of thinking for one day.

"Poor girl got no one but you to look after her," he said. "You wait for the police, you might never get your answer."

I drank another soda and went outside to my car. You got it right, Sid, I thought. The musician reads, interprets. I had to think. I had to read, interpret. Make sense of the cacophony of notes.

CHAPTER 10

I MADE THREE CALLS EARLY NEXT MORNING. First to Phil Lindstrom. I reached him at home. He said he was just about to leave for rounds. He'd seen Jordan twice in the past twenty-four hours. She was still in a coma, but also still stable. There'd been no real response to the antitoxin. No real response? Well, he said, I knew what that meant. He just didn't want to say it. He had to conclude the antitoxin was not working. Latest indications showed paralysis of her musculature had worsened. When I pressed him, he said another couple of days was about all we had. Then it would be all over. Then he used the "m" word.

We needed a miracle.

Pray, he said.

As if I wasn't already.

I told him I was working with Yvonne. We'd found a strain, and she'd sent it to the CDC. In the meantime, I was going back to the source to see what I could learn. I said I'd connected the strain to a person, maybe, and to a place, maybe, and that I was going to get more information today. Maybe. When he asked me to elaborate, I said I'd tell him the whole story once this nightmare was over.

Next I dialed Bruce Sanderson. I was going back to Philadelphia, and I wanted to see Alden Sherman. Would he please set it up? He wondered what gave me the idea I could call him any damn time of day. Just set up the meeting, I said. I was leaving in an hour. Please. And while he was at it, call Connely too, and tell him I was coming.

"He doesn't want to talk to you, Ben."

"Well, that's too bad," I said.

"He's hiding something."

"He's hiding a lot," I said.

I had one more call. I poured myself a second cup of coffee and dialed Sheila Pryzbycki's number. She was out of bed. That was a relief. I pictured her in a small, yellow kitchen, wrapped in a quilted robe, wearing her crown of perfectly big hair.

"What do you want, Ben?"

"A favor." On her desk, I'd seen pictures of her and her terrier. She wasn't great with people, but I figured she must have a way with animals. I explained that I had suddenly become a dog owner, that the dog needed temporary care while I did my work. Could she help me out for a few days? I braced myself for a lecture. Shouldn't we have thought the matter through before we brought this dog into our lives? Had we considered the dog's feelings? But I'd underestimated her. She just said to bring him over. She loved dogs and had the ideal backyard.

"You're sure?" I said.

A spoon clanked against a coffee cup. I heard her sip coffee.

"Rags'll enjoy the company," she said. "Won't you, my little honey-poo?" She talked it over with her dog for a couple of seconds. After listening to her I thought a dog's life wasn't so bad. It made me afraid that Buck might never want to come home.

I CAUGHT MY THIRD FLIGHT TO PHILLY that week at 9:00 a.m. Budget found me a brown Toyota Corrola with a sunroof and keyless entry. I was becoming a regular commuter. I drove north through town and hooked up with Highway 202 at Ambler. By 10:30, I was in Dellsburg Baptist's lobby. At the information desk, I breezed past the white-haired angels in their blue smocks. Down the hall toward administration were half a dozen suits with white Styrofoam cups in hand, remnants of the first coffee break of the day. On the surface, it was any hospital in the USA.

Sherman's secretary announced me when I walked in. This time, the big man kept me waiting fifteen minutes. I sat in a pumpkin-colored chair in his anteroom. I stood, then sat down again. I was running out of patience. More than anything, I had to keep control now. Be polite, I thought. Get what you came here for and then get home.

When Sherman came out, we made a perfunctory handshake. He showed me into his office, sat me down in front of his gleaming, empty desk. His face was flushed. He looked as if he'd taken a flight of stairs too fast.

"I know this is inconvenient," I said. "I appreciate your making time for me."

I told him I wanted to meet with Frank Connely. But before I did, I wanted to talk to him again. I wasn't here about the insurance settlement. As far as I was concerned, that was over. I said I knew there were delicate matters in Connely's past. I didn't care about any that. But I needed some information that only Connely could help me with, and I hoped Sherman would encourage Connely to cooperate.

Sherman patted the top of his head, smoothing his hair. His face was still flushed. Perspiration glowed on his forehead. He looked down at his phone. One of the lights was blinking. He excused himself and took the call at his secretary's desk. Another delay. I glanced around the room. Read. Interpret. There was a bookcase with a number of religious books. On one wall was a picture of Sherman with assorted dignitaries dressed in CEO fatigues, gathered around a golf cart. Signed by the governor: "Thanks for all your help." Another glossy, signed photo, this one in front of the White House.

Alden Sherman got around. He was a status-conscious man.

"All part of the job," he said from the doorway. "How do we get government to pay attention to the needs of hospitals?"

"Play golf?"

"It's more than golf." He moved behind his desk and sank into his chair. "Half the country's policy is brokered on a golf course."

And the other half, I thought, is just plain broken.

Sherman folded his hands and smiled a thin smile. He said he'd try to help me. He had a staff meeting in just a few minutes. It wasn't the best time. He'd accommodated Bruce Sanderson—and me—as a courtesy, because of the effort we'd put into the case. He could only give me a few seconds.

A few seconds, I thought.

"I need to talk to Frank Connely about Claudia Fraser," I said. "I think there's a connection between her and a friend of mine back in Detroit. This friend is in the hospital. She was poisoned."

"I'm sorry to hear that." He patted his hair again with the flat of one hand. "If you think there's a connection, why don't you talk to Claudia Fraser?"

"Because Claudia Fraser was murdered the night before last."

He drew in a breath and held it, then closed his eyes a second. He shook his head slowly, touched his hair again, then rolled up one shirtsleeve. He said he was sorry. Very sorry. She was a troubled soul. A licentious woman. Evidently her life had simply spun out of control. He wondered about the circumstances of her death. I told him I didn't have any details. If nothing else, I wanted to protect a dead Claudia Fraser from the moral machinery of this hospital. They might have further uses for her. I was determined not to be an accessory.

"But you see why it's important for me to talk to Dr. Connely. He might be able to tell me what other affiliations Claudia had with physicians."

"Affiliations, yes." He picked up the phone, dialed a number and waited. He rolled up the other shirtsleeve, picked up a pencil, and tapped it on his desk. Finally he spoke briefly, then set the phone back down. "He's not in the office yet."

A trickle of sweat was coursing down his left temple. The man was coming unglued right in front of me. I gazed over his shoulder. Outside, across the valley, a flock of crows was taking wing. Dark angels. I needed an angel to bring me some information, and fast.

I said, "What about Dr. Connely's professional life and interests?"

"He's a respected surgeon. He's operated on and taken care of a number of staff here at Baptist. He's an innovator."

"How so?"

"He has done ground-breaking work on voice disorders."

"What kind of work?" I asked.

"He treats vocal cords with a medicine that stops hoarseness. But you'd have to ask him to explain it. I'm not a doctor."

He'd reminded me of my disquiet at Connely's unduly large supply of Botox. He got it from a lab somewhere in Newark, I remembered. Was that the lab where the killer strain had been developed? It was worth a look.

I got up from my chair and shook his hand, both of us hoping it was the last time.

I STOPPED TO USE THE PHONE IN THE HOSPITAL LOBBY. I called St. Vincent's. There was no change in Jordan. Then I reached Sennett to see if he'd learned anything about Claudia Fraser. I told him I was in Dellsburg. Had he found out anything I should follow up on out here? He said he didn't know any more about Claudia Fraser than he had the night before, and what did I expect, miracles?

"I could sure use one."

"I knew you wouldn't sit still," he said. "I went to see Jordan this morning, Ben. I went. While you're in Pennsylvania playing detective. Do you see something wrong with this picture?"

Yes, I saw his point. But I was useless to Jordan sitting beside her bed. Here, at least, I might find out what had made her sick in the first place, and from there, find the antidote.

"What did Connely tell you?"

"He's not here. He's not answering pages. No one knows where he is."

"And that other guy?"

"Alden Sherman? He wouldn't know. And if he did, I get the idea he wouldn't tell me. He's real nervous about all this."

"So what makes you think Connely will be any different?"

"I don't," I said desperately. "But he's all I've got."

He covered the phone. I could hear him yelling for Knudsen to bring him something. "Here we go," he said. "I got that report you wanted. You didn't think I was just sitting here, did you? Mary Jane Connely died of respiratory obstruction. The husband refused an autopsy, and the patient's body was cremated."

"Anything else on the record?"

"The death was ruled accidental. No charges filed. The rest must have gone through the civil courts."

"Connely," I said through my teeth. "Where the hell is he?"

"Give me a minute. Let me check the police wire."

One of Connely's nurses was walking in my direction. She didn't look happy. She told me she was going out to lunch. She needed relief. She'd spent the last hour apologizing to patients for something she had no control over. Ordinarily the office ran like clockwork, but today it was a zoo up there. Werner was still up there, she said. Werner had the patience of two and a half saints. She zipped up her jacket, pulled on a stocking cap, and banged out the door.

Sennett came back on the line.

"You're not going to like this one, Ben."

"What?"

"There's a Dr. Frank Connely on the wire," he said. "Reported dead, victim of a one-car crash into the Delaware River. The police are listing it as an accident."

CHAPTER 11

I HUNG UP THE PHONE, stepped out into the waiting area, and dropped into a chair. Connely was dead, and I had nothing. Outside the hospital entrance, a man pushed a wheelchair down the walk. A red Jeep swung up the drive, too fast, then stopped suddenly. The driver was chewing gum and smoking. He glanced in the mirror and checked his stalagmite hair. The orderly loaded the patient, another young guy with spiky hair, into the Jeep, which jerked forward and sped away. I pictured the Jeep rolling down a hillside, the riders flying out of the vehicle.

Connely was dead.

And Jordan was losing ground.

My world was going nuts.

I went down to the cafeteria, ordered a coffee, ate a piece of pie. Doctors and nurses were coming together and breaking apart, all involved in living and working. For the glory of God, maybe. Or for their own personal reasons that were petty and grandiose, honest and suspect. They'd know soon enough about Connely. Most of them knew plenty already.

From the cafeteria, I took the elevator up to Sherman's office. The local press had assembled in the hall. Sherman stood outside his office door, making an announcement. I stayed in the background and listened as he finished up. He said Dr. Connely would be missed: a skilled physician, a humane individual who ministered to the needs of his patients. A respected colleague –

Respected.

Death, in its ironic way, would probably be good to Connely.

As the group of reporters filed away, I edged my way toward the office. When I caught Sherman's eye, he didn't look too happy to see me.

"No time, Dr. Dailey," he said. "Dr. Connely's untimely death has left us all in a state of shock."

"I just wanted to ask," I said, "if you knew anything about Frank Connely's contacts in Newark, New Jersey."

"Newark?" Sherman glared at me. "Newark," he said again, as if the word baffled him.

"I noticed in his office. He gets his Botox there." *Got*, I thought, but chose not to correct myself.

"Listen." He drew himself up and stepped toward me. Any touch of friend-liness had vanished. "I have nothing more to say. I have spent all the time on your investigation that I can. More than I should have. We have a terrible situation here. A tragic situation. I should think you'd know when it's time to back off."

"I know it's difficult."

"Extremely difficult. Now if you will excuse me, I have to attend a board meeting."

He backed into his office doorway, glared at me, then disappeared inside.

But what about the bacteria? I wanted to shout. The respected Dr. Connely had been no angel. He had been up to something, and now he was dead.

I took the elevator down, crossed to the professional building, and went up to Connely's office. An old woman, presumably one of his patients, stood outside his office door, dabbing her nose with a hanky. Inside, the office was cleared, except for the staff. Everyone was standing around, red-eyed or weep-ing. I knew scenes like this; E.R. waiting rooms, my own office, when I'd had one. The television on, sound turned down, medical drama on the afternoon soaps in progress. And the image of real loss. I went up to Mrs. Werner and of-fered my condolences. She was slumped in a chair behind the counter.

"So unfair," she said.

Yes, I agreed, life was definitely not fair.

She fiddled with papers on the desk. "They said he might have been forced off the road by another car. Into the river. Who would do such a thing?"

"Lots of crazy people out there," I said.

"He was so alive and vibrant. Interested in everything. His patients, his research."

She'd handed me my opportunity, so I jumped. "He seemed like he really cared," I said. "Really first rate. He was a doctors' doctor."

She brightened at this.

"You know he did research in addition to his practice?"

"Really? Where?"

"Somewhere in New Jersey."

"And what was it exactly?" I asked.

"I don't know exactly, but he told me he was trying to learn as much about the use of botulinum toxin as possible. He had a whole stack of articles from the lab in New Jersey. He showed them to me once. Too complicated for me."

"Do you have one I could see?"

"He kept a file in his bookcase." She went into his office and pulled down some reprints and handed them to me.

New techniques in the development of botulinum toxin. Bacteriological studies. I focused on the articles. At the bottom of two of them there was an acknowledgment, to Priscilla Wadsworth, in the research lab. The last one, on plating techniques for bacterial growth, closed with a standard disclaimer. In keeping with federal law, research from a private company had to be spelled out in detail. Connely's was being funded by a grant from the Elnor Corporation.

I went back to Mrs. Werner's desk.

"Do you think I could keep these reprints of Dr. Connely 's bacteriological studies? I found them very interesting."

The girl shrugged her shoulders.

"I guess it would be all right. After all, there's no one else to claim it."

"Thanks. I'll just make a phone call and get out of your way."

I went to the front office and asked to use a phone. The nurse showed me to a small desk at the side of the office. Fifteen minutes later I had the address and telephone number of Priscilla Wadsworth. Her research lab was sponsored by the Elnor Corporation at North Jersey Medical Center.

Bingo.

IT WAS A FIFTY-MILE DRIVE TO THE NORTH JERSEY MEDICAL CENTER.

At two o'clock, I swung out of Dellsburg and headed up the 206 toward Newark, through Lewisville, Lawrenceville, and Princeton. Under a clear, fall sky the western New Jersey countryside was fine, almost pristine. Further east, the landscape changed. Petroleum tanks, brown fields. Early modern toxic, I thought, not unlike Detroit. The place I wanted was off Highway 1 near the junction of the Hackensack and Passaic Rivers.

I found the Medical Center, a huge complex, spread out over fifty acres. On the surface, it stood as a symbol of defiance to the forces of decay that had seized the city. But there was a subliminal relationship: medical schools liked urban centers for ready access to indigent patients. An infinite supply of illness and trauma. Ideal for young physicians eager to ply their trade. An ironic twist on the parasite-host relationship.

I found the entrance to the medical center and pulled into the visitors parking garage. I guessed the lab would be attached to the main hospital, made a few inquiries, and was directed back out the front entrance and east, toward the low, tan building on the edge of the facility. I hurried along the sidewalk toward it, hoping she would be there. Hoping for no more surprises.

I looked in a few labs. It was a pretty standard research facility. Modular oscilloscopes, some electrophysiologic machines, and operating benches, probably for dog experiments. Next to each bench was a desktop computer. In the corner was a small, steel desk with a microscope and another computer.

I stepped inside a third lab with P. Wadsworth on the door. Immediately I saw a woman who could be no one but Priscilla Wadsworth. She wore a long, white lab coat with sleeves folded at the cuffs. But there was more to her than that. Buttocks rounded against the back of her coat,; the curvature, of her breasts made a symmetrical counterpoint. She wore glasses, which made her seem bookish, but her full lips were sensuous. She glanced up, giving me a look that said touch the right button and something might happen. It wasn't hard to guess why Frank Connely had come up here every three to four weeks. Research, my ass.

I introduced myself and told her I had been visiting Connely's office in Dellsburg. "I tried to catch him this morning," I said. "One of his nurses told me about his work here."

"Really," she said in a soft voice. The way she said it made me wonder if she knew he was dead.

"Really," I said. "She suggested that I stop by."

She sat on a bench, crossed one leg over the other, and gazed quizzically over her wire-rimmed glasses. I told her I was interested in Botox, its uses in diseases of the larynx.

"I'd like to help you," she said, "but Dr. Connely has given me strict instructions. No access to his lab."

"His lab?"

"His." She nodded. "For a couple of years now."

I walked to the middle of the lab, bent down, and looked at a computer screen. A login screen was displayed. The system was networked. She lifted her chin and seemed to tighten.

"I'm not here to steal anything," I said. "I need help."

She took off her glasses and wiped the lenses on her lab coat.

"Maybe I can help," she said. "Just now we're working on a new technique for electromyography of the larynx."

"I've heard of it." I cleared my throat. I could play expert. "Using unipolar or bipolar needles?"

She blinked. "Okay, you pass."

"I use Botox back in Detroit. I've talked with Dr. Connely about his work."

She put her glasses back on and adjusted her coat lapels. She had beautiful hands, long fingers. I wondered if she'd ever played piano. "We're two years into the project. Nothing conclusive, but I think we're getting close. And as long as the grant is alive, I have a job."

"Whose funds? Research money is hard to come by."

"A patient he worked on," she said. "Gave him tons of money."

"My kind of patient." I sat on the stool in front of the computer.

She dragged a stool next to mine and climbed on it, crossing her legs so the lab coat fell away from her knees. Legs. And just enough of the dark area above to tell me something. I looked up at her. She was smiling.

"Networked computers?" I nodded at the system.

"Yes." She laid one hand over the other. She didn't play piano anymore, not with those nails.

"Expensive," I said.

"His work is valued. When he got the money from his donor, Elnor matched the funds."

I looked around the room. Make this offhand, I thought. "Where do you do cultures and things like that?"

"Not here."

"No?" I said. A little too fast.

Priscilla looked away. A machine buzzed at the other end of the lab, and she crossed the room to reset it. When she came back and sat down again, her legs were a little wider apart. Maybe I was just imagining things. She also seemed nervous. Or maybe I was imagining that, too. She said she had a procedure to finish, which meant I'd really have to run along, if I didn't mind.

I said of course I didn't and got up to leave.

"Are you in town for long?" she said. She put her hand on my sleeve. I felt the slightest pressure in her fingertips.

"Maybe a couple of days. I'd hate to go home empty-handed."

"My friends and I sometimes meet in the city," she said. More pressure from those long fingers. "A place called The Original Sin. Down near The Village."

I said I'd heard the name. Who hadn't?

"Drop by tonight," she said. "Maybe we'll have something to talk about."

"Maybe I can do that," I said. Just the place to talk about bacteriology, I thought.

I stopped along the road and called St. Vincent's. Jordan was starting to spike temperatures. Not a good sign. I was going to page Phil Lindstrom but decided against it. In this situation, talking wouldn't do anybody any good. Let the doctor work.

I punched in Sennett's telephone number and waited. Connely's lab wasn't set up for bacteriology. That was clear. I didn't know how much Priscilla Wadsworth wasn't telling me, or what exactly she knew. So maybe I'd be looking into Original Sin.

When Sennett came to the phone, he said the M.E. had found something funny on Connely.

"Another tattoo?"

"How'd you guess?" He held a hand over the phone and spoke to someone. I pictured Knudsen's close-cropped head and eager eyes as I chewed my lower lip, impatience gnawing at me as the raven gnawed at Prometheus's liver. Was I getting literary in my panic and despair?

"Ben?" Sennett said. "Okay. We've got a flower tattoo on the right shoulder. Knudsen's doing a computer search on tattoos. Maybe something will come up."

"And I believe in the tooth fairy."

"You got zero out there?"

"I'll know soon," I said. "After tonight. I'm meeting Connely's research assistant, Priscilla Wadsworth." I decided not to say where.

"There's a lot going on here, Ben."

"Tell me about it. I've got a feeling of dread for all of this."

"Did I mean Jordan," he said.

"Yes. A general, all-encompassing dread. It's ugly."

"Fear is crime's punishment."

"Dostoevsky?"

"Voltaire."

"I'm impressed," I said. "I've got a reader when I need a crime stopper."

"Reading helps me think."

Think hard and fast, my good friend. We're running out of time.

CHAPTER 12

THAT NIGHT I DROVE INTO MANHATTAN by way of the Holland Tunnel and found a Holiday Inn near Broadway and 42nd Street. Down the street was a deli where I'd once had a dish of the best rugalach and schnecken I'd ever eaten. I returned and was not disappointed. Through dinner I watched a bald man at a table by the door have an argument with himself. In Hungarian. He smoked a pipe and gestured roundly at the people outside, as if questioning how they could disagree with him.

Welcome to New York.

I took a cab down toward Greenwich Village around eleven o'clock. Once in the cab I began to wish I'd asked Priscilla for a street address. I had to tell the cabbie I was looking for Original Sin. Did he know the place? He said he knew of it. Emphasizing *of*, in order to make a clear distinction between him and me. I was desperate, but not in the way he thought. At the moment, my idea of scoring was pinning Priscilla Wadsworth down on the subject of a new botulism strain and getting back to Detroit with an antidote.

The cab dropped me off in the meatpacking district, on a small side street, near the Hudson River. I walked toward the front entrance of a six-story brick building. Out front, in red neon letters, The Original Sin blinked on and off. A line popped into my head: There is no sin except stupidity. Oscar Wilde? I told myself to remember that one for Sennett.

The door was locked. I was about to take it as a sign and leave when the door opened, light streaming out onto the sidewalk. Stepping into the street was a man with a shaved head, a thick Fu Manchu, leather jacket, and motorcycle boots. He had three earrings in both ears, one of them a silver skull. From his looks Igor would be a fitting name.

"What?" he said.

"I'm looking for someone," I said.

"Who?"

"Priscilla Wadsworth. She told me to meet her here." I gave him my name. He looked at a clipboard. "When?"

I told him I'd met her that afternoon. Or did he mean when was I supposed to meet her? He looked me up and down, then frowned. I could see him searching his memory banks for just the right word.

"Okay," he said. He jerked a thumb toward the interior. "You're comped."

Igor stepped aside, and I walked past the heavy door. It slammed behind me. It was dark inside. The room had a low ceiling and was deeper than it was wide. Tables in the middle, at the far end of the room a stage. The air was thick with smoke, and the scent of perfume and gin hung in the air. Along the wall to the right was a long bar crowded with people, mostly young business types, men and women both. At the end of the bar I saw Priscilla. She waved me over.

Out of her lab coat, all trace of the schoolgirl had departed. The vamp remained, in full force. She wore a low V-neck sweater and tight, black leather trousers with stacked boots. Her eyes glistened behind blue-sparkled eye shadow, her lips looked wet and red.

When I reached the bar, she looped her arm inside mine and pulled me to the stool next to hers. Her breasts brushed against my chest.

"I'm glad you came."

"Charming doorman," I said. "Though a little too talkative."

"I told him to watch for you."

I stepped back and looked at her. "So, this is your after-hours look?"

"All work and no play," she said, squeezing herself a little closer, "you know what they say." I could feel the heat from her body. Her hand migrated downward, along my thigh. "What do you think of the place?"

I pictured Connely there, the good Christian doctor, with Priscilla's hand on his ass. What was that about hypocrites, being like unto whited sepulchers.

"A good place to catch up on your reading," I said.

"And catch the show."

"Show?"

"Maybe you'll want to audition."

Something told me not to expect Chekhov.

I ordered a beer and leaned against the bar, watching the mating game play itself out along the brass rail. Men in eight hundred dollar suits, Gucci loafers, and Tank Française watches. Women wandered from man to man, trolling for someone they liked. Apparently, as long as Priscilla was with me, I was safe. I was thinking hard. She must have heard about Connely's death. Did she care or was she involved? Her callousness in being here at all, along with her undoubted complicity in Connely's suspected criminal research in botulism strains, did not argue favorably for her innocence in his untimely death.

Or maybe mine?

The music changed, ratcheted up a few hundred decibels, and the lights dimmed. Priscilla pulled back from me. She seemed a little agitated.

"Tonight's amateur night," she said. "Some of us get to participate."

"Is that you?"

Something told me this would be more than a wet t-shirt contest.

"That's me," she said. "I've got to get dressed. Watch for me on the stage."

She disappeared through a side door at the front of the room. The stage lights flicked on and off, then settled into a continuous strobe effect. Onstage, one of Igor's colleagues carried a bench downstage and set it down. It was fitted with a metal frame, with ropes hanging from either end. He looked up and pumped the air with his arms, demonstrating his pelvic thrust. The crowd hooted in delight.

Shortly after, a young woman wearing a white shift and a black mask with slits for her eyes appeared at the side of the stage. She twirled around, giving us a good look. It was Priscilla. The howling gave way for a second, then rose again as two more women took the stage; one athletic, black, the other white and fleshy. Both wore soft-billed, leather Harley hats. Their black leather jackets were unzipped with nothing else on above the waist. Covering their legs were black, thigh-high stiletto-heeled boots. They faced the audience and swiveled their hips in a slow grinding motion, showing tufts of hair between their legs.

For a warm-up, they grasped on to each other, tongues in each other's mouths, gently rubbing against each other. Priscilla stood by dancing, waiting for her turn. She wasn't much of a dancer. The two women circled her, running their hands up and down her body, then removed her dress and showed her body to the crowd for approval. One kissed her on the mouth and moved swiftly down to her breasts. The black woman knelt in front of her, spread Priscilla's legs, and began massaging her. Priscilla backed up and sat on the bench. While one woman buried her face in Priscilla's crotch, the other tied her hands and legs.

I'd seen all I needed to see. I turned to the bar, held up my glass to the bartender. Next to me at the bar, a suit divided his time between watching the show and hitting on the woman with him. He had short, red hair and pink squinty eyes. He was so drunk and excited that his ears glowed. He was telling her he wanted it right there. He clamped a hand on the back of the woman's neck, swung her around, and bent her over the bar. His white shirt was soaking wet.

She turned to me and rolled her eyes. "Jane," she said, holding out her hand with some difficulty.

She might have been thirty. She had black hair, pulled back and tied, and wore a tie-dye shirt and tight pants. No bra. No jewelry. High heels.

"Ben," I said.

In the bar mirror, I could see a woman on stage wrap a whip around Priscilla's neck. The crowd was going nuts. Clothes were coming off. Couples were locking together. The fool was pawing Jane from behind. His face was bright red, his eyes glazed. I ordered a screwdriver for Jane. On stage two men had appeared, leather jockstraps accentuated by bloodcurdling painted faces, leather amulets, and motorcycle boots. I stared at one of them. His muscular chest was bare, with bulging biceps grasping around Priscilla from behind as his hands massaged her breasts. Under the red paint over his eyebrows, his eyes emanated an evil glow. I could have sworn that I had seen those eyes before.

"He's an accountant," Jane said, motioning over her shoulder. He was tugging on her jeans. She shrugged him off and kicked him in the groin. "I'll see him tomorrow in the office."

"Drunk and stupid," I said.

"Yes," she said. "Tomorrow he will just be stupid."

Priscilla had been lain face down on the bench. Her ass was elevated, her left side to the audience. The two men removed their jockstraps. One leaned over her from the back, the other took the front. Their female assistants brandished the whips, striking the men from behind. Not too hard, just enough to stimulate.

"What's your excuse?" Jane said.

"You might say this is research," I answered.

I took a drink and looked up at the mirror. The man at Priscilla's rear poured oil over her and began to massage her hips. He pulled her hips up, raising her from the bench. He was big and hard. The other man was giving it to her in her mouth.

"Want to see her bush?" The accountant. His jacket was off, his shirt and head newly wet. Someone had thrown a fresh drink on him. He reached around her waist and fumbled with her zipper.

"Fuck off, Andrew."

"Big, black bush."

The ape behind Priscilla was riding her hard. He had metal clips on his upper arms. Her flanks were streaked where he'd scratched her. Jane shoved Andrew away. Her pants were undone, slipped down over one hip. No underwear.

"What sort of research?" she said, pulling her pants back up.

"Tattoos." I placed a hand on the accountant's head and shoved him. He toppled over backward. "And bacteriology."

She slipped her pants back down an inch or two "Check this out." She turned away and showed me a small tattoo on her left cheek. From the floor, Andrew gave me a menacing look. I leaned down and examined it, ran a finger over the surface of her hip. All this fucking going on, and I was basically doing an office call, palpating the patient. It was a red, white, and blue butterfly. I straightened up and told her she could pull her pants back up. Across the room, Igor stared at me. Now why did such a nice homespun boy seem so interested in my every move in this place Priscilla had enticed me to?

"Patriotic," I said. I meant the tricolor butterfly.

Jane zipped up and shrugged. Said she regretted having it done. "The body is a temple, you know?"

They were doing Priscilla pretty rough. I'd seen raped women in the emergency room. I wondered if she had any idea how close she was to being criminally assaulted. The two women assistants were completely naked. They caressed the men's backs, masturbated with their whip handles. Andrew had pulled himself to his feet. He swayed, steadied himself, and raised his fists. A fighting accountant.

"Get your own date!" he said.

"I'm not your date, Andrew." Jane looked at me entreatingly. Could I do something about him? He staggered over and breathed on us. It was his best offense. Once again, I gave him a stiff arm. This time, he stayed down, splayed on the wet floor. I bought Jane another drink.

"As soon as I finish this one, why don't we get out of here?" she said.

I told her it was a tempting offer, but I couldn't.

"You here with someone?"

"The talent," I said, pointing at the stage.

As if on cue, both men pulled out of Priscilla and came on her back and in her face. Once he was finished, her partner in the rear pulled on his jock, jumped off the stage into the crowd, and made his way to the bar. The lights onstage died as those in the room came back up. The bartender handed him a pitcher of beer, which he lifted and began to drink. Beer sloshed down over his chest and shoulders.

So much for talking to Priscilla, I thought. So much for learning anything.

"Neanderthal," Jane said.

Beer ran down his arms, dripped from his elbows. It was when he set the pitcher down that I saw the mark. On his right shoulder, a round tattoo with a peculiar flower. I looked at his painted face

Across the room Igor was still watching me. After locking eyes with me for a long moment he stroked his tattoos and moved to the front door.

I bought Jane another drink and told her I'd be right back. I walked to the end of the bar, passing a half-dressed couple bent over a table. At the end of the counter I saw the men's room sign. I walked in and closed the door.

No windows, no easy exit.

I splashed some water on my face and walked back out. I decided a frontal assault was best, so I walked to the door. Igor blocked my way.

"No one leaves yet. Mr. Vic wants to see you after the show."

"Mr. Vic?"

Igor lifted his chin, gesturing toward the stage.

I looked to my side. On a tabletop stood an empty beer bottle. I knocked it to the ground, and it shattered. Igor's gaze flicked away from me for a moment, just long enough for me to give him a forearm shiver. My football coach would have been proud. Igor dropped to his knees. I kicked him forward into the table. I slammed open the dead bolt and raced outside.

It was dark in the street. Looking back, I saw the bar door open. Yellow light streamed onto the street. I kept running. I had no interest in talking to Mr. Vic.

The end of the street opened into an alley. I was getting ready to cut right when a man stepped out of the shadow and blocked my way. He held up a thin knife. The blade caught a little light from the wider street. I didn't know who he was, and I didn't care.

He rushed at me. I sidestepped, leg whipping his lower leg. I heard him crash to the ground, the knife clattering to the pavement.

I ran for the light of 10th Avenue. Light traffic, no yellow taxis, no crowds. No way for me to lose myself. I kept running, gaining another interminable crosstown block, then another.

I looked back again. Igor was not far behind me. Alongside him was an even bigger leather-clad man. I cut across 8th Avenue, avoiding two cars as I churned toward the 14th Street subway entrance. On the steps, I grabbed the railing and two-stepped it down, where I hurtled the turnstile and lunged into a train just pulling in.

The car was empty except for two black kids in Kangol caps. They looked at me with interest. I dropped into a seat, gasping for air. From the window I watched as the two men entered the adjoining car.

The doors closed. I stood up, edging to the center of the car. Aside from the two kids and a stocky man with a sack of groceries I hadn't seen in the corner, there was nothing between Igor, his friend, and me except a communicating door. It burst open. Igor ran a finger over his mustache and shook his head. I glanced beyond Igor, as if at someone behind him, and in the next fraction of a second pulled the stocky man's grocery bag off his lap, spilling the contents on the floor. He lunged forward, grasping at cans rolling away from him, shouting at me in Greek. Igor and his pal stepped back. I had already pulled the cord. The door reopened.

They rushed toward me, blocked by the man on the floor, now on his hands and knees. I stepped out on the platform. As suddenly as they opened, the doors closed again, and the train jerked forward.

CHAPTER 13

I RAN UP THE STAIRS, TAKING TWO AT A TIME. I was safe, but only in a manner of speaking, and probably only for the time being. My suspicion of Priscilla Wadsworth's motives in leading me to that club appeared justified. A clap of thunder broke as I dropped onto a bench, exhausted and drained. My hands were shaking. The air smelled of diesel exhaust. I'd moved that fast only a couple times since college. In life, just as in football, saving your ass is a great motivator.

I knew I couldn't hang around.

I walked back to the subway and took the E Train headed towards Queens. At 53rd Street I transferred to a 6 Train and rode to the Bronx and back. What was Mr. Vic's connection to Frank Connely and the botulism strain threatening Jordan and our baby?

I needed time to think about what I was going to do. I got back to my hotel room, dead-bolted the door, took a shower, and came out feeling almost alive.

Priscilla Wadsworth was involved. The man on the stage—Mr. Vic—was connected to Frank Connely, and to Claudia Fraser as well. The tattoo was no coincidence. I had to tell Sennett. It was late, but he'd have to understand.

When I had finished telling him about Priscilla Wadsworth, the sex club, and all that had happened, his silence made me wonder if he was fully awake.

"Well?" I almost snapped.

"I got a friend in homicide at NYPD," he said. "We'll pick up Priscilla Wadsworth and question her. There was another man with a tattoo?"

"It looked like the tattoo the Cass Corridor girl described."

"You're sure about this tattoo?"

"Sure enough."

"I want you to sit tight, Ben." He paused. "Do you think you can do that?"

"Sit tight?" I said.

"Stay there."

I ran over possibilities in my head. Jordan's condition. With a coma like hers, what was next? Respiratory distress syndrome, officially known as ARDS. 'A' for acute. I didn't have time to sit tight.

"And do nothing?"

"You're dealing with someone dangerous."

"I'm looking for antitoxin," I retorted. "And I'm starting to feel dangerous myself."

"Stay out of trouble." He knew it was useless to argue with me. "I'm flying to New York tomorrow afternoon. Earliest I can manage."

I gave him my address and phone number and hung up.

After a call to St. Vincent's—no news—I collapsed on the bed and fell asleep. The football nightmare returned. My last game, the pileup, the crunched feeling as my nose broke, then the dark void. This time Pop hovered over me at the hospital, squeezing my hand, begging me to wake up. I could see his gaunt face, parchment paper skin covering his cheekbones, coal-bright eyes glowing in their sockets. I tried to reach up to him, touch him, tell him how happy I was to see him. He was mouthing words I couldn't hear, probably telling me what a fool I was to play football.

I tried to tell him not to worry, it was just a game.

I managed another two hours of sleep. When I awoke, the sun was streaming through the window. I sat on the side of the bed and felt my legs ache from the night's exercise.

It was already eight o'clock. I dressed quickly. Before stepping out the door, I opened it slowly and looked both ways. I eased into the hall, having already placed the "Do Not Disturb" sign on my door.

The New York Public Library wasn't far from my hotel. After breakfast in the hotel coffee shop, I walked in just as they opened the doors, and I snared the first librarian I saw. She directed me to the proper location. I wanted to find out more about the death of Frank Connely's wife. I figured a Philadelphia newspaper would have something on it.

There were several articles in the Philadelphia *Inquirer*. The front-page story reported that Mary Jane Connely had died of unexplained reasons on an East Coast Airlines flight. Several other people, including her husband, had fallen ill, though not fatally. Food handling as a possible cause was mentioned. Subsequent investigations showed no contamination of the food served on the flight in question.

That was it.

No, it wasn't. There was another article about two years later. A small bit in the back of the paper. An out-of-court settlement between Dr. Frank Connely and East Coast Airlines concerning the tragic death of his wife.

Why had fourteen people survived, and one hadn't?

I faced the truth with a wary resignation. As much as I didn't want to, I had to see Priscilla Wadsworth again.

From a lobby phone I dialed Priscilla's lab. What would I say to her? Great performance last night? Was it you who set me up? Her phone rang a few times, then went to the answering machine. I hung up.

I tried Sennett. He was still in his office. I told him about Connely's settlement. He grunted in appreciation. Had Knudsen found anything on the tattoo yet?

An old woman in a blue scarf stepped up to the phone next to me. I looked her up and down. No way she was Mr. Vic, or Mrs. Vic for that matter. She was an old lady who needed to use the pay phone.

Sennett said they'd already done searches on tattoos. They'd worked with the FBI. "No one has seen or heard anything about this mark."

"What about Priscilla Wadsworth?"

"We checked her out," he said. "I'm afraid she won't be much help."

"Check again," I growled. "She's all we've got."

"Oh, we've got her all right. My NYPD friend says they found her in Van Cortlandt Park."

The woman in the scarf was digging through her purse looking for coins. I scooped as much silver as I had in my pocket and held it out to her. She poked at the coins in my hand, took the shiniest quarter and a dime, and mouthed the words thank you.

"Sodomized and strangled," Sennett continued inexorably. "Her right nipple was cut off."

"Florence?" the woman in the blue scarf asked.

"What else, Lieutenant?"

"The flower tattoo. The usual place."

"This is Edith," the woman said. "Has the exterminator been there yet?"

CHAPTER 14

SENNETT WAS COMING IN ON THE 4:30 P.M. FLIGHT. I said I'd meet him at his friend Lieutenant Ralph John Kincaid's office at the 32nd precinct. I'd hung up, almost deciding to do as he said, which was to wait for him and nothing else.

Almost.

I decided to call Herb Albright, my stockbroker in Detroit.

"Do you like olives, Herb?" I said.

"No money in food today. Technology's the hot ticket. Fiber optics. I got a few ideas."

Herb spoke in sentences of five words or less. He was usually doing five or more other things while talking on the phone.

"Ever heard of San Marino olives?"

"Best olives in the world. Got a pantry full."

Was I the only ignoramus in the world who'd never heard of these olives? I asked him if he knew what company handled them.

"I've got this program. Locates product." I waited a minute while he booted it up. "San Marino Olive Oil Company. Palermo, Sicily."

"Who's the U.S. distributor?"

"Landmark Industries. Big food supplier. I bought the stock a few years ago. People made big money. Forget Landmark. You're too late. I have another stock. Graphics imaging. Real potential."

"Where is Landmark's corporate headquarters?"

"Manhattan. You know something I don't?"

I said I might. I'd keep him posted.

Landmark was housed in a neoclassical modern building. Up on the thirty-second floor sunshine streamed through four circular windows, illuminating a huge Roy Lichtenstein painting from his comic strip series. It covered the entire wall in front of the elevator bank.

"Images of industrial America," a female voice said. "Symbolizing the urban landscape."

The receptionist was squinting at me from behind her marble countertop. I loved New York. Every waiter was an actor, every receptionist an art historian.

I said, "And you get to enjoy this every day."

"You here to find someone or look at the art?"

Then again, maybe she was just a receptionist.

"Find someone. What division of Landmark handles San Marino olives?"

"We have fourteen different divisions. Specialty foods division, cereal division, food services division, vitamins and food supplements division, et cetera."

"Try specialty foods," I said.

She looked it up. "Specialty. San Marino olives. Thirty-fourth floor."

I waited while she called upstairs. What was the reason for my visit? What was the volume of my store? Why didn't I contact a rep in my area? She explained these were security-related questions. Not just anybody could get upstairs. Well, my stores had been deluged with requests for San Marino olives, I said. I hoped to do a dozen cases or so a year. And I'd happened to be in New York, almost at the source. So I figured I'd stop.

She gave me a flat smile, and I panicked. Did anyone sell that many olives a year? Finally, she nodded toward the elevator, which I took to the thirty-fourth floor, stepping into a plush waiting area. Another receptionist was sitting behind a rosewood desk, typing on her keyboard. She looked up and smiled.

"Where exactly in the Midwest?"

"Detroit."

I sat down in a deep, leather chair and waited for a sales manager. They certainly were organized, I thought. I scanned their magazines for a second. The cover story of *Smithsonian* was about selling dinosaur bones for profit. Only in America. I reached for it just as the manager appeared.

Shirley Edwards was a trim, fortyish, African American woman dressed in a navy-blue suit over a white-collar blouse. Her face was pleasant and direct, a good face for sales. When I followed her back to her office, I noticed a limp.

"Aerobics?"

"Dance. I strained my Achilles yesterday. I forgot I'm not seventeen."

"Long live forgetfulness."

She smiled, lots of teeth and a crinkle at the corner of her mouth.

She got out a directory and thumbed through it until she came to the page she wanted. "We're in a couple of stores in your locale. The Gourmet Place?"

"Sure. Near Uniontown."

"Competition?"

"We're closer to Ann Arbor," I lied.

"If we sell specialty items in too many places, they're no longer special."

I told her I'd send a list of my stores when I got back, along with the name of my man in purchasing. When she mentioned volume, I said I really didn't know the specifics. My specialty was finding things. Which led me to the other reason for my visit.

"Do you have anyone who works here named Vic?"

She blinked for a moment, but her face didn't change.

"Mr. Vic?" I said.

"Last name?"

I said I didn't have one.

"We might have someone here by that name. I've never heard of him."

"It's a big place."

"And the reason you need him?"

I smiled, shook it off as if my request had been supremely unimportant. "My specialty," I said. "Finding things. I guess that includes people."

She led me back to the receptionist desk, where I took out a card and handed it to her. "Here's the phone number where I'm staying," I said. "It's probably a wild shot, but if there is someone by that name, could you give me a call?"

"Sure."

Well, If Mr. Vic was around, I'd given myself away, that was sure enough.

I ducked into a deli for lunch. When the waiter laid the menu down, I saw five blue-black numbers tattooed above his wrist. In surgery, I've reached inside a man's chest and held his heart in my hands, felt it stop and start. That never gets ordinary. It's a similar experience meeting a death camp survivor. Except the stop and start is in my own heart. I get an irresistible desire to touch a survivor. This man had fire in his eyes. I've met defeat, misery. This man was indomitable. My grandfather had eyes like that. A life that can't be extinguished.

I didn't open the menu. I took the Tuesday special: cabbage borscht and tongue, roasted and sliced thin. As I began to eat, he stood by the table, watching.

"Good?" he said.

"Good."

From his hands, it was great. He nodded approval and walked away. I felt as if I'd passed an important test.

While I ate, I decided what to do next: go back to the North Jersey Medical Center. From the phone in the back of the deli, I called to the center and asked for the head of pharmacology. I told his secretary I was doing research for Elnor Labs on another project and needed information on botulinum toxin. She said he had some free time that afternoon.

FROM THE INFORMATION DESK at New Jersey Medical Center, I was directed to the office of Professor Billingham, chief of pharmacology. He was on the top floor, in an executive's office overlooking the skyline of Manhattan. Not bad for a teaching professor. Other than the office, Billingham looked like every other academic researcher I had met: suspenders, Hush Puppies, and a pocket full of pens. He had the distracted look of a man with a hundred research projects that would never get done. When I shook his hand, I could tell he was nervous.

"You've come from Elnor?"

"Actually, Professor Billingham, I'm a doctor. The only thing I use from Elnor is enteric-coated aspirin."

The color seemed to come back to his face. "You tricked me."

"I need information about the botulinum toxin in your lab. Elnor sponsors the project. I figured it was the only way I could get in to see you without delay."

"How did you know who funded the work?"

"A journal article from Frank Connely's office."

Billingham grimaced. "The high-handed Dr. Connely."

"High-handed?"

"Pure genius, with encyclopedic knowledge of medicine and pharmacology, brilliant ideas. But he could be downright nasty. I came into the lab one time. He and his assistant were working."

"Priscilla Wadsworth."

"I must have interrupted him at a crucial moment, because he told me to… get the fuck out. I think they were…involved."

I asked him who controlled the grant money.

"He did. He controlled that, and he controlled Priscilla Wadsworth. He controlled everything."

"Have there been any significant discoveries?"

He sat on the corner of his desk. "I wasn't privy to everything going on in the lab. Elnor was paying big bucks to keep it going. The money they threw at the project funded a lot of other things we did."

Including his fancy office. I waited.

"Our papers are public," he volunteered defensively. "We're not hiding anything. Why all this interest?"

I told him I was treating a patient with botulism. She wasn't responding to normal antitoxins. "I have a hunch the strain of bacteria might be traceable to your lab."

"You've checked A through G?"

"Nothing works."

"Symptoms?"

"Neurologic. She's been in a coma."

I could see the scientist in him taking over. "Strange," he said. "Few people lose consciousness in botulism until late in the disease."

"Well, it happened here. It's almost a central nervous system-type reaction."

"Indeed."

"Does botulinum toxin have a central nervous system effect?"

Billingham shook his head. "Inject the toxin into any peripheral muscle, eventually traces will be seen in the brain. That's been shown with radioactive tracers in experimental animals. But there's never been an effect. By the time it gets to the brain, one of the arms on the polypeptide has broken off, rendering the molecule ineffective."

"So either my friend has something else going on, or the strain of toxin has a different effect than previously recognized."

"Friend?"

"Fiancée."

"I see."

"Can we go down and look at the specimens?"

Billingham looked perplexed, almost as if he had lost something that he couldn't replace. "They're gone," he said.

"I was just there yesterday."

"That was yesterday." He looked around at his office, as if knowing it would not be his to keep. "Elnor called this morning. They've closed the lab. Evidently Priscilla left without notice. Funds for the botulinum toxin project will be rescinded. The lab is stripped."

"Stripped?"

"Clean. And with it went a large part of my research money. When you called, I thought the company had had a change of heart. That's why I was so anxious to meet with you."

No wonder he looked forlorn.

"I'm sorry."

"That's life in research."

"I'm not sorry for you. You've had your perks. You benefited. I'm sorry for Priscilla Wadsworth."

As I got up to leave, I told him exactly how she'd gone without notice.

In the main lobby of the hospital, I saw Igor and his hulking buddy waiting for me.

To my right was the gift shop. I slipped in just as they split up and circled the lobby. I didn't think they'd seen me, but I wasn't going to take any chances. I bought a newspaper, then squeezed out of the door with my head down, looking for a security guard. One stood at the main entrance.

I introduced myself as a trauma specialist in the emergency room who'd just finished a tendon laceration on the auto accident that had come in from the interstate. I'd seen those two men, I said, pointing at Igor and his pal, rifling through the drug closet. They'd gotten away before anyone could catch them.

The guard unsnapped his holster and drew his walkie-talkie. By the time I reached the exit, he and two other guards were all over Igor.

I CALLED ST. VINCENT'S FROM A PAYPHONE near the Manhattan side of the Lincoln Tunnel. It took a minute, but I finally got Phil Lindstrom on the phone.

He gave me Jordan's condition—worse—and said he needed that bacteria, fast.

Not what I wanted to hear.

"We can't get her off the ventilator. The fever is spiking more regularly. It's almost as if the coma was induced by the toxin. It's not supposed to happen that way, Ben."

"The lab?"

"Nothing. We've even had the CDC here in person. We can't match this strain with anything anyone has seen. If something doesn't happen soon, I'll want to try that laser treatment we talked about."

I had a brainwave—illumination born of desperation?

"Call Dellsburg Baptist Hospital in Pennsylvania," I said. "Get the bacteriology report on a Mary Jane Connely, if you can. She died a few years ago from botulism. I think the strain that killed her is the one we're looking for."

Phil was nonplussed by my suggestion, but he said he'd call.

I hung up in a rage of futility. My only hope was finding Mr. Vic. Jordan's only hope was my finding Mr. Vic. He was connected to Connely. But what kind of hope was that? Mr. Vic wanted me dead.

I had to get some good news or I'd lose my mind.

I called Bruce Sanderson's office. Sheila answered, and for once, she sounded happy to hear from me.

"That dog of yours is so smart," she said.

"He takes after my side of the family."

"He knows exactly where everything is in my house."

"Sheila?"

"And he listens so good."

"Sheila!" I said. "Is Bruce in?"

"He's sick today." It was an accusation.

"I need documents from the Connely case."

"Yeah?"

"The complaint faxed with Connely's curriculum vitae."

From the pause on the other end, I could tell I was stretching my welcome. "I've got a hair appointment," she said. "I can only stay until five."

"It's life and death, Sheila."

"Bruce is going to have to pay for this. He gets mad about overtime."

"I'll pay the overtime," I said. "Please? I'll let you keep my dog another week."

Her tone sweetened, though somehow that didn't seem like the right word. "You found my weakness," she said. "You won't take advantage, will you?"

I said she was safe with me. I gave her the information I needed and told her I'd get her a fax number within the hour. I shrugged off the guilt of lying to her. At this moment, was anyone safe with me?

CHAPTER 15

I WAS ACTUALLY EARLY FOR MY MEETING with Sennett at New York's 32nd precinct. When I asked for Lieutenant Kincaid, the desk sergeant pointed me toward a bank of offices in the back hall on the right. I shouldered my way back there, past a couple of officers with their prisoners. It occurred to me I could have been in Chicago or Detroit. Like illness, crime looked pretty much the same all over.

Kincaid was a medium built man with thick, brown hair cut short. He had the neck, arms, and shoulders of a body builder gone on vacation; great, but no longer grotesque. His handshake appropriated your hand. Sitting next to him at his desk was a familiar face.

"Can't stay away from the police, can you?" George Sennett asked.

"My grandfather bribed border guards to get out of Russia," I said.

"A family trait." Sennett laughed out loud. It broke the ice. "Let's talk about Priscilla Wadsworth."

"This will help." I held out a slip of paper.

I explained that we'd need some papers from Detroit. While we waited for the fax from Sheila at Bruce Sanderson's office, I reviewed everything I knew about Priscilla Wadsworth and Frank Connely. Kincaid sat through the narrative without moving, his face expressionless, inscrutable.

"Their deaths are connected to the girl in Detroit," he summed up, except that it sounded like a question.

"Yes," I said. "No doubt."

I glanced at Sennett. No help. Kincaid's face was a mask of doubt. So the ice wasn't broken after all.

I pointed out that the tattoo was the connection.

Kincaid wondered if I knew who this Mr. Vic was.

"The guy on the stage at the Original Sin had the same tattoo. I can't prove yet that he was Mr. Vic, but I suspect he is." Then there was the lab.

"Whatever was in that lab must have been important," Kincaid agreed. "We were over there a little after you were. We dusted for prints."

"What about the club?"

"Closed down. Everything gone. The lease on the place was to a John Doe. A dummy. I admit that has a highly suspicious appearance."

I told him about my close encounter in Newark with Igor and his friend at the North Jersey Medical Center that afternoon. Kincaid listened, nodding. Good God, what does it take to galvanize these people? The woman I loved was spiking fevers. Every breath counted. Mercifully, just then my fax came through: information about Frank Connely's trial.

Kincaid didn't seem impressed. He said they needed to do things by the book. A serial killer was nothing to play around with. They'd look at prints, cross-reference victim information, take a look at some tattoos, put a new detail on all the sex clubs they knew.

"How long?" I asked.

"Two hours, two weeks. Who knows?" He leaned forward. His chest was like a cement wall. "Crimes like this are the most difficult because the killers are usually perversely smart."

"Lieutenant, I don't have two weeks to wait."

He remained impassive. Quietly, gently, he began to squeeze my balls. Metaphorically speaking, of course. New York was *his* town, he said. It was *his* investigation. I was a private citizen. If I were contemplating rogue action, I'd get one warning.

"We have lots of cells in Manhattan," he said. "I'm happy to keep you there to protect you from yourself."

I could feel the fire in my face. "Lieutenant, I've got a critically ill, pregnant woman back in Detroit who is going to die unless I find the bacteria that caused her illness."

Sennett said, "and he has a way of finding things, Ralph."

"I'm sorry about your patient." Kincaid eased back in his leather chair. "But I don't come into your operating room and perform surgery, do I? I'm warning you. If you get in the way of my investigation, I'll be all over you."

He and Sennett exchanged a long glance. The result of that silent communication meant that I owed Sennett another one. Kincaid opened a desk drawer. He handed me a cell phone.

"'Star five' gets you a direct line to my sergeant's desk. His name's O'Leary. I'll tell him to cooperate with you."

"It may expedite matters," Sennett said.

"O'Leary," I repeated.

"Just outside my door," Kincaid said. "The guy who sent your fax. It's almost as good as getting me."

Outside the station I gulped cold, damp air. It had just rained. The streets were still wet, which somehow made the city smell clean. Miracles were possible. I folded the pages of Frank Connely's file and put them in my jacket. Maybe there was a clue there. I didn't expect Mr. Vic to suddenly pop out of the pages. But perhaps I'd find something. At the moment I had nothing else to go on.

I went down to the corner. The guy with the hot dog stand was just about to close. I got his last dog, cold and overcooked, but it was enough for dinner with the way I felt. I sat on a bench near the police station, took out Connely's file, and read the complaint again. It was mostly boilerplate. I reviewed his CV, turning automatically to college class and medical school. When I downed the last bite of hot dog, I got up from the bench and walked back to the police station. I'd decided to take the captain up on his offer and have O'Leary do something for me.

He was sitting outside Kincaid's office, a mountain of paper on his desk. I asked him how late he worked.

"Midnight," he said. "The real action starts just about when I get off."

There was a jar of candy on his desk. "May I?"

"Tension relievers." He handed me the jar.

"Your dentist calls them his mortgage payment."

"We could use some more help," he grumbled. He picked up a handful of papers and dropped it. "This is the stuff they don't tell you at the academy."

I held up Connely's CV. "Maybe this will be a little out of the ordinary. I've got a couple of things I need you to look up." I gave him the papers and told him what I wanted. He looked up with a wise-ass smile that said, *another piece of paper?* I explained that Kincaid had granted me three favors. I considered showing him my magic phone, but it wasn't necessary. He grunted and said that what I wanted would take a little while.

I reached in his candy jar and took another tension reliever. "These things work," I said.

NEAR 50ᵀᴴ AND MADISON, I stopped in front of a sports memorabilia store, with a display of signed Heisman-Trophy-winner footballs in the window: Hopalong Cassidy, Leon Hart, and Tom Harmon. I'd met Harmon once. Handsome and rugged, he was the epitome of the Heisman winner, and I had idolized him. I wanted the Heisman too. That's why I'd played. As a kid, I'd always added my name to that list. Now that I looked back, it seemed like such a fruitless goal. So far, the only Jew ever to get the Heisman was Fred Goldman, and he got it through the death of his son.

The thought was disturbing. It reminded me of the child Jordan was carrying. My child. The thought of being a father flooded my mind with a strange feeling of pride. A need to love and protect a family I had never had.

I looked back into the store. Would it be a boy? When would I buy him his first football? Or maybe a girl. Would she like sports, or would I buy her dolls and dresses? My thoughts turned back to Jordan and my child, both clinging to life in the intensive care unit. I could not let them die. Never.

I started walking again. At the corner there was a small children's store. I had to walk in to look, to see what it was like. An urge came over me to buy something, a present for my unborn child. I looked around, but nothing seemed right. I was about to leave when my eyes fell upon a shiny object near the window of the store. It was a tiny, silver rattle, maybe an heirloom. I bought it and put it in my pocket. I don't believe in luck, but somehow I needed a talisman. I don't think the storeowner understood why I didn't want it gift-wrapped.

It took another fifteen minutes of walking to get back to the hotel. By that time, my mind had cleared. When I got off the elevator on the fourth floor, the hallway was deserted. I was ten feet from my door when I noticed the "Do Not Disturb" sign lying on the carpet. I knew I'd left it on the doorknob. I figured I had two courses of action, and staying around was not one of them. Just beyond my room was the stairwell, behind me the elevator. I backtracked to the elevator.

When the elevator car door opened, I jumped back on, counting the seconds it took for the door to close. Exiting, I almost ran over a couple in the lobby waiting to get on. Back on the street, I started to breathe again. I was tempted to call O'Leary. But they would play it by the book; wait to pick up the assailant, wait to interrogate the assailant, wait to release the assailant. A whole lot of lost time. This might be my chance. If there was someone in that room, I needed to find out who he was, where he came from, and who sent him.

Down the street I saw a small market still open.

I went down and bought a roll of aluminum foil, a bottle of Drano, and a wide mouth plastic bottle of Coke. Outside the store I opened up the plastic Coke bottle and emptied the contents down a convenient drain. Then I tore open the aluminum foil box, balled up and stuffed as many small pieces of foil as my pen could force through the opening. I put the cap back on the bottle and walked back to the hotel carrying my little grocery bag.

This time I took the stairs.

The stairwell was well lit and empty. My footfalls echoed. At each turn of the stairs, I expected to see someone, but I was alone all the way up. At the fourth floor landing I stood in front of the door and listened for a moment. It was dead quiet. I opened the door a crack and looked. I was right next to my room. There was an end table against the wall. If this was going to work, I'd have to be quick.

I opened the door and entered the hall. Inside my jacket I found my room key wedged between some paper. I pulled it out and laid it on the table. I took out the Coke bottle, set it on the table, and removed the cap. My hands were trembling the way they had when I'd done this the first time, some thirty years before. I opened the Drano and slowly poured it into the bottle. It began to foam and hiss. I laid the bag and Drano can on the table, put the cap back on the Coke bottle, and crawled toward the door of my room. As the gas started to accumulate inside, I gave the bottle a few hard shakes, put my key in the door and shoved it open. I tossed the bottle inside the room and ran for the stairwell. Behind me, I heard a muted explosion, and then yelling from inside the room. By then I was leaping down the steps three at a time.

When I emerged in the main lobby, I pretended to be as nonchalant as a frat boy proud of the mayhem he'd caused. Near the front door, I settled into a chair behind a newspaper and waited. In a matter of a few minutes, he appeared. It was Igor's friend, the goon I'd last seen in the lobby of North Jersey Medical Center. There were white spots all over his leather jacket and black jeans. As he stormed past the bell captain and out the front door, I got up to follow him.

I wasn't a professional, but how hard could it be?

Harder than I expected. He moved like a fullback through the crowd, straight down the street and toward Broadway. I tried to stay within fifty feet of him, dodging New Yorkers, who also moved like fullbacks, as I moved through the crowd. At Times Square, I moved a little closer, watching for his spotted jacket. His head bobbed in and out of sight on the sidewalk in front of me. He swung down Broadway.

Take it to the goal, I thought.

On Broadway, his pace picked up. I moved closer. A few blocks later he turned off onto a side street, then into one of those old, beat-up buildings in New York that should have been condemned years ago. I waited a full five minutes at the end of the block, then cautiously strolled past.

On the directory outside the entrance was the name: Apex Laboratory Supplies.

CHAPTER 16

I STOOD ACROSS THE STREET FROM APEX a full fifteen minutes, watching for my goon. When he didn't come out, I passed in front of the building and glanced inside. A security guard was just inside the entrance. I reached the edge of the building and looked along the length of the alley. There was a delivery entrance with access from 35th Street. Some trucks were backed up to open freight doors. An open invitation for me. I jogged down the alley toward the trucks. In the cab of the first one, the driver was fast asleep. The second truck was empty. I opened the door, climbed in the cab, and swiped the driver's uniform jacket and company cap left on the seat. I took his clipboard, too. I pulled the jacket on and strolled to the rear of the truck. A uniformed guard emerged from inside. I nodded at him, reached in my pocket, and took out Kincaid's phone.

The guard walked to the edge of the dock. "What's up, Mac?"

I pointed at my watch. "Six o'clock," I said. "Apex delivery. How long before they unload me?"

"You a scab?"

I assumed a do-I-look-like-a-scab, insulted expression. "It's my kid's birthday," I said. "I want to finish my run and get the hell home."

He frowned at me for a second, then pointed inside. "Seventh floor." So much for security.

I climbed up the loading dock and headed through the freight doors. At the end of the ramp, just inside the receiving area, I saw a "Staff Only" sign. An empty locker room. Twenty or thirty steel-clad lockers lined one wall. Inside were uniform overalls, some of them with nametags. I pulled off the trucker's jacket and cap and laid them on top of the clipboard. In James Carlson's locker, I found another hat and a pair of maintenance overalls with a name tag. I quickly pulled them on. Then I grabbed a mop and bucket, lowered my head and stepped back out of the dock. No guard. I wheeled the bucket toward the interior of the building.

Two large doors opened on a brightly lit corridor. I rolled down the cement floor to a bank of elevators at the end of the hall. I tugged my cap lower on my face and pushed the up button. When the door opened, I got on and pushed seven. I thought of Kincaid. If he could see me now, I'd become a guest of the city so fast my head would spin.

When I exited the elevator, my eyes took in the reception area. It was in good shape, with handsome marble floors and mahogany moldings. James Carlson obviously did a good job. In the middle of the room was an elegantly styled, art deco reception desk, where another uniformed guard was posted, this one staring at a bank of television screens. I made my way with my mop and pail toward the desk. The guard looked up at me and shook his head.

He said, "What's with you guys?"

"What?"

"Second one of you in the last hour. Somebody's mother coming?"

"Spots." I motioned toward to elevator. "Spots on the floor near the elevator."

"Your buddy lick-dab was here. Little lick, little dab, and you have to come back and clean up after him." He chuckled, obviously pleased with himself.

"He's a little distracted today." I told him it was his kid's birthday and he was rushing things a little. I drew closer to his desk and peered at the security screens. "Did you see that guy in a black leather jacket? Black jeans with spots on them?"

"Yeah, I seen him. He looked like one of them dingoes, or what do you call them. Hyena. He was here ten minutes ago. Had an appointment. Dressed like that. Goddam dingo or something. He had a pass, so I let him in. Why?"

I rolled my bucket away from me, then brought it back. "He stopped me," I said. "Asked directions."

The guard looked down at his records.

"He looked strange," I said.

"He's legit. He had an access card to the lab. Even had his thumb print, so if he wasn't supposed to be here, we'd catch him."

"Hyena," I chuckled. "That's a good one."

"Goddam right."

I looked around, picked a direction at random and headed down a corridor to my left, hoping I'd find the research department without my ignorance being noticed by the guard. Around two more corners, and I'd found it. I wheeled my bucket down the hallway, past a series of wooden doors with frosted windowpanes, black lettering on the front. Director of Supplies. Research Technician. Plating.

I rounded another corner, staring down at the blue and red tiled floor. At the end of the corridor, a door was open, lights switched on. I moved toward it, mopping, looking up from time to time. As I approached, I took in the setup. It was a lab, all right. Much the same as hundreds of medical labs I'd seen, including Connely's and Priscilla Wadsworth's at North Jersey Medical Center. I was about to walk in when I heard a rustling behind the door. I flattened myself against the wall beyond the door.

A man rushed out, not seeing me, and the lab door clicked shut. Tall and thin, he wore a long raincoat and a brown felt hat. Under one arm he carried a mass of papers. He stopped in front of the elevator and got on as soon as the doors opened. After he was gone, I kept mopping, trying to control my heartbeat, watching the lab door. A few minutes later I heard footsteps inside the lab. They approached the door. It swung open, and I watched feet and pant legs go past me. It was my friend Mr. White Spot. He continued down the hall, ignoring me, and took the elevator down. The lab door clicked shut.

Alone at last, I thought.

I tried the doorknob, hoping. I'm not very good at illegal entry. The knob turned, and the door opened. The place was in disarray. To the left, there were several incubators in the corner, all empty. In the center of the room, cardboard boxes were stacked on the floor, and on desks. Someone was getting ready to move in or move out. A few Hewlett-Packard computers sat on the floor next to the door. They looked like those I had seen in Priscilla's lab.

Next to the incubators was a small refrigerator. Inside I found agar plates and several test tube racks. I slid each rack out and examined it. In the third rack, I noticed a turbid fluid in one vial. "Botox - Type I." Next to this vial was another one, labeled simply "antitoxin."

I had it.

I had the same bacteria that had infected Jordan. I pressed red stoppers tightly on the tubes. This stuff was too lethal to spill, too important to lose. I was about to put the vials in my jacket, when I thought I heard a muffled voice in the hallway. I put the vials back in the refrigerator. In a back corner of the room, I'd already noticed a large wooden box, a shipping container. I jumped inside and brought the filling straw down over me. I left enough room so I could see through the wooden slats.

In a moment, Mr. White Spot entered. He looked around, as if to see if he had forgotten anything. He pulled off his jacket and tossed it on a chair. He wore a tight black t-shirt. He was muscled and tattooed. Neither phenomenon relaxed me. After a few seconds, he went to the refrigerator, opened it, and leaned over to peer inside. *Don't take it*, I prayed. Now that I had the bacteria, I couldn't let it get away. I contemplated what I would do. Stand up and show him Kincaid's telephone? The guy probably had a gun. And there were those arms of his. I heard a guttural grunt as he said something to himself, then stood up, put his jacket back on, and moved toward the door. He stood there five full minutes. When nothing happened, he strode down the hall toward the elevators.

My mop and cleaning supplies. God, what an idiot I was. Maybe I thought of myself as Holmes, but if so, I was also my own Watson.

What kind of janitor would've left his equipment lying around? His suspicions were not allayed; he lingered out in the hallway, looking for me. Doors opened and closed. He made another swing through the lab. My legs were cramping terribly. Finally, after fifteen minutes, I heard the elevator bell.

I climbed out of my hiding place and listened. I walked to the door and looked down the hall. All clear. I brushed straw off, went to the refrigerator, and grabbed the vials. It was life and death. I checked the stoppers again, then shoved them into my jacket.

I left my bucket and mop in the hallway. Bad janitor.

My footsteps echoed on the metal steps in the back stairwell. At the bottom, I banged my shoulder against the door, a fire escape. It swung open. I jumped into the alley. I took off the overalls, threw them in a trash bin, and started running.

I RODE THE SUBWAY UNTIL 7:30 P.M., reining myself in fiercely, thinking of Jordan spiking a fever. I had to be sure we were safe. At every stop, I felt my gut clench as the doors banged open and people rushed onto the train. No one looked at me, nobody was following me. I was totally alone, with Jordan's life in my hands. Finally, I let myself act once more. Another fifteen minutes got me back to the 32nd precinct, where Kincaid was still in his office.

"What do you want?" he asked brusquely.

I set the vials on his desk.

"What's this?"

"Toxin and antitoxin," I said. "I found it in a lab near 35th Street."

"There aren't any research labs around 35th Street."

"Maybe not officially, but there sure as hell is an Apex Lab in an old building there."

"Apex?" He reached for the vials. A muscle jumped in his jaw. "This is the stuff you were looking for?"

"Let's not open it, unless you're interested in shortening your life."

"You're sure this is it?"

"I'm virtually certain, but I need to get it tested," I said. "As soon as we know for sure, the antitoxin can be sent back to Detroit. It's the only thing that will save my fiancée."

He said they could have answers in hours. There was a state-of-the-art bacteriology lab at his disposal, in place as part of their terrorist protocol. Given something concrete to work with, Kincaid was all business. I liked the urgency in his voice, and I liked how he took over. The next thing, he said, was to go have a look at this Apex lab. I suggested he might look for a man in spots. "Spots?"

"Yeah," I said. "He looks like a hyena."

For a fraction of a second, something happened to Kincaid's face. On any other man, I would have called it a smile. On him, I thought it was prelude to a sneeze. "Good," he said.

"Work," I added. But he wasn't going to give me that much, not yet. He snorted and took the vials out.

While he was out of the office, I picked up his phone and dialed Phil Lindstrom in Detroit. I told him I had the stuff. It was probably Type I Botulism.

He whistled. "What we need is an antitoxin."

"There was a vial labeled antitoxin. The police are checking it. They should have an answer soon. If it's the right stuff, they'll have it up there within hours."

"Let's hope you got it in time."

Hope was all I had.

I hung up the phone in the lieutenant's office and sat back in the side chair. Kincaid walked back in with Sennett. I hadn't even thought about whether he'd still be there, but I found that his not having bolted back to Detroit gave me a warm feeling inside. They'd checked for an Apex Medical. Someone named Veronica Paschein was the lab tech. A squad car was on its way to pick her up.

"If she works in that lab," I said, "chances are she'll be dead soon."

"That thought has crossed our minds," Kincaid said.

I looked at Sennett and stood. "Once I get the antitoxin, I'm out of this."

"You're already out of this," Kincaid growled. "You could have been killed over there."

"Whoever was waiting for you at the Holiday Inn," Sennett said, "they weren't looking for medical advice."

"I'm not going to worry about it right now. When I get back to Detroit and Jordan is safe, I'll deal with whatever happens."

"Just protect your backside."

Kincaid picked up his phone. "I'm sending O'Leary with you. He'll take you to the airport."

"I've never had a police escort before." I handed him his phone.

"Keep it for the moment. You never know. Give it to O'Leary when you board the plane."

O'Leary had his hat on when I got outside. He handed me a manila envelope as he came around his desk.

"Here's the papers you requested."

The fax. I looked inside the envelope. Six sheets. I'd look at them on the flight home.

O'LEARY CALLED AHEAD TO THE HOLIDAY INN and told them we were coming. The bell captain met us at the front entrance. Would we follow him, please, and see the hotel manager? When we stepped in his office, the manager rose behind his desk. He wore the *de rigueur* maroon jacket. He pushed back a shock of thin hair and thrust a hand out for me to shake.

"The staff," he began, "wishes to apologize for what happened to your room."

"What happened?"

"Apparently a bomb went off."

I tried to look concerned.

"The room is a shambles, I'm afraid. If any of your personal property is damaged, we will be glad to pay for it."

When I told him to forget about it, he tapped a finger emphatically on his desk and said, "No." He insisted that if anything was damaged, he would personally reimburse me.

He wouldn't take no for an answer. Instead, he wrote out a slip of paper and handed it to me. "Have a complimentary dinner in our gourmet room."

The bell captain escorted us up to the room. Workmen were already tearing the place apart. I was surprised by how much damage a Drano bomb could do. And yet Mr. White Spot had gotten out alive.

Once I collected my things, O'Leary followed me back to the elevator, down to the lobby, and out onto the parking deck. I pointed out my sedan.

"'Follow you out of the city," he said. "Those were the lieutenant's words."

I pulled out the key. I was about to squeeze the keyless entry when I felt his hand on my wrist.

"First law in a protective situation: never trust nothing." He popped a gumball in his mouth and took the key ring from me.

"We never know what's in a car. In a case like this, we get behind this concrete pillar and reach around to point the opener."

He touched the button. There was a sudden flash and explosion on the driver's side of the car. Glass shattered. Then came a flash. I could feel the wind go out of me. The concussion drove us both against another car.

I must have blacked out for a moment.

When I struggled to my feet, I saw the car engulfed in flame and smoke. I looked around for O'Leary. He was sitting upright on the cement deck, his hands grasped around his neck. His face was purple. As much as he tried to breathe, no air was getting in.

The gumball.

I slipped behind him and lifted him to his feet. He was big, easily two hundred pounds. He wobbled on his feet as I got my hands just under his sternum. With a quick pull, I jammed my balled fist into his abdomen. Nothing happened. I gave it another try, this time a little harder. His diaphragm chugged and a reddish projectile shot out of his mouth.

He wasn't breathing. I laid him back down on the parking deck, lowered my head to his mouth, and started mouth-to-mouth. His eyes were open, and his color was awful. "Come on, O'Leary," I yelled. I could hear sirens in the distance.

I continued breathing. After an eternity, fire trucks and EMS arrived. I looked up as three paramedics piled out of the van.

"This man needs to be intubated," I yelled. "Now!"

They rushed to my side with their kit. One EMT, probably no more than twenty-two, pulled out an intubating laryngoscope and a cuffed number eight tube.

I stopped mouth-to-mouth as they clamped a mask on his face and started squeezing air into him. O'Leary was still blue. The tech pried open his mouth.

"I can't see the airway," he shouted.

"Pressure," I said. He looked up at me with uncomprehending eyes. "Put some pressure on the front of his neck." I took my thumb and forefinger and pushed backward on his Adam's apple. "Do it like this."

I picked up the scope and started to intubate.

"What do you think you're doing?" the EMT said.

"I'm a physician," I said briefly. "If you want this man to die, go ahead and do it yourself. I'd be glad to tell everyone that I can find exactly what happened."

He rocked back from O'Leary.

I grabbed the EMT's right hand. "Keep some pressure on his neck!"

I picked up the scope and put it back in O'Leary's mouth. This time, with pressure on the neck, I could see the larynx and the opening to his airway.

"Tube!"

The EMT handed me the plastic number eight, and I gently passed it through O'Leary's vocal cords into the trachea.

"Hook the tube up to the bag," I instructed, "inflate the cuff and keep squeezing."

Slowly O'Leary's color began to come back. I hoped he hadn't been anoxic too long. I looked over at what was left of my rental car. The fire department had put out the fire. As the techs lifted O'Leary into the ambulance, I thought about Kincaid.

I figured this episode would really cement our relationship.

CHAPTER 17

"**A**RE YOU PLANNING ON HANGING AROUND?"
Kincaid had been on his feet the whole time in intensive care. It was almost midnight. He walked from one end of the waiting room to the other. He feinted before a chair, as if about to sit down, then came back to himself, remembered O'Leary, and returned to his work of waiting and worrying. He was willing O'Leary to be all right. Every other lap or so, he'd look down at me. I was sitting next to Sennett.

It was the second time he'd asked me the question.

I told him again that O'Leary had grasped my hand as they loaded him into the ambulance. For the second or third time, I said I hoped he'd be okay.

Kincaid hovered over me like a skyscraper.

"The city," he said. "Are you planning on hanging around the city?"

Ryan O'Leary, I'd learned from Sennett, was Kincaid's nephew.

When the doctor came out, I was relieved by his expression. He had a tic—a twitching jaw muscle, and thinning hair. Though little more than half my age, he'd probably attended too many middle-of-the-night soirees to bother trying to impress anyone with a portentous frown.

He went straight to Kincaid. "Your guy is going to be all right."

I looked at the floor and shut my eyes.

O'Leary'd regained consciousness, seemed to know where he was and had full control of his body. The doctor turned to me. "Are you the guy that kept him alive?"

I nodded.

"The EMT told me what you did. You saved his life."

Kincaid shook hands with the doc and dropped into a chair across from Sennett and me. Well, we were out of one patch of woods.

"He was right," Kincaid said to me, pointing to Sennett. "Trouble seems to follow you."

"My specialty," I said. "It's on my resume."

"So it's okay for Ben to go?" Sennett said.

"Yes," Kincaid said. Then he realized Sennett was joking, and added, "Unless he'd like to write parking tickets."

"What about the car?"

Kincaid said he had already talked with an investigator. They couldn't find the source of the explosion, which indicated the work of an expert.

I stood up and offered my hand for Kincaid to shake. In it was his cell phone. "If you're lucky, they'll bomb my plane."

"I've arranged another escort. You're not traveling alone."

When I began to protest, Kincaid stood up. "He found the Fraser woman, didn't he? He found your car, didn't he? He can find you. And he will."

"You're the boss," I said.

"Do you know how long I've been waiting to hear those words?" Kincaid said. "And thanks, Dailey."

La Guardia Airport. Back in hell again.

I stopped by the rental car outlet and reported my mishap to the agent. He looked perplexed as he scanned his sheet for exclusions. Car bombing wasn't on his list. I wasn't in the mood for two hours of wrangling. Instead, I told him to check the contract. I had taken the full insurance,

Sennett and I made our way through security lines. Watching those guards stare at X-ray screens, I wondered how many weapons passed undetected. Then I thought about the bomb that had almost killed me. By the time we reached our gate, I was nauseous. I reached inside my jacket looking for gum and found the fax I had jammed inside. Frank Connely 's academic and medical history.

The longer I looked at it, the more I wondered.

I got up, went to a pay phone near the gate, and called St. Vincent's. They'd received the antitoxin hours before, confirmed by the NYPD lab. Now only time would tell if it would take, if we'd gotten it to Jordan in time. Another twenty-four to forty-eight hours would tell the rest of Jordan's story.

"You can't fly home with that telephone, Ben," Sennett grinched.

"Just one more call."

I called Penn State University information and got ahold of Alumni Services. Sophie Wandurski answered the phone. I told her I was from Michigan and looking for an old friend. After three minutes of questioning she convinced me that Frank Connely had never matriculated at the university.

By this time I could hear my plane being called. Sennett's hand was on my shoulder.

"Doctor's orders," he said. "You're coming with me."

"Let the police do their work, right?"

He rolled his eyes. He was right. Hearing myself, I was tempted to slam myself upside the head.

Somehow both Sennett and I refrained from doing me grievous bodily harm. Two hours later, we landed in Detroit.

CHAPTER 18

"FACTS," SENNETT LIKED TO SAY. "NOT HUNCHES."

Next day I walked into Sennett's office empty-handed, ready for a lecture on letting the police do their work.

"Jordan?" he asked roughly.

Once again, I was moved. "Still in a coma," I said. "No change regarding the baby."

"What about the stuff you found in New York?"

"Antitoxin," I said. "It'll take a while to see if it works."

"How long is a while?" His voice rose in exasperation. Coming from him, I appreciated it.

I said we wouldn't know for a couple of days.

We were silent for a minute.

"Well?" he said at last.

"Connely was never registered at Penn State."

"Penn State." He shook his head. "What made you think he was?"

"The deposition," I said. "I testified for him in a malpractice lawsuit. His CV came with the case packet."

He reached out his hand, and I passed him the fax.

His voice rumbled. "Graduated 1975. Penn State University. Let's call again."

"You're wasting your time."

Twenty minutes and three calls later, we had no evidence of Frank Connely.

"He couldn't practice without credentials," I said. "And he was a skilled physician. He did some sophisticated things."

"Stranger things have happened."

He claimed to have trained at the Medical College of New Jersey. We called there. No one had ever heard of him there, either.

"We'll find out who he was. It'll just take time."

"How much time?" I said. Sennett shook his head.

I was out of my chair and at the door.

"Ben," Sennett yelled. "We'll take care of it."

I STOOD ON THE STEPS OUTSIDE THE POLICE STATION to collect my thoughts. I'd made quite a scene, stomping off. Now what was I going to do? I had no leads. Sennett was right. It was police work. I decided to go back over to St. Vincent's and see Jordan one more time before I did anything rash.

Jane Flowers stopped me outside Jordan's room in ICU. I had known Jane for years. She was one of the best nurses I had ever worked with. Just having her in the same room with Jordan was comforting. One of the lab techs was drawing Jordan's blood.

"What's going on?" I said.

"Dr. Lindstrom wants you to call him."

We walked up the hall to the nurses' station. I waited while Jane got him on the phone.

"Ben," he said, "I think Jordan may have turned the corner."

"What?" My breath was coming in short gasps.

"The antitoxin seems to be working. Her vital signs have improved. The baby's looking good, too."

I drew in a long breath. "Are we out of the woods?"

"Not yet. There's still a chance of infection."

"When will we know?"

"Forty-eight hours," he said. "I know this is agony, Ben."

"Agony." I knew Phil was doing his best. I had to wait. We all had to wait. I thanked him and hung up.

I turned back to Jane.

"Dr. Dailey?" she said.

I touched my eyes. "A little dust," I said. They were wet.

She laid a hand on my arm and whispered something. I didn't hear it. I was crying suddenly. She slipped an arm around me and held me. I'd seen her do it before. "Thank you," I whispered in her ear.

I stumbled out of ICU and back down the hallway. Doctors, nurses, orderlies, everyone going somewhere. All so purposeful. How could they look so blasé when, at any moment, their lives could begin to unravel?

Forty-eight hours. I knew how long forever was. Forty-eight hours.

IT WAS A LITTLE AFTER TWO. I decided to cut across the warehouse district and head for Gus Katsopopoulos's diner, a place that served the best Detroit version of a Coney Island hot dog. I was relieved to see the lunch crowd from the downtown business offices had dissipated. When it came to Coney dogs, Gus was a local god. Just the thought of one made me hurry.

It felt good to walk. How many years had I walked hospital hallways, walked the soles right off my shoes? Suddenly, that part of my life was over. Now here I was. And where was that, exactly? On the streets of Detroit, hungry for a hot dog, free to go and get one. Things weren't all bad.

There were only a few people left at the counter. I slid onto a red plastic-covered stool.

Gus set a coaster in front of me. "Doc, how you been?"

"I'm alive."

"That ain't so bad, is it?"

"Depends on how you felt before you felt that way."

"Always the philosopher." He picked up a glass of water, swirled the ice, and took a drink. "I had a cousin. She went to some fancy university out east. Studied Zen Buddhism."

"How about a Coney, Gus?"

"Works at Nieman's selling dresses. How do you like that? Best salesperson they got."

"Extra onions?" I said.

"Think she uses her philosophy to sell clothes?"

On the television at the end of the counter, CNN droned. I told him that at one time, I had thought some of us chose our lives and some were thrown into their futures. Now it looked to me as if we all got a little of both.

"My father wanted me to be a doctor," he said. "In the old country, there was much respect."

"Your father didn't know about malpractice, Gus. Or HMOs. Or insurance companies."

"He wouldn't have cared." He set a Coke down in front of me and glanced at the TV. Sports edition. Highlights of college football from the previous Saturday. What a country.

"He comes over to the house now, he spends the day at the pool, and he says I'm making a good living." He smiled and shook his head sadly. "But I should have been a doctor."

On TV, they were plugging Saturday's game, Ohio State and Michigan. The twenty-ninth anniversary of the Buckeye's national championship. It wasn't exactly the anniversary of world peace. Gus touched the remote, raising the sound. The announcer claimed every member of that championship team would be there for this year's possible national championship game. As the segment closed, they flashed each college's insignia. I was looking at the Buckeye emblem for a moment or two before my brain caught up with my eyes.

"I need to use your phone, Gus."

"In the back," he said. "Something serious?"

"I've got to see a man about a nut."

The OSU insignia. I had seen a Buckeye nut, and recently. Frank Connely had had a bronze Buckeye nut on his desk. It was too crazy, but maybe Frank Connely had been a graduate of Ohio State.

Through Columbus information I got OSU alumni relations. Could they give me some information on a past graduate, I asked?

"What is this regarding, sir?"

"I'm over at the med school," I said. "I'm trying to find a student who graduated in the mid-seventies to invite him to the class reunion."

"The student's name?" the voice replied.

"Frank Connely." I spelled it for her. I heard her keyboard click. She covered the receiver and spoke in a muffled voice. My heart sank.

"Doctor?" she said. "The only Frank Connely we have is Frank J. Connely. And this Frank Connely never graduated from Ohio State. He was a football player back in the late fifties."

I came clean. "I'm looking for a man of that name who never graduated, but who claims to be an Ohio State alumnus. You don't have any current information on this person, do you?"

"No, I'm sorry. But try the athletic department."

CHAPTER 19

I GOT HOME AT ABOUT THREE IN THE AFTERNOON, intent on calling the athletic department in Columbus. The quiet in the house seemed unnatural. I finally realized it was because there was no Buck yapping at phantom intruders. I didn't like the feeling. It was too quiet. I knew living alone was never going to be an option again.

I flicked on a light, walked into the study, and sat down at Jordan's desk. The slanted rays of the fall sun filtered in through the front window, specking motes of the dust in the air. I looked at the old roll top that Jordan had retrofitted for a computer. She'd found it at an antique fair. I'd been the lucky one who got to carry it back in my car and squeeze it through the front door.

As I waited for the computer to boot up, I glanced around the desk. I knew where Jordan kept her PalmPilot and her calculator. They weren't there. I glanced around the room. Jordan was meticulous. Unlike me, with her everything had its place.

I got up from the desk and looked at the drawers under the bookshelves. Things were tossed aside. Not enough for casual observation, but enough for anyone who knew Jordan.

Slowly, I got up from the chair. Someone had been in this house. Looking for something. My heart was beating as I walked out the library and up the stairs. From a glass case along the upper hallway I removed my Al Kaline bat. I walked slowly to the bedroom and flicked on the light. No one there. My eyes fell on the antique dressing table under the mirror. I could almost see Jordan sitting in front of it, brushing her hair. I looked at the row of drawers. The one in the center looked partially open. It was the one that held her cosmetics.

I walked over to it and pulled it open. Everything was out of place. I was convinced now.

Bat in hand I walked into the bathroom. No one there. Back out into the hallway. That's when I heard the noise. I froze and listened. I was right. There was a sound at the back door. Just a click, but it was enough for me. Whoever wanted me dead hadn't given up yet. I headed to the stairway. Then I heard another click of the bolt, this time a little louder. It was the second lock. Someone was working the door. *Shit. Here we go again.*

I crept from the foyer, through the back hall, into the kitchen. I could hear a rustling.

I leaped into the kitchen and saw the back door ajar. I raced toward it and pushed it open.

It was cold. My breath hung in front of me. I kept my back close to the house and came around to the side driveway. I stepped forward onto the pavement, prepared to fight, and collided with him. He got me in a bear hug, put a reverse chokehold on me, and we went down on the ground.

FIRST, I STRUGGLED AGAINST THE HANDCUFFS. Then I tried explaining to the cop that it was my lawn where he was planting my face. Finally, one knee between my shoulder blades, he dragged my wallet from my pants. After a second or two, I heard a dry chuckle and an embarrassed apology. I was more relieved than pissed. He helped me up, apologized again, and explained that Sennett had ordered a car to cruise by on regular intervals. When he'd seen someone at the door, he'd reacted.

I went back inside and called Sennett. I told him I was glad to see he was watching over his constituency. "You're like the Mounties, you always get your man."

"'Except I don't ride a horse."

"Yeah, and you don't always get the right guy."

"Police work is never perfect," he said. "Like an elevator ride. Sometimes you get the elevator—"

"Sometimes you get the shaft. How about the guy that got away? How long had he been there?"

"He couldn't have been here too long. Our guys were moving around the side of the house when you came in. They didn't see you arrive. When you left, they thought you were the intruder. We found his footprints. They didn't get a good look at him. Is anything missing?"

"Jordan's cellphone. A few other miscellaneous things. Nothing of any apparent significance."

"Did she back it up on the computer?"

"Not here, but at the office."

"I'll check it out."

"I appreciate the effort. Just make sure your guys don't mug my friend, Jerry, when he comes over tonight."

"Oh, yeah? What's he look like?"

"Six-three, two-twenty-five. 10th degree black belt in karate."

"We'll be sure to make nice."

It took about ten minutes for my nerves to settle down. Then I picked up the phone and dialed the Ohio State Athletic Department.

A lady answered in a singsong voice. I pictured Aunt Bee from the old Andy Griffith series.

"Yes," she said, "there is a record of a Frank Connely back in the late fifties. He played for a year and then left."

"Would anyone know his whereabouts?"

"Well, the only link to anyone that far back would be Coach Stig Hunter. He retired fifteen years ago but still lives in Columbus. Most people go to him for stories about the old days."

I got his number from her and dialed him, introducing myself as a physician in Detroit.

"I hope that I'm not bothering you," I continued.

"Are you from the HMO?"

"No, sir."

"Checking on my benefits?"

I hated HMOs as much as any civilian. I told him so.

"Parasites," he said.

I agreed. I listened patiently as he vented for a moment. Finally, he said, "What can I do for you?"

"I'm trying to make a connection with someone from Pennsylvania. I think he played football at Ohio State. Someone in the sports information office suggested that I call you."

"It must have been Cindy Summerfield. She's always telling people that. As a matter of fact, she's got all the memories. All I got is age. Who was the guy anyway?"

"A doctor."

"Doctor?"

I braced myself, thinking we'd veer back to HMOs. "His name is Frank Connely. I understand there was a player by that name in the late forties or early fifties."

"I remember the name." Silence, a long one. "Nice guy. He played a couple of seasons and then transferred. Erie State, if memory serves me. One of those players who saw he wasn't going to play much."

"Can you tell me anything else about him?"

"I think he coached in Pennsylvania." I heard a rattling sound in his voice.

It sounded like the beginning of a cough. I realized he was laughing. "They may go," he said, "but they're always Buckeyes at heart."

I was doing the math. It didn't add up.

"Always a Buckeye," he said again.

"So this Frank Connely would be in his late seventies now."

"I should think so," he said. "Yes."

"The Frank Connely I'm looking for is much younger."

"You're sure he played for Ohio State?"

"I saw a bronze figurine on his desk. A buckeye nut."

"Never seen one."

He changed the subject, asking if I'd ever played football.

"College," I said. "Then I got injured."

"Where'd you play?"

"Michigan."

The cough-chuckle started up again. "Were you any good?"

"I too was one of those players who saw he wasn't going to play much."

"But they said you had potential?" he said. Cough-chuckle. In football-speak, that meant hamburger.

"A punching bag for the first string," I said.

"Was your injury serious?"

"I got knocked out, suffered a little amnesia, headaches. After that it never seemed so important."

"Injuries are part of the game." An easy comment if it wasn't you.

"I knew that. I still like the game, just not in the same way."

"You Michigan boys did good for yourselves," he said. "I could never hate you the way Woody did."

"You only hated us one Saturday a year."

"Those days," he reminisced. "We went crazy. Pounding players on their helmets, yelling at them, stirring them up into a frenzy. Sometimes things went a little too far."

Like Woody Hayes giving a player a left jab to the throat, I thought. "Now I see things a little differently."

"It's not an easy job."

"Coaching is the best worst job in the world. During the season, Coach Hayes went over plays and planned strategy for hours. Once the season was over, we recruited until February. Then the letters went out, there was a short break, and spring practice started. The only rest you had was May and June." He went quiet. We sat there together. "I regret the time away," he said. "My wife died shortly after I quit coaching. Cancer. In the end, I learned that football doesn't hold the meaning of life. It was just a game."

"You shouldn't punish yourself."

"When you lose, you question yourself first. At least, the honest player does." I liked this old man. I thanked him and told him I would have enjoyed playing for him.

"Listen, I have to run. We've got an alumni thing in Ann Arbor tomorrow," he said suddenly. "But I think you're barking up the wrong tree. You must have a different Frank Connely." He must have been in a hurry, because I didn't get a chance to say goodbye.

I hung the phone up and stared at it for a moment. There's more to a voice than what it says. I should know; it's my business. And Stig Hunter's voice, as he denied knowing of a bronze buckeye nut, had spoken differently from his words. I thought I'd call Cindy Summerfield.

"WE TALKED EARLIER," I BEGAN. "But Stig Hunter told me to call back."

"Greatest offensive line coach we ever had. He's a living link to the greatest days in Ohio State history."

"Indeed," I said. What I wanted to say was, "Enough! Football is a game. Get it? G-A-M-E."

"Have you ever seen a bronze figurine or statue that was in the shape of a buckeye nut, with flowers around it?"

"Sure. Sounds like the Buckeye Victory Stone. Coach Hayes gave those to players on the championship teams. Why?"

"I'm looking for a guy who had one. His name is Frank Connely. The only trouble is no one seems to know who he is."

"It shouldn't be too much trouble. Coach gave that trophy away to the '68 team and a couple of teams in the mid-70s."

"Do you have a roster you could fax to me?"

"Sure can."

"Photographs?"

"Sure. Team picture or individual shots?"

"Both," I said. "If it isn't too much trouble."

"No problem. It'll take a few minutes."

I gave her my fax number and thanked her, then added, "I appreciate your help, even if I am from Michigan."

"Forget it. In the end we're all Americans, aren't we?"

"Even this Saturday?"

She laughed. "Well now that you mention it..."

AT FIVE O'CLOCK THE PICTURES STARTED rolling off the fax machine. My hunch had been wrong. Wait, I told myself, sternly. You went through a lot to get this dope. At least let Jerry have a look at it before you give up.

Jerry showed up twenty minutes later. I showed him the photos.

"I've got a hunch. I think this guy Connely played ball. I think he played on the '68 state team. I thought maybe you'd spot something I've missed. Anything, anybody."

Jerry studied the photo again. Like me, he was taken back thirty years. It was like he had seen all these men before and was reliving past experiences. In his case, back to haunting memories. I regretted the necessity, but my life—and Jordan's—were still in danger.

"This guy. Jackson Carpenter." He pointed to a picture of a young man with dark hair who didn't look anything like the doc I had defended in Dellsburg.

"He's a defensive back. He looks like he could have played the left side of the line."

"I've seen him before."

"Jerry, you probably saw his face just before he turned off your lights on the safety blitz."

"Maybe," Jerry said quietly. This time of the year never was good for Jerry.

"We're still going to the game on Saturday, aren't we?"

"You bet. Listen, I have to go. Sorry I couldn't be more help."

"That was a quick visit. What's the hurry?"

"I wasn't expecting the photos. You know."

The memories of the car crash. I knew. I walked him to the door. "Jerry, if you see a couple of guys in a car out there, don't worry. They work for me."

"You're kidding? Bodyguards?"

"No, just friends."

I closed the door and went back to the study. I looked at the football photos again. I looked at Carpenter. Maybe it was suggestion, but this time something in his eyes seemed to register. For no reason, except that doing something was better than doing nothing, I called Sennett and asked him to look up Jackson Carpenter. He got back to me twenty minutes later.

"Jackson Carpenter. He grew up in North Allegheny, Pennsylvania. Graduated Ohio State University in 1971. No wants, no warrants, pretty much a clean record."

"Pretty much?"

"College nonsense. Drinking. Girl trouble that Carpenter and another guy got into."

"Any idea what the girl thing was?"

"They're careful at the university about disclosing such information," he said. "It's a 'protect the student athlete from future problems' issue.

"Their words?"

"Kids do stupid things. Nobody wants to penalize them for the future."

"Should football help you escape the consequences of criminal behavior?" I theorized aloud.

"It's a great game."

"Build a hospital. Do something for humanity. Grow up."

"If you haven't played," he said, "you can't understand."

"You?"

"Middle linebacker. Middle Tennessee State. I never miss a game on TV if I can help it."

"We ate teams like yours for lunch at Michigan."

"Yeah? What does an old, broken-down doc like you know about it?"

I let him drag it out of me. Played both ways. Fourth string. I'd received a service letter for lasting the whole four years. "The first time I got in a game," I finished, "I got my bell rung good. It knocked some sense into me."

"I still like it."

"I might have an extra field pass for the game on Saturday. If you're such a football nut, maybe you'd be interested?"

"Ohio State vs. Michigan? Greatest game of the year. I'd give anything to be down on that field, dressed for the game, feeling the emotion again."

"Pick up your ticket at will-call. They're under Jerry Brooks' name. And see what you can find out about the girl trouble in Carpenter's background, please? It's my shot in the dark."

I HEADED FOR ST. VINCENT'S, Sennett's man following in the car behind me. As we left, another squad car pulled into the spot vacated by the first. It was a queer mix of feelings—the security of being protected, the annoyance of being followed.

When I got to the ICU, what I saw through the room window was better than I could have imagined. She was breathing on her own, eyes closed. I turned to a beaming Janie Flowers.

"We removed the tube this afternoon. Breathing on her own is a good sign. Dr. Lindstrom says she might wake up in a day or so."

I gowned up and went inside the room. Her hand felt great in mine, and her skin color was excellent. It really seemed she had turned the corner.

"The baby?" I asked Janie.

She said so far there were no problems, despite everything. "I need to ask you something," she said. "Did you send a Dr. Connely in for a consult?"

"No." I was stiff with fear and attention in a moment.

"It was during the shift break," she said. "He came into the ICU. Claimed that you had asked him to come in and consult. You personally, he said. I didn't like the way he acted. You know how you get a feel for certain people?"

"Yes."

"And I'd never heard of him before. I said could he please hang on while I called you to verify."

"It's okay, Jane. Believe me."

"And he left. Just like that. So I called security."

"And?"

"They couldn't find him."

"Police?"

"Security said they'd call."

I picked up the phone and dialed Sennett. I told him someone is trying to pass themselves off as Dr. Frank Connely.

"I'll send a detective over to talk with the nurse. In the meantime, we can protect Jordan. No one will come in or out of that room without proper identification."

I waited with Jordan until the officer arrived, then went back to my car and drove home.

The headlights from Sennett's man flashed in my rear-view mirror. I stopped in front of the house and waited for the officer to get out behind me. He checked with the other officer who had been watching the house then came over to my car to give me the all clear.

I was afraid. Afraid to go into my own house. And afraid someone might harm the only person in the world who meant anything to me.

When I opened the front door and stepped into the foyer, my foot slid on a piece of paper lying on the limestone floor. I hit the light switch, bent down, and picked it up.

In clipped newspaper print pasted on the paper, I read: "He discovereth deep things out of darkness, and bringeth out to light the shadow of death."

CHAPTER 20

I STARED AT THE PAPER, WONDERING WHAT the absurd inscription meant, my anger boiling to the surface. Sennett and his protection were a joke. Nobody could prevent a determined nutcase from getting at his victim. My collar felt tight against my neck. I needed to get out. I needed to be on my own, protecting myself.

I put the paper in my pocket then looked around, under the table, in the corners. Nothing. I flipped the wall switch and turned on the lights to the front room of the house. To anyone looking from the outside, it was business as usual. Upstairs, I put a few things together in an overnight bag, then went back downstairs, careful to leave the lights on.

Outside the back door, I turned away from the driveway, toward the back lawn of my neighbor. It was cold. The wind sounded in the few leaves remaining on his oak tree as I passed beneath it. Across his yard, I made for the street again. Everything was as I had left it. The cop sitting in his car across from the house, my Wagoneer parked five or six spaces down. It was early evening, and the streetlights had just come on. I stayed at the edge of their light until I reached the back of the car.

There was a quick flash of light as I opened the car door. I climbed behind the wheel and closed the door softly. The cop hadn't moved. I started the engine, put the car in reverse, and backed out toward the intersection, the only illumination coming from the streetlight on the corner. I rolled around the corner, made a U-turn, and was gone.

The feeling was almost exhilarating. Now all I had to do was stay alive.

I drove toward the western suburbs. Just outside Ann Arbor, I pulled into a gas station, filled up, and grabbed a bag of pretzels. From an open-air telephone near the highway, I called Sennett.

"I'm best on my own," I said. "I felt like a trapped animal there."

"It's better to be a live, trapped animal than a trophy on someone's wall."

"Maybe."

"This isn't kid's stuff, Ben."

"That's why I left." I told him about the package and the inscription.

"So you've got a killer on your tail who's working for God," he said. "Do yourself a favor and come back."

"Not right now. I have a few things to do."

"You mind telling me where you're going?"

"Let's just say I'm checking on our tickets for Saturday's game."

"The stadium?"

"The vicinity."

"I'll be here for a while and then I'll be home." I could hear the resignation in his voice. "Keep alive until after the game, will you?"

I FOUND STIG HUNTER STANDING near the front door of the Varsity Inn. He was a little fatter than the man in the picture I'd been looking at, but the face was the same. The receptionist had pointed him out to me.

I introduced myself, referring to our earlier phone conversation. There was a moment of hesitation. Then he asked me if I wanted a drink.

The hotel lobby was a sea of scarlet and gray. We found our way to the small bar off the lobby. At the first table we passed, two guys with massive arms and bellies were proclaiming their allegiance to Ohio State. They were flanked by guys half their size. On the table in front of them were three beer pitchers, all of them full. I motioned Hunter toward the back, to a table with vacant seats near the window.

A waitress came and took our order, two diet sodas. We looked at each other and smiled. Two old guys who knew the score, or at least some of it.

He faced the problem my presence implied. "I thought we had decided your man wasn't a Buckeye."

"I wanted to talk about Jackson Carpenter."

A frown crossed his face. "Could have been one of the best I've ever coached."

"Could have been?"

"He quit after his freshman year."

"Any reason?"

"Just one of those things, I guess. Wasn't for lack of love for the Buckeyes. He was a fanatic." It didn't sound like a compliment.

"Did you keep in touch?"

"Nope."

"One of the few you didn't keep in touch with?"

"Yes." Hunter nodded. I thought about the lucky young men whose lives he'd touched.

"Why not Carpenter?"

"There was no chemistry between us." He shrugged. "It happens."

"Was it the incident with those girls?" I had touched a nerve. I knew it from the look on his face.

"Look, Doctor, I don't gossip about my old players. Good or bad, they were my boys. Why are you so damned interested?"

"Someone has been trying to kill me." I filled him in quickly. He listened, then said he didn't think there could be any connection, but under the circumstances, he'd humor my questions.

"Jake Carpenter," he said, "was one of the greatest disappointments in my career. He came to Columbus from outside of Pittsburgh. We had a number of good players from there. I knew he was going to be great from the moment he set foot on the practice field. He had quickness and instinct. It's something you can't teach."

Same as a surgeon, I reflected. Or a detective.

"You can help a guy get stronger," Hunter said. "You can get him to run faster. But quickness and the killer instinct, you either have it or you don't. We teach players how to use that killer instinct. That's a coach's job. But it's like nuclear fuel. You can use it, but you have to control it."

"Carpenter?"

"No," Hunter said. "A coach gets to know a person pretty well. He had a fundamental character flaw. He didn't want to win; he wanted to dominate anyone and anything that was in his way. He didn't care how."

"The episode with those girls. Was that the reason he left?"

"He didn't have the discipline to play for us. Coach Hayes was a smart man. He knew he couldn't conquer this kid."

"What do you mean?"

"On the football field," he said, "you could see it in his eyes. He wanted to kill, do bodily harm. A defensive back can create a lot of mayhem."

"What ever happened to Carpenter?"

"One day he came and turned in his jersey. That was it. Coach Hayes would only stand for toughness. He drew a line in the sand. If you crossed it, you were done."

"So he quit? It didn't make sense. I never knew anyone who was too mean to play. Something had happened off the field to expel Carpenter, and I needed to know what it was, despite Coach Hunter's noble intention to keep the skirts of Ohio State clean.

"What about Carpenter's buddy?"

"Who?"

"The other guy who was caught with those girls."

"Never knew what happened to him." He flinched slightly as he spoke.

"You wouldn't remember his name, would you?"

"Naw, too many kids over too many years."

Stig Hunter, a complete fact book on Ohio State football. He never forgot anything. And now he couldn't remember a player who'd figured in a police case.

His reluctance to tell me the truth spiked my urgent curiosity all the more.

CHAPTER 21

Cocktail hour was over and the lounge was full. I headed toward the door, where three or four silver-haired men were huddled near the entrance. The first one to meet my eyes looked like an ex-cornerback, fifty pounds overweight now. He had a friendly, open face. I tried him first.

"Do you remember Jake Carpenter?"

The smile vanished. "Yeah, we know him."

"Is he here?"

They all shook their heads in unison. The one in the back stepped forward. "We haven't seen him in the last few years."

I stuck out my hand. "My name is Ben Dailey. I'm doing a story on the '68 Ohio State team." The one with a hearing aid gave me a vacant look. "Carpenter's name was on the roster," I said, a little louder. No one answered. Finally, the fourth man spoke. He was big like the rest, with curly, red hair going gray and the eyes of a man who didn't take crap from anyone.

"I knew Jake. What about him?"

"I'm trying to locate every kid in that team picture. Nobody seems to know where he is. I thought maybe he had a friend."

"Jake didn't have many friends on the team. The only guy I ever saw him hang out with was this kid they called Billy Bob Frank, or just Tiny. I guess they went to high school together."

"How do you remember that after thirty years?" I asked conversationally.

"You don't forget someone you caught in the fraternity house with those girls, doing that kind of stuff. I remember him all right. I'd have beat both of them to death if the boys here hadn't been there." With the intensity in his eyes and the size of his fists, I believed him.

"Look," I said desperately, "do you remember anything else about them?"

"Yeah, I saw them at a couple of frat parties. All they used to talk about was their high school football team, the Allegheny Steelers. I know that's the name because we always used to razz him about how a carpenter could be a man of steel."

"Anything else at all?" Their eyes had narrowed. By now it must have been pretty clear I was no small-town journalist writing a stale old-champions story.

"Yeah. They loved their high school coaches. They always talked about them and how they had died in a car crash. They used to talk about them like they were gods. It would've made you like those two if they hadn't been so low down."

"What happened to Carpenter?"

"They kicked Jake off the team the next year. We never saw him again. Look, mister, this here is a reunion. I don't want to spoil any more of our party, if you know what I mean."

I knew what he meant. I apologized for disturbing them, thanked them, and left them to rehash fonder memories.

I MADE MY WAY DOWN STATE STREET, past the small shopping district, and onto the main campus. The graduate library was still open, a few people milling around, the stacks relatively empty. At the circulation desk, a librarian was checking her computer.

I told her what I was looking for.

"You're going to tax the system with that one," she said.

I told her I had faith in the university.

A few minutes later she came back, a printout in hand. Circulars, she said, were on the second floor. Ask for Dolores. I folded the paper she handed me and took the stairs two at a time up to the second floor. I wasn't in the mood for elevators. The entire second floor was filled with twelve-foot, metal shelves, packed from top to bottom with books and journals. The kind of rat-maze I usually loved. Tonight it felt like a tomb.

Dolores was waiting as I approached. I handed her the slip of paper.

"It'll be just a sec," she said, then disappeared into the stacks. She came back with a disc in her hand.

"Pretty lonely up here," I said.

"Especially on Friday night." Dolores handed me a disc. "Especially on Friday night before Ohio State."

"Double especially." I looked at the disc for a few seconds. "Want to show an old man how this works?"

Two unoccupied Gateway computers sat in a reading area in the middle of the room. Delores sat down behind one, slipped in the CD, and turned on the computer.

I wanted to find Jake Carpenter's friend. I knew he'd gone to Allegheny High School in western Pennsylvania. I looked up the newspaper from the area, *The North Allegheny Record*.

I asked for the CD with the newspaper on its records. It didn't take long for it to appear on the screen.

"Fifty years of *The North Allegheny Record*," Dolores said matter-of-factly. "Here, let me help you. I'll click on 'Find' under the edit column. Now what are the key words for your search?"

"How about 'coaches,' and 'automobile crash.'"

She tapped in the name and searched the records. An article came up on the screen, "Local Coaches Die in Car Crash." The year was 1966.

"Magic," I said.

"If you need anything else, just call."

I started reading.

Last night Allegheny High School coach, William Frank Kanaly, and his assistant, Stefan Cowles, were killed in a one-car crash off Route 22 near the Standard Station at Old Main. The car apparently lost control on the icy pavement and hit a telephone pole, instantly killing the two men.

Kanaly had recently been the center of attention in an undisclosed incident at the high school involving members of his football team. Both men were exonerated, as were the members of his team.

The article went on for a while, ending with this:

A service for the two men will be held at St. Simeon's Church on Thursday, February 12.

I clicked "Find" and tapped in both of the men's names. A second article appeared: "High School Football Team Under Cloud of Suspicion."

The Allegheny High School football team has come under suspicion after anonymous accusations from two female students at the school. The Record has learned that the girls claimed they were assaulted at a party following North's 62-0 drubbing of neighboring Punxsutawney.

Police said they were investigating the matter. So far, no charges had been filed, and the students involved remained unidentified. Coach Frank Kanaly declined to comment on the alleged incident.

I sat back and looked at the screen. It was quiet, library quiet. Almost too quiet. Up the aisle from me, Dolores's chair squeaked. A reassuring sound. I hit "Find" once more, bringing up one more article, dated December 11, 1965, "Students and Coaches Cleared of Wrongdoing in Sexual Assault Case."

Frank Kanaly and Stefan Cowles were cleared of any involvement with accusations made by two female students from Allegheny High School. Furthermore, the young women dropped their charges against the unnamed football players.

Interviewed after the decision, Kanaly stated that "reckless accusations on the part of two students have done potentially serious harm to myself, my family, Stefan Cowles and his family, and the football program at our school. It is our hope that we can put this behind us and move on."

One more for the home team?

I clicked "Find." Nothing.

Back to Dolores. "What about back issues of the *Michigan Daily,* 1968?"

"Right around the corner, on CD." She crooked a finger and led me to the spot, where she pulled out a small file with discs. "Here," she said. Campus newspaper, 1968. We walked back to the computer, brought it up on screen.

Ohio State vs. Michigan, 1968. I typed in the commands and soon the first article appeared. Dolores patted my shoulder and showed me how to enlarge photos. There was a lot about Woody Hayes and Bump Elliot and the show-down taking place. Michigan hadn't won since 1964, and it didn't look as if it would this year. Players on both sides were quoted. I recognized names I hadn't seen in years. I could feel myself getting drawn in by the words, by the simple facts of the time. I was starting to relive the time, my heart rate picking up, my palms sweating. In the background, a phone rang. Dolores answered, then hung up. I heard her walking down the corridor.

I read through pre-game hype, articles about stars on both sides.

Click, find. The Game.

Headline: "Buckeyes Turn Wolverine's Roses to Thorns." I read every word. The game came back to me in small vignettes. There were statistics, coaches' comments, pictures. On the last page was a small photo near the bottom. I squinted at the screen, trying to make out the scene. Point, click, enlarge. It didn't work.

"Dolores?"

I got up from my seat, rounded the corner. She wasn't there.

"Excuse me?" I said. "Dolores?"

A book clattered to the floor. I wasn't alone.

At the end of the room, a large man dressed in a dark overcoat and ski mask came around the corner of the stacks. I ducked behind Dolores's desk, searching for a weapon. Anything. I looked around the desk. He reached inside his coat and pulled out a revolver. I couldn't see his face. I imagined him smiling behind the mask as he raised the gun. I did not intend to die this way—that was my knee-jerk response. I turned back to the desk and saw the cord. On the small black cone-shaped handle, in white letters, *Security.*

Grab, pull, live.

I yanked the cord as hard as I could. There was a shrill, wailing screech. I bolted for the stacks. As I did, I heard him push the desk out of his way. I ran the length of the stacks, straight for the door and the stairs beyond. As I reached the stairwell, two dull thuds exploded above the alarm, rattling the metal stanchions just as I flew past them.

WITHIN SECONDS I WAS OUTSIDE AND ALONE, the late November cold stinging my eyes, heart pounding. Squad cars pulled up at the side of the building. In the gathering darkness, I slipped into the back of a crowd assembling near the library entrance. After ten minutes, a couple of officers came out, all smiles, writing the incident off as another college prank, big game nonsense.

I decided to go back to the Varsity Inn, trying to stay close to groups, crossing from one side of the street to the other. At the Inn, I found the lobby crowd had thinned. I called Stig Hunter in his room and apologized for disturbing him. Instead of being angry, he almost seemed glad that I had called. He agreed to meet me.

I waited for him in the bar.

When he sat down, he ordered a diet soda. He seemed a little more drawn than when I had seen him before.

"There was more to Jake Carpenter, wasn't there?"

He nodded.

"When you're a coach and you recruit someone, they're almost like your kid. You know what I mean?"

"You mean you feel a responsibility."

"The night they got caught with those two girls, I got called down to the police station. It wasn't natural what they did."

"What do you mean?"

"I mean they used Coke bottles on them. I had to hush it up. And then I learned about the other stuff."

"What other stuff?"

"He and his buddy. We never learned the full extent of it. No one did. We just didn't want to embarrass the football team. It was a deal we made. He quit the team, and we kept quiet. I never forgave myself for doing that and for misjudging Carpenter. I wish I had never gone to his high school."

"Everyone misjudges someone in their life." I thought about my own troubles after Jimmy Scotten died. "What about his friend, the kid he called Billy Bob Frank?"

Hunter looked at me blankly. "I don't know anything about this Frank kid. All I know is that there was evil lurking in that boy Carpenter. I should have done something, should have said something."

"Maybe he is all right."

Hunter just shrugged his shoulders.

"One last thing. Do you know anything about Stefan Cowles?"

"I remember him. He coached at Allegheny back in the sixties," he said. "A good coach. He had a couple of looks from some guys that Woody knew. But then there was that high school thing."

"You mean the scandal."

"Ruination by innuendo. Once the papers got hold of it, it was all over."

"Did Jake Carpenter ever talk about Cowles?"

"No," he said.

Silence.

"Coach?"

"I've had a hunch," he suddenly said, his words rapid, as if to get them out before he repented. "Carpenter bled scarlet and gray. My bet is that he'll be on the field for the reunion of that team. He was a Buckeye through and through. That's the main reason I'm not going on the field. I just don't want to see him."

"That's a pretty big hurt for you to have over a kid that never even graduated the program."

"Maybe, but I don't want to see him."

Right now, neither did I. But I knew that I had to go to the stadium tomorrow and find him.

I was about to get up when Hunter put his hand on mine.

"Thank you. I've wanted to tell someone this for thirty years. Just saying it makes me feel better."

"It's okay. I understand. It's just a game. But sometimes sports takes all of us into places we don't want to be. Tell you what. If I was a kid, I'd like to have you as my coach."

I got up and walked back to the lobby. It was close to eleven o'clock. I was beat. And I had no desire to go back out. At the front desk, the same receptionist was on duty. He was cheerful and earnest, happy to inform me that he'd had a cancellation. King-size bed, non-smoking? He tapped computer keys, swiped my credit card, and I was in.

Room 320 was at the end of a long hallway. As soon as I got inside, I doubled-bolted the door and wedged a chair under the doorknob. The window overlooked State Street. People outside were shouting and singing. I perused the crowd, then closed the curtains and turned on the TV. On ESPN the so-called experts described what was going to happen tomorrow. Ohio State against unbeaten Michigan. Everybody had an opinion about the game, illustrated by slides and game tapes.

Local networks, same show. The Big Game.

I shut the TV off, disgusted that so much was being made of so little. I picked up the phone and called St. Vincent's in Detroit. Jane Flowers was still on duty. Jordan was making progress. A guard was posted outside her room. I lay on the bed looking up at the ceiling, wondering why someone was still trying to kill me. The more I tried to guess, the more I came up empty-handed, my mind a blur of chases, gunshots, and newspaper clips. Fragments of a story that made no sense. Exhaustion finally overtook me, and I fell asleep.

The dream came to me again. In the tunnel, ready to take the field. Excitement bursting through me. Lights, cheering fans, the huddle before the game. For the thousandth time, the coach called my name, pushed me toward the field. This time the dream seemed more real.

Numbly, I took my three-point stance, staring between the helmets of a two hundred and thirty-pound guard and a two hundred and eighty-pound tackle.

I saw the tackle glance to his left and nod as my eyes danced back and forth. Over the din of the crowd I could hear them yell at me.

The quarterback started his call and did a head bob with a slow cadence to draw us offside. *Don't bite, Dailey.* Then the center snapped the ball. My key was the running back.

"Trap left!" the linebacker yelled again. I moved to fill the hole.

By this time the center was on me. I raised my hands up and pushed him off. The back was coming. Suddenly, I saw them, my adversaries from the other side of the line. Double-teamed, one went for my leg from behind in a chop block. The other used a forearm shiver under my chin, snapping my head back and knocking off my helmet. I could feel myself collapsing helplessly as I saw the back run toward the hole. Out of desperation I reached out, grabbed his ankle, and brought him down.

Then the pileup. The muggers weren't done. I felt a clawing fist in my stomach. Then an elbow smashing into my face. I felt a searing pain, a snap, and then blood trickling down my face. Stunned, I lay flat on the ground for what seemed like an eternity. People gathered around. One of them stood hovering over me with blood dripping off of his taped right hand. I saw him bend down for a moment.

I looked up at his face, a white skeleton barking out words, rows of teeth clacking against each other. I stared at him, felt myself go limp, felt a sense of helpless vertigo as in the moment just before a fall. He wore a black robe, held a gavel in his hand, ready to strike.

I woke up in a sweat. It was four in the morning.

I knew that was all the sleep I would get. I turned on the lamp and sat up in bed, thinking I'd take a shower. I couldn't get rid of that last image stuck in my head, the skeleton image signaling, looking directly at me.

It sounded like the title of a football murder mystery: *Death Calls the Play.*

CHAPTER 22

IT HAD BEEN THIRTY YEARS since I had stepped on the field. The Big House, the largest college stadium in America. A storied building with the ghosts of hundreds of memories still lurking in its corners. They had redone the edifice since my time, adding ten thousand seats and putting a bright yellow and blue trim around the top of the stands, an effect the locals called "the halo."

The alumni traditionalists made them take the artistic trim down. Too bad. I thought it was an interesting touch, a little garish for my liking, but art is perception.

I lost myself in the crowd walking from the Varsity Inn. It was easy to do, a fact that made me feel both safer and more careful. I was invisible. But so was whoever wanted me. A silent attack, and he would be gone. As I got closer, I felt my heart rate increase, a headache gathering strength behind my eyes. It was more than fear.

Jerry arrived early at the stadium and met Sennett and me at will-call. He was waiting for me with a frown on his face.

"Biggest game of the year, and you're late?" he said.

I told him what had happened the night before in the library.

"Okay," he said. "We're out of here. Nothing is worth dying for." I knew that statement must have taken all of his willpower. The same as it had taken for me to come to the stadium.

"Relax, Jerry. We're investigating a crime. On duty."

We walked back around the stadium and into the Victors parking lot. It cost $10,000 to park there. The lot was full. Sis, boom, buck. Behold the power of football. The tailgaters were wrapping it up. One last shrimp and lobster, one last martini, and one last high-five by people who'd probably never felt real contact in the game.

My knees seemed to wobble as we approached the guards at the entrance.

"You all right?" Sennett said.

"Headache," I lied. "Let's go."

We passed the guards with our field passes and headed down into the tunnel. It was eerily quiet. I knew there were 100,000 fans on the other side. Up ahead someone was whistling. It reverberated in the tunnel.

Jerry stopped for a moment. He shook his head.

"What's the matter, Jerry?"

"Did you hear that whistling?"

"Yeah, why?"

"It reminded me of something. Something I've forgotten and can't place." He shook his head. "Forget about it."

We started walking, our footfalls reverberating, a sound that echoed in my memory, our breaths making thin vapor trails in the light at the entrance to the field. I'd been there so many times, pumped and ready to run onto the field. Now we were only three ex-jocks looking for a killer.

"Bring back memories?" Sennett asked, almost enviously.

"I wish it did. I've forgotten most of it. Doctors say I wanted to forget."

Sennett shook his head. "How could you forget this?"

We stepped onto the edge of the field. Most of the 100,000 fans were already in their seats. Banners flew, placards rose above sections of the crowd, fans hoping to be seen on ABC. We shoved past groundskeepers toward a spot near the tunnel. Sennett was engrossed in the spectacle, the grass, the masses, the flags. Then came drums, the band, a roar erupting as they high-stepped onto the field, trombone players waggling their instruments in the air, percussionists beating a cadence as the band formed a block "M" and moved down the field, the drum major throwing his baton over the uprights and catching it on the other side. The sound was deafening. The crowd went wild.

The PA system crackled, and a voice echoed across the stadium. From the tunnel, a hundred men in suits and topcoats moved onto the field. Opponents first. It was one of the few niceties in the game. They lined up in two parallel lines, holding the scarlet and gray Ohio State University insignia, forming a gun barrel to shoot the team onto the field. Near the edge of the grass, I recognized one from the group I'd questioned the night before at the Varsity Inn, from the '68 team. In the tunnel, the OSU team was working itself into a frenzy, jumping up and down, crashing helmets. When the captain gave the signal, they ran the gauntlet of ex-Ohio lettermen.

The old timers stayed for a couple of minutes, enjoying the sight.

Suddenly, Jerry was pulling at my sleeve.

"It's him."

"Who?"

"The guy in the photo."

I looked but saw no one.

"He walked back down the tunnel."

I craned my neck, thought I saw a beard, dark hair, sunglasses. Then nothing.

"How'd you know it was him? I asked urgently.

"That look. I know I've seen it before. He seemed so calm." Jerry's eyes were wide like he'd seen a ghost.

With so many people in the stands, we didn't stand a chance of finding him. Michigan took the field, and the Big House rocked. It was pandemonium, delicious and frightening. While captains lined up for the coin toss, I watched the tunnel. Kick off. I watched the tunnel and the sidelines. Kick return, end zone. Futile.

"Watch the game," Sennett said. The wave was moving around the stadium. Sennett was into the moment. The whole gestalt.

Michigan up the middle. Two-yard gain. I said, "Jerry thought he saw something."

"What?"

He clapped and cheered. He was morphing into a college freshman right before my eyes. Michigan up the middle. One-yard gain.

"I don't remember it being this cold when I played," he complained.

"You played in the south. Fair weather football."

"You call hurricanes fair weather?" he shouted. He shook a pair of gloves out of his pocket and pulled them on. "We played East Mississippi State two days after a hurricane came ashore. That was the day we took home the coveted Rattlesnake Trophy."

"Rattlesnake?" Option play. Quarterback keeps. Dropped behind the line of scrimmage.

"I suppose that's not to be confused with the Water Moccasin Cup?"

Sennett didn't laugh.

Two minutes later Jerry tugged at my sleeve.

"Ben, that guy. I've seen him before, and it wasn't from those photos. He was the one whistling before. It was the tune that made me remember."

"Remember what?"

Jerry told me. I tugged Sennett's sleeve.

"Lieutenant, we've got to go back to Detroit." Sennett looked at me as if I were crazy.

"You mean leave? It's Michigan against Ohio State!" I told him what Jerry'd just told me. "Shit, my damn luck."

"Only shallow men believe in luck."

"Call me shallow," he snarled as we moved toward the exit.

CHAPTER 23

AT HALFTIME THE CITY WAS EMPTY. There was no one else left in town, except for the few "study geeks" cramming before exams. Sennett took State Street south and headed for I-94. Clouds were rolling in from the west. In a short time, they would be raining on the winner's parade. Jerry and I followed Sennett in our cars.

Green signs flashed as we flew past them. Belleville, Willow Run, Romulus, Metro Airport. We passed the five-story high statue of a Uniroyal tire. Only in Detroit. Ahead of us, across the evening sky, lay the Rouge plant stacks and their effluents and, beyond that, the beginning of the Detroit skyline.

My office was in St. Vincent's medical office building. With the magnetic siren light flashing on Sennett's car, we made it in record time, arriving at the front door just in time to see, on the guard's TV, Michigan deflect a pass on fourth and ten, defeating Ohio State.

The guard, who gave everyone a hard time, seemed disappointed when the lieutenant flashed his badge. By the time we reached my office, Jerry seemed to be hyperventilating.

"You okay?" I asked.

"Just out of shape." I didn't always trust Jerry's assessment of his medical well-being. After all, he'd played a whole game in high school with a broken leg.

I walked to the back of my office and into one of my examining rooms. In the corner was a television monitor on top of a computer. I switched on the monitor and activated the computer. When the list of exams came up, I found the one I was looking for.

I brought it up on the screen and looked at the two white vocal cords. One looked a little redder than the other.

"Okay, sir," I could hear my voice in the background. "Sing something. Anything."

His voice came out strong.

"*Goin' to Kansas City, Kansas City here I come.*"

I switched off the machine.

"Familiar?"

Fear and anger came over Jerry's face.

"Same voice. Who is he?"

"Steve Waring," I read the name. "He came and saw me a few days ago. A disease called spasmodic dysphonia."

"What do you know about him?' Sennett asked.

"Not much. He came in from the East Coast. First time injection."

I went up to the file cabinet and pulled out his chart. I gave Sennett the address and phone number. He went to my outer office and dialed the station. Within a couple of minutes, Sennett came back with the expected news—Steve Waring didn't exist. Phony address and phone number.

I told Jerry I would drive him home. He was pretty shaken up by hearing that voice again after all these years. All those years since the night Timmy Steel had died, in that car driven off the road by two Buckeyes.

I got in the car and opened the door for Jerry. As I did, I took some things off the seat. I felt a hard, plastic object. And once again things came together.

JERRY ASSURED ME HE WAS GOOD TO DRIVE, and I let him convince me. I raced back to my office. In the video room, I popped in the VHS tape. It was the one I had gotten from Frank Connely's office. Soon a pair of vocal cords appeared on the screen. I listened as Connely spoke.

"Okay, Steve, sing into the microphone." "Kansas City" came back on the soundtrack.

"How can you be sure it was the same guy?" Sennett asked skeptically.

"Look at the left vocal cord. It's the same reddish discoloration. Couldn't be anyone else."

"Might not stand up in court. How do we get an ID?"

"Connely had a nurse named Werner. I bet you'll find her in Dellsburg."

A search for Sue Werner in Dellsburg came up empty. There was a Werner in nearby Arlington. Bingo.

"Mrs. Werner," Sennett said, "This is Lieutenant Sennett from the Detroit Police Department. We need some information from you."

Twenty minutes later she'd gone to Frank Connely's office and called Sennett back. I got on the other line.

"Dr. Dailey has a tape from your office. Do you remember giving it to him?"

"Sure. It was from one of his early cases."

"Did Dr. Connely have a system for labeling them?"

"Yes, Lieutenant, it's right here. Each tape was for a separate patient. While he knew he was going to have to streamline the system, he wanted to separate them in the early studies."

"How many cases were there?"

"About twenty or twenty-five."

"Mrs. Werner, this is Dr. Dailey. It's extremely important that we find the right one. Do you have the VCR in front of you?" I knew this could take hours, but what choice did I have?

"Sure."

"We're going to need you to help us." I explained what we were looking for. When I told her it might help understanding how Dr. Connely died, she seemed eager to help.

I could hear her rummaging in the background for the tapes. She came back to the phone, a little out of breath.

"This is crazy. Everything is strewn around in the cabinet. I can't understand it, I'm the only one who knew about the tapes. I never left anything so cluttered. It's going to take me hours to straighten it all up and find the tapes you need." My heart sank.

"Are you sure that tape was with them?" There was a pause.

"You know, there was a tape on my desk. I couldn't remember how it got there, but with all the commotion with Dr. Connely's death I never put it back. Let me take a look."

We waited for a couple of minutes that seemed like hours.

"Here it is."

"Please put it in the VCR, and see what comes up," Sennett said, calmly.

In the background we could hear Connely talking. I could hear someone speaking on the tape, but couldn't make it out. Werner came back to the phone.

"There's nothing special on this one that I can tell. Dr. Connelly asked him to sing a few bars and then recorded his vocal cords."

"Can you tell me what he was singing?"

"That old tune we used to listen to as kids, you know, 'Goin' to Kansas City.'"

"That's the one, Mrs. Werner. Can you tell me who it was?"

"Let's see. That would be Steven Coles."

"Do you remember Mr. Coles?"

"Sure. He was an old friend of Dr. Connely's. He used to call him regularly. In fact, he was our first Botox patient. Dr. Connely just couldn't seem to get it right. They decided to get another opinion."

"Do you know who Dr. Connely sent him to?"

"No. It was someone in the Midwest. I know that."

"How?"

"Because Mr. Coles mentioned that he was going to stop in Toledo on the way back."

A chill went down my spine. Sennett thanked her and hung up.

"Lieutenant. There may be a connection here. A Stefan Cowles was one of the coaches who died in Allegheny."

"What are you talking about?"

I explained. I pulled the copies I'd made of the newspaper articles from my pocket. Sennett looked them over. "Cowles and Kanaly," he ruminated.

"Say that again, Lieutenant."

"Cowles and Kanaly."

"That's it, Lieutenant. Kanaly. Get it?"

"Get what?"

"Coles and Connely. Cowles and Kanaly. Too close for jazz, don't you see? There has to be a connection."

Light dawned in his eyes. "We know who Coles is," he said, his usual phlegmatic manner failing to conceal a trace of excitement.

"Then let's check out our Dr. Kanaly."

Within thirty minutes, several sheets of paper came rolling out of my fax machine. I picked them up and stared at them in disbelief. Then I picked up the phone, motioning for Sennett to get on the other line. When the receptionist at the Varsity Inn answered, I asked for Stig Hunter's room. I wasn't surprised to find him there.

"Didn't go to the game, Coach?" By this time, he knew my voice.

"I'm an old man now. Too much excitement."

"Or was it the fear of running into Steven Coles?"

"What do you mean?"

"Steven Coles, a.k.a. Jackson Carpenter."

There was silence.

"Why didn't you tell me the guy Jackson Carpenter, also known as Steven Coles, M.D., hung around with someone named John Hunter?"

"He's my brother's only child, and he was dying from lung cancer. What was I going to do? Let him suffer more?"

"And football is power. Football rules, even when it comes to disciplining two kids like Jackson Carpenter and your nephew. No blemishes on the almighty team, right?"

"What do you mean?"

"I mean you used the power of the football team to cover for him, right?"

"I couldn't let John take the fall. He was a good kid. Just needed some time to straighten out. I knew I was right. Look, he even went to medical school."

"Being a doctor doesn't make you a good human being."

"Maybe, but from my perspective I did right. I made a deal with the university. I got Carpenter to quit, and John had to do community service. John went on to do something good with his life, and my brother died knowing his kid was all right."

Sennett decided to intervene.

"Look, Coach, this is George Sennett. I'm a lieutenant in homicide, Detroit Police Department. When is the last time you saw Connely?"

"I saw him at the funeral of his wife. A terrible tragedy, dying like she did. He looked so distraught. I worried about him."

"There's no use worrying about your nephew now. You know he died in a car crash three days ago?"

"Yes. And you think that Jackson Carpenter had something to do with it."

"I think Carpenter may be behind a lot of things. We need to learn more about him. It's clear that Coles and your nephew were close in college. What we don't know is what their deal was. I think you're the only one who might be able to fill that in."

"They had a few things with girls. I told the doc." Sennett had conducted too many interrogations to let him get by that easily.

"There's something else, isn't there?"

"Someone had gotten wind that they might be involved in a death somewhere. Nobody ever proved it."

"Was it true?"

"All I know is that I talked with John. I straightened him out and that was that."

"What was his relationship to Carpenter?"

"I think Carpenter was the sick one. That's why I was glad to get him off the team. He and John played on the same high school football squad. They were bosom buddies since they were small kids. John idolized Carpenter."

"Why did John change his name to his high school coach's?"

"If Carpenter did it, then John would have followed."

"By the way, do you know how Connely's wife died?"

"Yeah, some kind of infection they said. Food poisoning on an airplane I think."

"Botulism?" I asked.

"Yeah. They never talked about it in the papers. But John told me that after the funeral."

After a few more questions, Sennett let him go. I said goodbye. In spite of the fact that he'd been willing to let me die to keep Connely's secret, I felt sorry for the old man. I felt sorry for anyone who'd outlived everyone and everything he'd ever believed in.

SENNETT CALLED HIS OFFICE. I WATCHED him writing furiously as he listened. He was frowning as he hung up slowly.

"You picked a pretty solid citizen to chase. Steven K. Coles is senior vice-president of Phillips and Dalbeck. They're a large conglomerate out of Chicago. On the board of directors for his church, Evanston Baptist. President of the Optimist Club. President of the local Chamber of Commerce. Active in community affairs. This guy is a Boy Scout."

"Steven Coles has to be Carpenter. Phillips and Dalbeck, huh? If you want to know about a company," I instructed, "you should talk to a broker."

I called Herb Albright and asked him what he knew about Phillips and Dalbeck.

"One of the biggest corporate takeover companies in the country."

Could he tell me what they owned?

"They own so much, it would take two weeks to put it all down on paper."

"Who is the CEO of the company?"

"Alfred Simpkins. He's at the main office in Chicago."

"Let's get him on the phone," Sennett sighed as I hung up.

Sennett got his number through his desk sergeant and dialed it quickly. The man on the other end seemed annoyed at the call.

"This is Al Simpkins. Who am I speaking with?"

"Lieutenant George Sennett, Detroit police."

"This had better be important, lieutenant."

"I need some information on a Mr. Coles, one of your VPs, I believe."

"In regard to what?" he replied.

"There is a possibility that Mr. Coles may have been involved in a series of serious crimes." There was a pause at the other end.

"I have nothing to say without an attorney's advice."

"Excuse me, Mr. Simpkins," Sennett said. The edge in his voice would have sawn lumber. "But this may be a matter of life and death. We would appreciate your cooperation."

"Until I know what this is about, nothing doing."

"Your employee, Steven K. Coles, is a suspect in several murders. We have reason to believe he may be on his way to commit another."

"Impossible," Simpkins snorted. "Utter nonsense. I have no more time to waste. Good day, Lieutenant."

The phone clicked.

Sennett's jaw muscles clamped tighter. In twenty seconds, he had Knudsen on the line.

"Call Chicago P.D. Ask for Captain Marshfield in homicide. He's an old friend of mine. Tell him it's regarding a murder in Detroit and that Simpkins may be involved. Tell him Simpkins resisted questioning. Ask Marshfield to put him in the holding tank until his mouthpiece arrives."

As good as done, Knudsen assured his lieutenant.

"Why wouldn't he talk with us?" I wondered aloud.

"That's what I'm going to find out," Sennett grunted wrathfully.

"How?"

"We're going to put this sombitch's balls in a vise and let him meditate on the meaning of cooperation."

"And how does that help me now?"

"What?"

"We have to get Coles, before he gets to me."

"How do you propose to do that?"

"You heard what Coach Hunter said. If he wants something, he'll get it. On his terms."

"What are his terms?"

"This guy won't bite with all those people around," I said. "If you want to catch a fish, you need bait."

"What are you getting at, Dailey?"

"I mean me. I'm the bait."

"What do you have in mind?" he asked cautiously.

"Call Knudsen back and ask him to check out Landmark Industries in Manhattan. See if they know about Mr. Coles."

Knudsen got back in ten minutes. No one at Landmark Industries had heard of Steven Coles.

"Who'd you talk to?" Sennett said.

"A guard on duty at the building. He went through the roster of employees."

"Anything else?" he asked.

"He said I was the fourth policeman he'd talked to today. They had a hit-and-run death outside the building early this morning. An employee was killed."

"Did you get a name?" I said.

"Edwards, Shirley. Black female, about five-ten –"

"I know her," I said. "She works for Landmark. Head of distribution. That was her day job." I told Sennett I was pretty sure she'd been one of the women on the stage at The Original Sin in New York. Priscilla Wadsworth, Claudia Fraser, now Shirley Edwards.

"Now what?" Sennett asked me after hanging up.

"We're playing defense," I said. "This guy's running circles around us. How do you control the running game?"

"Put eight men on the line. Smother the SOB."

"Right," I said. "He doesn't want Jordan. He wants me. Jordan was an accident. I have something he wants. I can identify him. Without me the cops could question him forever and never make a case. He's too smart."

"So, what do you propose?"

"I've got to face this guy on the line. I'm the target."

"I can't let you do that, Ben. We have procedures."

"I'm the bait, remember? He wants me. You guys show up, and he'll find some other way to kill Jordan and me. This guy is too smart for a police net. He's probably here right now."

"All the more reason we go in with you."

"Hinckley shot President Reagan on national television," I said. "He was surrounded by cops. I'm going to see Jordan," I added, casually. "Why don't you wait here for me? I'll be right back."

In his face suspicion warred with a natural, male reluctance to cross boundaries. "You get a ten minute start," he said at last. "Just remember you might not see me, but I've got your back."

"Why, don't you trust me?" I asked, all innocence.

He chuckled grimly. "About as far as you could carry a football. Just make sure you don't leave the hospital."

"I'll make sure you know where I am," I said with some bravado. The truth was I didn't know."

CHAPTER 24

M Y SHORTCUT TOOK ME THROUGH the emergency room side entrance. There was a guard I recognized standing by the door.

"Coming through the back tonight, Dr. Dailey?"

"First rule for survival," I said. "Never show your face in the ER. They might find something for you to do."

He winked at me. "Especially tonight. Two auto accidents. People running all over the place. I heard them yelling for a head and neck surgeon."

Dammit, why did I stop?

I turned the corner and looked into the trauma room. Sounds of commotion came from behind the drapes. I pulled back the drapes and glanced inside. A young man lay on a gurney, arms thrashing from side to side, blood gushing from his nose. Two nurses and a doctor were trying to settle him down. Blood was coming from his throat and his nose. I could see why the doctor was frustrated. This was not going to be easy.

I stepped over to the gurney. "Get a Robinson catheter, umbilical tape, and a bottle of half-inch iodoform gauze," I said. Everyone turned toward me. The older nurse recognized me. I turned to the emergency room doctor, Bill Julliard. "Light, good suction, and a quiet patient. That's what you need to stop this."

He pulled back, giving me access to the patient.

"Valium?"

"Do it," I said.

I put on a paper gown, mask, and gloves. The nurse returned with the things I needed. Julliard injected the sedative while I put the instruments on the table. The patient's struggle grew less intense. The bleeding persisted.

Once my headlight was in place, I rolled a cloth into a ball, along with the umbilical tape, long cotton strings used for tying off the placenta. When I was done, the two strings came out on opposite sides of the ball.

"Hold his head still," I said. While the younger nurse held the patient's head, I inserted the red rubber catheter through his nose. "This is tricky. Give me the metal tongue blade. Let's open the patient's mouth and have a look." I aimed my light, saw the red catheter tube hanging down in the back, blood flowing freely in his throat. In a matter of minutes, the man would either exsanguinate or asphyxiate. Neither was a good choice. I reached in with a hemostat and grabbed the catheter, pulling it out of his mouth. I tied one of the cotton strings to the end of the catheter and pulled the end back through the nose. The edge of the pack was resting on his lips with the other string hanging out the front. I opened his mouth and propped it open with a black rubber bite block. His mouth was open just wide enough to accommodate the pack. I fed the catheter again, tied the other string to it, and drew it through his nose.

"Here we go." I pulled harder on the second string, and the pack disappeared into his mouth. I pulled again. As I did, I put my finger inside his mouth, pushing the pack behind his nose. The flow of blood stopped.

I packed about a yard of the yellow tinted iodoform gauze into his nostrils and tied the pack off.

"He's not going to bleed for a while, Bill. You can see what's wrong with him. But we better take some blood to make sure." I drew two large syringes and put one on the tray next to the patient and the other in my coat.

Julliard looked relieved.

I took off my gown and gloves and set them down on the table. My jacket and shirt were spattered with blood. I'd need a change of clothes.

I left the emergency room and turned into the employees' lounge, where I found an empty locker and changed into a pair of green scrubs. In these clothes, I could be a floor sweeper, a nurse's aide, or a surgeon. I put on a bouffant cap, a mask, and paper boots for my shoes. I was now free to roam the hospital with impunity. I was about to leave when I remembered the syringe in my coat. I stuck it in my scrubs and walked out.

In the hallway, I grabbed another cleaning cart outside the door. My second gig as a janitor in three days. Was the cosmos trying to tell me something? I leaned over the cart and pushed it down the hallway. Coles or Carpenter, or who-ever the hell it was, would be waiting for Ben Dailey to come to Jordan's room.

I didn't think he'd be looking for a floor sweeper.

I PUSHED THE CART ONTO THE ELEVATOR and rode to the third floor. It was 9:00 p.m. The hallways were empty. The sound of my cart and the squeak of my rubber-soled shoes echoed down the long hallway that led to the intensive care unit. I took out the dust mop from the cart and started cleaning the white tile floor. Every now and then I took the syringe out and dropped a spot of blood from the needle on the floor.

Outside a staff conference room, two male residents in scrubs stood talking in hushed, animated conversation. The subject had to be football. A beeper went off, and they were gone.

If I was going to bait the wolf, now was the time. I pushed the cart up to the conference room. Just inside, on a coat rack, hung some white coats. I took one, instantly becoming a doctor. I left my cap and mask on the cart and put the syringe in my coat. In a few minutes I reached the ICU, fifteen glass cubicles arranged around a central nursing station. Above the desk of the station, several cardiac monitors registered patient status. I glanced toward Jordan's room. Outside the door, sitting in a chair, was a uniformed policeman.

I walked up to the room.

"Can I see your driver's license, sir?" Sennett had drilled these guys well.

"I don't have my wallet."

"Your name?"

"Dailey, Ben Dailey," I said impatiently.

He looked at his list and then at a picture Sennett had provided. He motioned me inside.

Jordan was sleeping. The tube was out. The color had returned to her face and her auburn hair cascaded around it. She looked wonderful.

The nurse who was standing by the bedside turned toward me. "She's doing better."

"Is Jane Flowers off tonight?"

"She called in sick."

I looked at her for a moment and then looked back at Jordan. "As long as she's sleeping, I won't wake her up. I'm going to get a cup of coffee. If she wakes up, tell her I'll be back in a few minutes."

"No problem."

I walked out of the ICU. If the fox was in the hen house, I would soon know it. I turned the corner and walked back to my cart, where I took off the white coat, put the syringe in my pocket, and started to push my dust mop again. All I had to do was wait and mop the floors.

IN THE NEXT HOUR, I cleaned every inch of the hallway on the third floor. Sennett had not found me yet—if he was following—but I was painfully conscious of having no ID tag. A few people came down the corridor, mostly residents. Then the shift changed. They came in groups, nothing out of the ordinary. I turned away as they passed. When things settled down, only skeleton crews remained on the floor. It was the graveyard shift.

At around midnight I saw him. Tall, black-haired, athletic, and probably in his mid-fifties. He got off the elevator and came down the hall. He wore a white coat, a stethoscope dangled from his right pocket. There was assurance in his stride, as if he'd made midnight rounds thousands of times. As he passed, I turned away from him and rotated around my cart, glancing up at him as I did so.

White coat or not, there was no mistaking those eyes. It was Coles, or Carpenter, or whatever the hell Satan's name was this week. Once he was fifteen or twenty steps beyond me, I stored my mop on the cart and followed him down the hall. All the rooms were quiet. As I walked, I dropped some drops of blood as I walked.

I looked over at Jordan's room. The guard was gone. Coles was in there, leaning over her bed. He had something in one hand. It looked like he was holding the IV line with the other.

"Stop!" I yelled, running toward Jordan.

He turned around. I saw his eyes, closer this time. Evil, serpentine eyes. Seeing them so clearly, at that instant, my pulsed raced, anger flushing through my body. Coles flung away the IV line and sprang for the door, nearly colliding with me. Once in the hallway, he sprinted down the corridor.

I lunged through the doorway to Jordan's bedside. I had reached her in time. Whatever deadly substance waited in that syringe on the floor would not hurt her now. I looked around for a moment. *Where was the guard? Where was Sennett?* I dashed out the door and looked up and down the empty hallway.

By that time, Coles would be on the elevators, or far gone down the stairs.

I walked down to the elevators and looked up at the numbers. Both were on ground floor. Then a light blinked. One elevator had gone all the way to the basement, down to the research wing.

CHAPTER 25

I PUSHED OPEN THE DOOR TO THE stairwell and dropped some blood from my syringe, first outside the door and then on the steps.

I walked down the stairs slowly, nothing but the slap of my shoes against the steps filling the silence. The further I went, the more I knew there was no turning back.

At the first landing, I stopped and listened. I looked up and down. Down, I thought, against reason, despite the common sense voice telling me that if I went far enough, I would find a killer. I turned and took the next flight, straining to hear, to sense a presence. I rounded the next landing. A dark object rushed at my face. Sharp pain.

Then nothing.

I AWOKE IN A DARK ROOM. I was sitting. Something opaque was tied around my eyes. My forehead ached from the blow I'd suffered, but aside from that I felt no pain. When I struggled to get up, I found my hands and legs tied to a chair.

"Hello, sleeping beauty," a voice said.

I felt fingers grasp my blindfold as it whipped off my eyes. I squeezed them shut against the piercing light. Once my pupils adjusted, I realized that I recognized this hateful face before me. My friend Igor. I looked around the room. We were still in the hospital. But where? A number of machines against the wall. The laser storage room.

Igor wore a white coat with an ID badge, the name carefully obscured by the overhanging collar. He'd shaved his conspicuous facial hair.

"Taking up medicine?" I said.

"Why not? I have the degree. Bacteriology and toxicology."

"That's why you work in a sex club."

He smiled and shrugged. "It's all part of the grand plan."

"I'm disappointed in you," I said. "You'd think a man with a background in toxicology could do better than guns and car bombs. Very crude."

"You want crude?" He said. He pulled back and sank a fist into my stomach, knocking the wind out of me. "I could have killed you a dozen times. But the boss wants you to look pretty."

He circled the room, sizing things up, making sure there was no escape. He turned and watched me straining to see how I was tied, struggling to get free.

"I love watching people suffer."

"We're onto you," I gasped, trying to pull air back into my lungs. "Two dozen cops are on their way to the hospital right now."

"No fear," he said, holding up his ID. "I'm a doctor."

"Ever hear of code seven?" I said. "Hospital procedure requiring all employees to validate their identities. Cops'll be combing this building in a few minutes."

"They'll never look for you here, in the basement. In a room with a bunch of machines." He pointed over to a gurney in the corner. There was a body bag on it. "By the time we're done with you, you're going to be *code dead.*" He placed a strip of duct tape across my mouth, checked the tape holding me to the chair, then crossed the room to the door. "Sit tight," he said. He opened the door, pushed the lock button on the handle, and walked out of the room.

My mind raced from one question to another. Jordan. Was he climbing the stairs to her room right now? Or looking for Coles?

I had minutes. To my left, I saw the Sharplan 1100 laser against the wall, its articulated arm lying on top of the machine. I dug my heels out in front of me and felt the plastic chair move slightly. It was four feet away. *Move, man. Move.* I leaned my whole body toward my feet. The chair jerked forward. I lunged, and the flimsy chair wobbled, almost tipping onto the floor. *Don't panic,* I coached myself. *Go slow.* More cautiously, I reached my heels out in front of me and scooted another couple of inches. Slow movements, my calves aching with each inch I gained.

After a few minutes, I reached the machine. Now what?

Someone had been testing it. It was plugged in. The key was in the switch. But without a free hand, there was no way I could turn on the machine. I maneuvered the chair around to the corner of the machine, lowered my head to the side of it, and dragged my mouth and the tape across the sharp corner. It gouged the skin on my cheek, but the edge of the tape lifted. I slid my cheek along the machine again, caught the corner, and this time tugged harder. The tape gave under the pressure, exposing my mouth. The salty taste of blood coated my tongue. I kept at it. Gradually, I was able to uncover my mouth.

I bit down on the key and rotated my head. Nothing. I tried the other way and felt the key turn in the switch. Lights on the control panel flashed. A fan inside the machine whirred as it came to life and began to warm up. *Too loud,* I thought, watching the door for Igor. I stretched my body as far as I could to lean across the machine. My nose nudged a black button that read Laser Activate. I'd seen Lindstrom work this thing. I remembered his instructions. I pushed myself toward the power setting, jamming my nose against Wattage Control. When the setting read 40 watts, I stopped.

Sweat stung my eyes. My vision was blurred. I had to find the beam. I dug in my heels and dragged the chair around to the front of the machine, where I saw the faint red glow angling to the floor from the arm. Controls. On top of the machine, the foot pedal.

I bit down on its cable and pulled the pedal to the edge of the machine. Another pull and it crashed to the tile floor. The sound seemed deafening to my agonized caution.

The pedal came to rest against the base of the cabinet. My right foot could slip right over it. I scooted into position in front of the laser, held my hands in its path, while watching over my shoulder. I stepped on the pedal and waited. Pain like a hot knife seared my back and the smell of burning flesh nauseated me. I jerked my foot off the pedal, tried to calm myself, then tried again. Two more excruciating burns. Finally, the beam lined up with the tape across my wrists. My calf muscles spasmed as I pressed down on the pedal. Smoke rose over my shoulder, but this time it was the tape burning, not my flesh. Two minutes and I was free. I pulled the tape off my face, freed my feet, and stood up. Unsteady on my feet, I ran to the door, twisting the knob, pulling, fumbling to unlock it. Nothing. A toolbox lay open by the door. I examined the knob. He'd reversed it, key open inside, button lock outside. The door was locked from the outside.

Igor, I thought, *you're not as dumb as you look.*

I looked around for a phone and found one on a desk in the back. No dial tone.

I staggered back to the door. For a wild moment I considered bashing it with my shoulder. It was a metal door, in a concrete basement. Who was I kidding? These lasers were my only weapons, the CO_2 and Yag.

Lindstrom had told me Yag was the most powerful. I turned the machine on and searched for the clear plastic fiber. I assembled the mechanism, remembering Lindstrom's demonstration. With the fiber inserted, the machine powered up. I held the pistol grip holder in my hand and cranked the power setting up to a hundred watts. It wouldn't go any further. My eyes followed the beam to a spot on the linoleum floor as I pushed on the hand control. A black area appeared on the tile. Charred tile. This sucker was deadly. But for accuracy I had to use it at close range.

I leaned back against the wall and breathed. All right. Let him come.

After a few minutes, I heard footsteps; then the doorknob clicked. The door burst open and Igor entered, carrying syringes and a tourniquet. He looked around quickly, saw the empty chair, then searched about the room until he found me in the corner.

"Aren't you clever?" he said.

I held up my flimsy gun. "Don't come any closer," I said, feeling pretty ridiculous.

"Are you going to shoot me with your pop gun?" he said.

"Laser," I said.

"You're subtle, Doc," he said. "I'm not."

He reached into his back pocket and pulled out a black stiletto. With a flick of his wrist, a six-inch blade opened with a flash. "I was going to drug you and slit your wrists. It looks like we'll have a little fun instead."

Igor took off his coat and threw it over my chair, revealing massive shoulders and forearms. I wanted to rush at him, but I was tethered by my laser to the machine. He sauntered toward me, tossing his knife from hand to hand.

When he was three feet off, I took a step forward and pointed my big old laser gun at him. It seemed like aiming a peashooter at a grizzly.

"I know lasers," he said. "You can hurt me, but you can't kill me. Besides, I'm too quick for you, Doc." He took the next step. I tried to fire the laser, but I couldn't get a shot off. And he was fast. He pinned me against the machine and raised the knife to my throat. With all my strength, I kneed him in the groin. He yelled out in pain, relaxing his grip on my arm. With my free hand, I grabbed the hose attached to the CO_2 gas cylinder. I ripped the hose free from its coupling on the laser. A rush of air exploded at the end of the hose, two hundred pounds per square inch. When Igor jerked his head away from the sound, I swung for his mid-section, doubling him over and giving me an opening. I jammed the hose into his ear canal.

He screamed in agony and clutched the side of his head, staggering backward. I hit him with my shoulder, knocking my back against the machine. His head snapped back, and his eyes went blank. He crumpled to the ground.

I used plenty of duct tape, hands and elbows behind him, feet together. I was pretty sure I'd ruptured his eardrum, but I felt unrepentant, somehow. I finished by taping his mouth shut. He'd be pretty noisy when he woke up. One down, but the tough one still to come.

I'd finished taping Igor when I heard a sound at the door. I looked up to see a figure standing in it.

It was the face of Steven Waring. My patient and, now, my executioner.

WARING. COLES. JACKSON CARPENTER OR MR. VIC.—take your pick. The same evil eyes I had seen at the sex club, in the graduate library, in my own office.

He seemed larger than I remembered, more powerfully built: six foot two, two thirty-five. His stance was athletic, the jutting jaw a look of power. Black hair, thick black moustache, brutal hands that could snap you in two. He had a gun.

"Mr. Waring," I said. "Or is it Mr. Coles?"

"Call me whatever you like, asshole." He lifted his gun and scratched the side of his face. "You're going to be dead soon anyway."

"Your buddy was thinking the same thing."

Igor was conscious. He squirmed on the ground, groaning. Coles frowned, pointed his pistol at him, and squeezed off a headshot. Igor lay still. Blood started from the bottom side of his skull, forming a dark pool on the floor. I had never seen a person killed like that.

"I finish what I start," Coles said. As he spoke, he moved toward me, keeping himself between me and the door.

"No way to treat a loyal employee," I said.

"He was expendable. I've no use for excess baggage." He kicked a chair out of the way.

"Like Shirley."

"Flotsam and jetsam."

"Is that what Claudia and Priscilla were?"

"You've got a big mouth," he said.

"It runs in the family." I took a step back from him. "I inherited it from my cousin, Kievel, from the old country. They had plans for him at Auschwitz. He talked his way out." I was in front of the CO_2 laser. Its articulated arm hung down at the side of the cabinet. There was no CO_2 left, but the arm might be useful.

"Talk all you want. There's no escape."

"Why did you murder those women?"

"I had to close up shop and get rid of the evidence. Especially Claudia, after she tried that scam with the videotape. Then you got nosy."

"So, the olives were meant for me, huh?"

I slipped behind the machine so it stood between us. He scratched his cheek again with his gun. Suppose he didn't have a gun, I thought. He could still break me in two like a toothpick.

"You've made a lot of people dead," I said. "Beginning with Frank Connely's wife. Was she your first?"

"Who's counting?"

"Believe me," I said. "Someone's counting. They're going to get you, Coles."

"So you found my name out," he said, closing in on the CO_2 laser. "How?"

"You know how. From the videotape. It was your one slip-up. When you came down to see me to fix your voice, you never figured I would use that tape. Now it's your only identification. You couldn't find it in Connely's office. That's why you came after me."

I could see the anger in his eyes. He put the gun in his pocket. "You know," he said, "I was just going to shoot you. But I'd like to make you suffer a little bit first."

"Even if you kill me, it'll be too late. We've got Simpkins."

"You mean Steinberg," he said. "Fucking kike. I'll shut him up next."

The word came at me like a punch in the gut. It was worse than physical pain. I recognized that snarl, the intonation.

"The same way you killed Jerry Brooks' friend?" I said. I took a step to my left, keeping the machine between us.

"What?"

"Ohio State vs. Michigan, 1968."

"Our greatest game." He smiled. "Buckeyes forever."

I reached across the machine toward the laser arm. As I did, I kept talking. The mention of the game seemed to divert him momentarily. "Then you remember," I said. "After the game. A couple of guys driving back down US 23 with Michigan plates. You ran them off the road."

"What are you talking about?"

"It was you," I said. He looked for a second and then smiled.

"I remember now. Those two black guys in the old car. Man, I gave them some shit, didn't I."

"You even sang them a song, didn't you?"

"How'd you know?" He seemed surprised.

"From the videotape. It was the same one your buddy, Connely, had in his office. My friend Jerry Brooks was the guy that lived. He remembered the song."

"You mean 'Kansas City.' That's my victory dance. After we pushed them off the road, I saw one of them was dead and the other was messed up. I kind of like to sing to them. Call it a farewell serenade. Just like with our coaches."

It took me a moment to register the confession. "You?" I said, stupidly. "You two killed your high school coaches. Why?"

His eyes were stormy with remembered wrath. "They thought they were going to punish us over those two high school whores," he snarled. "Kick us off the team for next season. And for what? We couldn't let them get away with that."

"Your Buckeye teammates said you idolized your coaches," I ruminated aloud. "And you even took their names." I shook my head, understanding beyond me.

His teeth showed in a wolf grin. "You know what they say. It's a fine line between love and hate."

My mind came back to the present. "That tape was the only thing you couldn't erase, wasn't it?"

"No problem now. I've got the eraser in my hand." He waved his pistol menacingly. He didn't need to overplay it. I was already terrified.

My hand rested on the laser arm. I drew it slowly closer to me, felt the resistance in the mechanism. It was now or never. When Coles shoved the machine to the side, I pulled back hard on the articulated arm and let go. It snapped like a bowstring and caught him flush against the cheek. He was stunned, but not hurt.

"Sonofabitch." He touched his cheek and looked at his hand, then rushed at me. I tried to duck, but he was too quick. His fist jammed into my stomach, knocking me to the ground. I felt his forearm against my Adam's apple. He sank all his weight on the arm pressed against my airway. I struggled to roll out from under him, but he was too strong. I swung my head wildly from side to side. It was no use.

I began to relax into his attack, felt myself drifting away. In the grayness enveloping me, I suddenly saw my grandfather. "Why waste your time with this football foolishness, Ben?" In the haze of oncoming death, one thing stood crystal clear, with a clarity I had never known. I realized that of all my sins on earth, quitting on myself had been the worst.

One last time I opened my eyes. At my side hung the Yag. I reached for it. In one motion, I swung it upward and fired the beam directly at the middle of Coles' left eye. His head shot backward as he clawed at his face. I was no match for his strength, but I kept my hand on the button and the beam focused on his face.

"My eye!" he screamed.

He dropped his hand, wildly reaching for the laser. I aimed at his eye again.

"I'll kill you," he said, getting to his feet and backing away.

"You wish, asshole." I rushed him and grabbed the front of his shirt. Left jab, right hook, and a football forearm shiver to the jaw. Coles' head snapped back against the sharp edge of the laser cabinet. He groaned, then reached for the back of his head. He looked surprised when he saw blood. He went for me like a mad bull.

I went low this time, grabbed him, and threw him off balance just long enough to backsweep his leg. As he went down, I dug my heel into the back of his leg. He cried in pain, holding onto his knee.

"That was for me," I said. "And this one is for Timmy Steel." I bent over him, pulled back my arm, and crashed the heel of my hand into his nose. I could hear a cracking sound as the bones separated. Blood poured down his upper lip.

He had slumped to the floor, his back against the laser. I thought of that picture of Muhammad Ali standing over Sonny Liston. That's how I felt. Then I remembered the photograph I'd seen in the *Daily*, just the other night, an image that had haunted me for thirty years—me lying on the field, an OSU player standing over me. Coles. I'd tucked it in the back of my mind after that, too painful to know, too awful to extract.

But this was more than just me. I thought of Jerry and Timmy Steel. One of them lying dead in a field off Highway 23. For what?

What would my grandfather have said to such a man?

I looked down at Coles now. I'd never felt such hatred. I wanted to finish him. I walked over to the door to gather my thoughts. I opened the door and looked down the hall. Nobody. It was just Coles and me. His kind had killed my relatives. He had killed Timmy. Now I could take my revenge. No courts, no lawyers. Real justice.

I walked back in the room. From the toolbox on the floor by the door, I took out a hammer and tapped its blunt end against the palm of my hand. There was blood on my hand from breaking Coles' nose. All right, I thought. Now was my time. Justice was mine. No one could fault me. I knelt over him and raised the hammer, looking down at his expansive forehead. I saw my grandfather rushing with outstretched hands, gasping, then falling to the ground, clutching his chest. I was still a college kid. Not trained, not smart enough to help him. Could I do this now? Shouldn't I?

Blood dripped down Coles' face. I'd destroyed his nose.

Enough.

I lowered the hammer. If I killed him, it would be the start of another nightmare. I wanted to be done with them.

I backed away from him. I walked back to the toolbox and dropped the hammer. I found a fifty-foot length of electrical cord to tie him, thinking about what lay ahead. The authorities would punish him. He'd find an attorney to spare his life. He'd get a prison term. But I'd get something in return: my life restored and my family alive. Surely that was good enough, certainly better than murder.

I was straightening the cord when a voice shattered the silence.

"Ben!"

I dove to the left and heard a crash reverberate through the room. Coles had pulled his gun.

Then came a second crash. Coles had rolled to his left as Sennett's bullet missed. I heard Sennett curse, then the clatter of his gun hitting the floor.

Coles rose slowly, holding the gun in front of him, while focusing his good eye on me. I looked toward Sennett. He was down, clutching his upper left arm.

"Okay, Dailey. You first and then your buddy."

He raised his gun and pointed.

"You killed Connely, didn't you?" I asked, trying to stall for time.

Coles gave a malevolent smile. "Sure, hit and run on a desolate highway. Perfect timing. Now it's you."

There was a sound behind him. He turned toward the door just in time to see Jerry snatch Sennett's gun from where it lay. There was a slight hesitation, the hesitation of the cornerback defending the fly pattern. As Coles whirled to shoot, fire erupted from the end of Sennett's Smith and Wesson. The clip emptied into Coles' chest. He was dead before he hit the floor.

In the ensuing silence, the remnants of gun smoke wafted to the ceiling of the room. I looked over at Sennett. He was getting up slowly, holding onto his arm.

"Don't worry," he just grazed me. Good thing he couldn't see."

By this time Jerry was standing over Coles's motionless body. He was dead but the look on his face—the swollen eye, the blood-smeared nose, and a cruel, twisted smile—would live with me forever. I looked up at Jerry and searched his eyes. The ghost was gone. The nightmare he had lived with for thirty years would never come again.

"The lieutenant here called me to come back down again." Jerry grinned at me. "Seems like you didn't want no police help, but he figured he'd follow the blood spots. If that ain't you all over, Dailey. Hotdog to the end."

"I heard that. Now I've got to live this down with the guys at the station," Sennett growled. "Following you by 'breadcrumbs' and then missing at close range. I won't hear the end of it. They'll call this the Hansel and Gretel case," Sennett growled, struggling to a seated position against the wall.

I knew I could never hold my own against the two of them together. The best face-saver would be to pass out.

So I did.

CHAPTER 26

Sanderson's desk was cluttered with food and papers. As we talked, he picked up French fries and munched absently. Watching him reaffirmed my notion that, if I were to do it all over again, I might choose preventative medicine over surgery. Surgeons wave their magic wands and cut out disease, sometimes they even cure it. But stopping an affliction before it started, now that would be miraculous. Selling Bruce on prevention would take a miracle.

"Have you ever heard of Throckmorton's sign?" I said.

He lifted and dropped a sheet of numbers in front of him. That meant "No."

"It's an infallible sign on an X-ray. The penis always points to the lesion."

He squinted up at me. "This a joke?"

"If I took one of you right now, yours would point at your brain." Sanderson actually looked down at his crotch trying to figure out what I meant. Puzzled, he looked back at me and shrugged.

"You're a walking time bomb, Bruce."

He picked up a can of root beer and drank. He said, "I've invented a whole new lifestyle. It's called the HSD. High Schmaltz Diet. The five basic food groups are corned beef, chopped liver, egg yolks, French fries, and mayonnaise. Stay on the diet six months. If you're still alive, nothing can kill you."

Preventative medicine would be too hard.

He pointed at my expense report. "$200 for neck massages?"

I showed him my throat, where the black and blue marks were just starting to fade. "I could have let the maniac kill me," I said. "It would have been a hell of a lot cheaper, until you take into account the malpractice award, the attorney fees, the court filings on appeal, and—"

"Okay," he said. "I'm just doing my job." He reached under the desk, pulled out a checkbook, and swept his lunch and a few papers out of the way. Documents drifted lazily to the floor. "We made out good, didn't we? I got orders to cut you a check today."

"I've never seen your company so eager to pay."

"When the police went back to Coles' apartment in Chicago, they found all kinds of things. Coles had everything written down. These two guys had been planning this for years. Kill both wives, collect the insurance, and run for the islands. There's an eighty-five-foot sloop in their names down near St. Bart's."

"How'd they get started?" I asked.

"When Connely's girlfriend discovered the new strain of botulinum toxin, they couldn't resist."

"Enter Elnor Pharmaceuticals," I said.

Sanderson nodded. "Connely saved partially used bottles of the toxin in his office. When he had enough, he convinced Claudia to plant it in the food. Enough to make the other passengers sick, enough to kill Connely's wife. The insurance settlement gave the good doctor $2.5 million dollars. He should have taken the money and run."

"Live off the misery of other people, and you will never be poor."

"True," he agreed calmly. "Coles' divorce lawyer had kept rights to her estate for Coles. Coles' ex got sick and showed up in Connely's office. Old friend helps old friend? Connely told her she needed to have her tonsils out. She trusted him. He killed her by putting a stitch through her carotid artery. It takes two weeks for the suture to erode. The vessel ruptures, and the patient dies. But when the guilt got to Connely and he caved on the stand, Coles decided all the money was better than a confession from Connely."

"The sex club?" I said.

"Insurance money from killing their wives wasn't enough. They opened the club in New York, lured prospective investors—respectable citizens only, afraid of scandal—then blackmailed them. Simpkins told us everything. He saw you in the club." Bruce picked up the discarded sub and took a big bite. I thought back to that night. Simpkins must have been the businessman getting dessert.

"But why'd they try to kill Jordan and me?"

"You were the only person who could connect Coles to the lawsuit, the club, and the botulinum toxin. You had his videotape. He knew that would implicate him if you made the connection between the two tapes. When you started nosing around Delaware Baptist and talking to Alden Sherman, that convinced him that you had something."

"Sherman was in on it?"

"Coles needed a squeaky-clean hospital to lure the pharmaceutical company to do clinical trials. So he brings pious old Sherman to The Original Sin. We found some pretty wild videos in Coles' apartment in Chicago. Nothing like a choirboy for some old-fashioned Sodom and Gomorrah, if you get my drift."

"And then he started killing everyone."

"It was only a matter of time before he got rid of them all, including Connely. The girls he murdered were lookouts. When he didn't need them anymore, they were history. All he needed was to kill you, and he was home free. It was almost the perfect crime."

"I still don't understand why you're opening up your check book so quickly."

"According to Pennsylvania law," he raised a hand to his mouth and burped discreetly, "when a criminal act causes a wrongful verdict, the defendant is entitled to treble damages. Connely was in on this thing, so we went back to his estate and got our money back. The rest went to Connely's wife's family."

I thought about Stig Hunter. He wouldn't have taken the blood money if it had been offered. I looked down at the remains of Sanderson's lunch.

"So your company is happier than a pig in slop."

"You bet," he said. "And I'm up for a promotion."

"I'd better hurry to the bank while you're still in a good mood."

"So you get expenses. Right? Who did you tell me to make the other check out to?"

"The Stanford Alumni Association." With that I got up. I was about to walk out when I turned back to my corpulent friend, half hidden by the mess on his desk.

"You know, Bruce, you really—" Then I stopped, looked at the smile on Sanderson's face, and realized I was only a doctor. I had done all I could for Bruce.

Sheila had Buck ready in his traveling cage. She handed him over reluctantly.

"I'll miss him," she sniffed. "If you ever need a sitter..."

"Thanks, Sheila. Consider yourself his godmother."

As I went into the sunshine, I reflected that I no longer felt as if I owed Bruce Sanderson anything. If I ever had.

Jordan was a wise woman.

WE WERE SITTING IN THE STUDY listening to Paul Desmond play *Desmond Blue*. Jordan, five days out of the hospital, was wrapped in an afghan, resting her feet on the ottoman, her head against the chair. A floral pattern. I always thought she picked colors to match her hair. She was beautiful. Beneath the blanket, the beginnings of a telltale bulge in her stomach.

She sat forward and laid her hands on her stomach. "When will it move?"

I got up from my seat and knelt down beside her. She took my hand and put it on her stomach.

"It's too early. Give it time. He'll be a football player soon enough," I said.

"He? You sound so sure." She laughed. "Besides, I thought you hated football?"

"I still like it, just not like Jerry does. For him, it was a form of sublimation."

"Are you in session, Dr. Freud?"

"Sublimation. He took his bad thoughts and made them socially acceptable through football."

"If everyone could do that, I'd be out of work," Jordan mock-grimaced.

"Gandhi said all crime is a disease and should be treated as such."

"Does that make the police practitioners of medicine?"

"When I visited Sennett, he told me he's going back to work next week. He used that exact word. He needed to get his medicine back on the street."

"And how about you?"

Buck was nudging my leg. I cupped my hand under his mouth and shook his muzzle.

"Healing the public comes in different forms, Jordan. I'm a doctor, I was trained to heal."

"I understand." She extended her index finger and traced the bruises on my throat. I really believed she did.

She got up from the chair and led Buck toward the kitchen. "I'll take him out. I'm tired of sitting around. Do you want a sandwich?" She and Buck disappeared into the kitchen. I listened to her talking to him and realized how much I cared for her. For an inveterate loner like me, it was both frightening and inexpressibly soothing.

But I still had to get over one final hurdle: one thorny, little burr I had to get out of my hide.

Todd Pearson.

I stared ahead at the bookcase in front of me until my eyes caught sight of the familiar letter dangling off the edge. Pearson, Sommerby, and Wright. How many times in the last two days had I walked by it, read the envelope, set it back down? Analyze that, Dr. Freud.

I had to know. I pulled the letter out and started to read:

> *Dear Jordan,*
> I've settled the matter between Mr. Sid Blanton and his landlord. There will be no condemnation. His space will remain intact as long as he has the club.
> By the way, Anna and I want to thank you for the beautiful wedding gift. We can't wait to hear about your new arrival. My best to Ben.
>
> *Your friend always,*
> *Todd Pearson*

Jordan walked back in and saw me reading the letter. "Oh, I forgot to tell you. It's good news for Sid, isn't it?" I looked up at her, holding the puppy, and smiled. Quietly, I reached inside my jacket pocket and pulled out a shiny, metal object. It made a clacking sound that gave Jordan a start.

"Playing rattlesnake today?"

"No, it's a present for the baby. I got it in New York."

She reached for it, just as the phone rang. I'd played this scene before. This time I let it ring.

GENE RONTAL, M.D. was born in Detroit in 1944. After attending under-graduate school in Ann Arbor, he obtained his medical degree from the University of Michigan. Following his medical school training, he pursued a career in head and neck surgery at the University of Minnesota. Upon completion of his residency he returned to Detroit where he has practiced since 1972. The author of numerous scientific publications, he has lectured widely on a variety of subjects involving diseases of the head and neck. He also has been quoted in many lay publications including *Scientific American*, *National Geographic*, and *The Wall Street Journal*. Currently a professor at the University of Michigan, Dr. Rontal lives in the Detroit area with his wife, Ellen, and has two children, Sara and David. *A Lethal Dose* is his second published work, following his first novel in the Ben Dailey series, *Sterile Justice*.